THE MATCH FAKER

RUBY BARRETT

CONTENT WARNING

Content Warnings

This book deals with themes of parental neglect, mention of previous abusive relationships, secondary character with cancer diagnosis; and, contains explicit sex scenes.

To my perfect match
xo

PROLOGUE: JASMINE

January

My nipples could cut glass; an unfortunate feature of Canadian winters, not a bug. There's a certain kind of frigid that only exists in Toronto in January. The wind off Lake Ontario slices between buildings, hardens frozen snowbanks into dirty, jagged peaks, and cuts through all three of my layers, turning my fingers into popsicles and my nipples into razors.

If I had any sense, I would have at least stuffed my thick mittens into my bra. They make it impossible to grip the flimsy plastic handles of my cupcake carrier, so I can't even wear them. But all my sense flew south for the winter. Because it's *sensible.*

From somewhere in the depths of my thrifted baby alpaca wool coat, my phone vibrates twice in quick succession. Standing here, shifting from foot to foot while I wait for my light to change, I'm close to the glass building of Haüs Interiors, so I'll save myself the trouble and respond to the texts when I get inside. And warm. And out of these cursed, secondhand, three-inch heeled booties. They're beautiful, but they're deadly on ice, entirely inappropriate for the windchill and far too expensive to be purchased at market cost. I work with a lot of rich people, though—my boyfriend, Mitchell, included—and my thrifted finds help me play the part.

As I join the throng of commuters crossing the street, my phone buzzes again, a call this time that tickles somewhere around my hip bone. My breath clouds around me as I huff.

I'm not answering you, Jade.

My sister is just mad that I wouldn't let her misappropriate one of Mitchell's birthday cupcakes. For a man in his early thirties, Mitchell is weird about his birthday. He wants attention but he doesn't want it to seem like he wants attention; a by-product of being the only child of a wealthy family, I guess. I wouldn't know.

Jade's one goal in life is to antagonize him. When we started dating two years ago, her favorite tactic was to call him the wrong name. Usually something like Michael or Marshall, sometimes Mickey. Now, she takes a more passive-aggressive approach, like "forgetting" that he was staying over and calling bylaw on him when he parked his car a little bit too close to a fire hydrant. Or like eating his leftovers. Or stealing his birthday cupcakes.

She's not malicious, just protective. In her defense, I haven't done a great job of picking partners in the past, between the boyfriend who casually asked if I'd be open to "showing" his colleague "a good time" and another one who assumed that since I had a breast augmentation at eighteen that I had "daddy issues" and "no self-respect." The daddy issues may have been accurate, but I still dumped him. That's why I wish she'd choose to see Mitchell's good qualities. He's never said anything that unkind. He's hardworking, and he's conventionally attractive like all those actors named Chris. Maybe he's a little boring, but not everyone can be funny, and there are more important things in life than laughter. Like stability. And Mitchell is rebar.

Our future is easy to imagine. We enjoy each other's company. His family likes me—which is good since his parents are co-owners of Haüs Interiors and our bosses. In another six months, we'll be engaged. Then married in a year. After that things will be easier, life will be perfect.

Because Mitchell is the perfect match for me.

My phone vibrates again, this time multiple messages in quick succession. "Jade," I growl, the sound hanging in the cold air in front of me.

I put the cupcakes down on an empty bus stop bench. The move is gentler than my mood calls for, but the baked goods don't deserve to suffer because of another sister squabble. Especially these cupcakes, with their perfect dollop of lavender icing, candied lemon slices, and sprinkle of lavender sprigs on top.

Commuters peer at me from inside the fogged glass of the stop's enclosure. That alone is a sure sign that it's freeze your tits off cold—when the weather-hardened Torontonians would rather brave a urine-soaked TTC bus stop than stand outside. I pat myself down for my phone, grumbling under my breath about little sisters. Finally, I find the device tucked into the inner pocket of my coat, my body heat the only thing keeping the early gen iPhone functioning in minus thirty windchill.

A bus pulls up, the brakes squealing, and the people in the bus stop rush the door before those on the bus can get off. The driver shouts at the crowd to make space and cabs honk at the delay in the early morning commute. Someone on the bus starts yelling, their words indecipherable but the frustrated tone clear.

All of it is muffled, like I'm behind a pane of glass, every sensory input organ devoted to processing the name on my phone screen.

The calls, the texts, weren't from Jade. They were from Mitchell. In the time it takes for me to input my password, a million scenarios run through my mind. Mitchell texting is not alarming. It's the calls. Mitchell never calls. Even with his sales clients, he'd rather meet in person than talk to them on the phone. If he's gone as far as to contact me this way, then that means there's been an emergency.

Or worse, he thinks I forgot his birthday.

My hands shake as I jab at the text message icon, alight with its glaring red bubble. Jade would tell me I'm being ridiculous. Rationally, I know that I am. It's just that his birthday has to be perfect, nothing can go wrong.

I have to be perfect. For him.

I take a deep breath to quell my panic. His birthday will be perfect. I made sure of it. I made *myself* perfect. For the last ten years, that's what I've done. Molded myself into the perfect girlfriend, the perfect catch. Jade hates it. I've lost friends because of it; but they don't know what I know. That in the span of a day, your entire world can come crashing down. Your father can leave and take with him your mother's sobriety, your tuition, and any semblance of family you had left. For the last decade, I have done what he couldn't: I've sacrificed.

I've sacrificed my dreams of working for the Royal Ontario Museum as the textile curator. I dropped out of school. Found a full-time job so then-twelve-year-old Jade could move out of our family's home and in with me while she finished grade school when it became clear our mom couldn't provide her with stability and our father only had eyes for his mistress.

I started as a sales associate at Saks, modernized the booking system for their alterations department. From there, I worked as a personal stylist for the rich women of the GTA. Then I made the jump to interior design assistant at Haüs. And sure, maybe thirty-two feels a little old to still be an assistant. Maybe it's not the BA in Art History from U of T, the MA from NYU, the PhD from London Met. Maybe I'll never receive the Veronika Gervers Research Fellowship. But I'm proud of what I've done for Jade and myself. She's going to university debt-free and she's going to be the best goddamn therapist there is; she's had enough practice on me and my issues.

And yes, I've dated men from a certain tax bracket while doing it, chased the lifestyle I grew up with, and I adjusted some qualities to make myself more desirable to them. So, sue me.

If I can't get what I want, shouldn't I get what I deserve? Stability, security. The right to fall asleep at night without worrying about tuition and groceries, rent and back taxes.

The acrid scent of exhaust stings my nose as the bus pulls away. It's official, my fingers are in stage three of frostbite. Even so, I take another steadying breath. I am the perfect girlfriend, the perfect partner. Mitchell's call was probably a butt dial and the numerous texts various expressions of excitement for his birthday.

"You're worrying over nothing," I say to myself now that the crowd from the bus has dispersed and open our chat.

> Mitchell <3: hey babe.

> Mitchell <3: i tried to call you. this is really hard to say over text.

> Mitchell <3: i know you were really excited for my birthday and stuff. and if you don't want to come in to work today, i totally understand. my mom said you can use one of your personal days.

> Mitchell <3: but…

> Mitchell <3: gah this is so hard!!! i think we should see other people, ok?

> Mitchell <3: like…i think we should break up.

I read the words over and over again. Haüs Interiors is down the street, I can see it from here. And Mitchell is *there*. His parents ordered breakfast for the whole office as part of his birthday celebration. Heart pounding in my ears, I look around, waiting for him to jump out and tell me I'm the latest victim of a hidden-camera practical joke show.

The city around me gets blurry as my eyes fill with tears. Clearly, my body knows what my brain has yet to understand.

With a deep breath in, I rack my brain for a suitable response, but what is there to say?

My co-worker boyfriend dumped me minutes before I was scheduled to arrive at work, where I'll have to be *nice* to him because it's his motherfucking birthday. Where I'll have to spend most of the day with him since I am the head designer's—his mother's—assistant. His mother, who knew he was going to do this since she's already approved my personal leave.

How do I respond to what is arguably the most embarrassing thing that has ever been routed through a cell phone tower?

Hot, angry tears fall. Normally, I'd be embarrassed to cry in public, but at least the tears are warm. I have worked so hard—so fucking hard—to be perfect, to be good enough.

He couldn't even do me the courtesy of breaking up with me in person.

I am not perfect. Not the perfect daughter or sister. Not the perfect girlfriend.

That makes me angriest of all. After all the work I've done, all the sacrifice, it's still not enough. It never is.

My phone vibrates again as another text comes in. The screen hasn't locked yet, and I see the message from Mitchell right away.

> Mitchell <3: i hope we can still be friends :)

That's when something breaks in my brain.

A scream tears out of me, a sound between a battle cry and a sob, as I lift my phone over my head and spike it onto the ice-covered ground, where it shatters into pieces.

Kind of like my pride.

1

JASMINE

February

Zara Afzhal is perhaps the finest person I work with at Haüs. Since the worst moment of my personal and professional life, Zara is the only person who hasn't avoided eye contact with me, or gone conspicuously quiet when I've walked into a room, or suppressed a giggle after I've walked past.

"Hi, Jasmine," she says from behind the receptionist desk as I step into the office after lunch.

Normally, I'd eat at my desk. As Anaïs's assistant, I work closely with her, yet she insists I sit with the team in the open-plan, bullpen-style office. Naturally, that has made lunchtime incredibly awkward.

The noon sun reflects off the glass buildings around ours, illuminating the minimalist white and gray decor of our foyer, making the space golden and hazy. Sunbeams reach toward the mostly open workspace beyond the front desk and filter through the spiral staircase that leads to the private office on the second floor, giving the impression that this place is a honey-colored paradise rather than a washed-out prison for my dreams.

Swallowing back the unease that bubbles up inside me each time

I step through the front door lately, I tap the salt and slush from my consignment designer booties.

"Anaïs and Butch want you to go straight up to their office."

"Oh." My heart stumbles and I stop dead as the door clicks shut behind me. A meeting with Anaïs is nothing unusual. A meeting with her *and* Butch? Not good. Not good at all. The last time an employee met with both of them, privately, he was fired. He messed up all the papers on Butch's desk, yelled obscenities while he stormed out, and supposedly took a dump on Anaïs's BMW's hood. I didn't witness the last one though.

I grimace at the box of six gourmet donuts I picked up to enjoy with Jade tonight. It's probably unprofessional to arrive at an ominous work meeting with baked goods in a box emblazoned with the words *Glory Hole* across the top.

"I'll take those," Zara says. Her heels, most definitely designer and *not* sourced from a consignment website called Luxury Flea Market, tap on the concrete flooring as she comes around the desk. "Leave your coat here, too. I can take it all to your desk."

"Thank you," I say, voice shaky. Before I hand over the donuts, I pull two out. A vanilla sprinkle and a s'more. Anaïs won't eat it if it's not gluten-free, dairy-free, and locally sourced, but Butch is a trash can for baked goods.

As I climb the stairs to their joint office, I am almost certainly rocking a terrible case of toque-head, and I have to pee. This isn't how I wanted to be fired: a laughingstock with my control top nylons squeezing my bladder. A chill runs down my spine while, somehow simultaneously and inexplicably, my armpits sweat.

Oh, how far the perfect fall.

The tap of my heels on the stairs echoes in the stark space. As I ascend, I tell myself I won't, but it's no use. Holding my breath, I glance at Mitchell's office. The members of the sales team have offices rather than cubicles, and his is one of the first behind the reception desk. He's not there. Probably at a client lunch or a job site.

My calves scream as I reach the top of the stairs. Curse these booties and workplaces where everyone is "family" yet aren't treated like family unless their blood runs as blue as those in power. Because I'm balancing the donuts in napkins in both hands, knocking on their office door with my forehead may be my only option. But then Anaïs opens the door from the inside, her smile glowing, her hair glowing, her skin glowing.

Anaïs is aglow.

"Jasmine, darling. *Viens*," she purrs. My name slips off her tongue, *Jasmeen*, in her impeccable French accent. It curls around all her English words, her lips pursing, her eyes casting upward when she whispers a quiet *how do you say*. But Anaïs isn't French or even Quebecois. She grew up an hour north of Toronto in a very anglophone suburb and went to French immersion high school.

At least dating Mitchell had one perk: access to his parents' secrets.

Butch rises from behind his desk as Anaïs shuts the door behind me. He cups my elbows, air kissing both cheeks. "Hey, doll." When he pulls back, he only has eyes for my donuts. "Are those…?"

"I picked them up at lunch."

"You're an angel." He grabs two plates off the bar cart set up with a vintage coffee grinder and a French press and places them on the low coffee table in the seating area between their desks.

As Anaïs's assistant, I'm typically busy running errands to the garment district for fabrics, organizing her schedule, or managing her Instagram account. I spend a surprisingly small amount of time in their office and now my eyes can't help but snag on the details. Her side of the office is what I imagine Le Petit Trianon looks like. Delicate and elegant with gold leaf accents. Instead of a computer chair she sits in a hand-carved armchair upholstered in blue silk. Her laptop is set up on a traditional ladies writing desk. Each piece is beautiful, but they must be murder on her back.

Butch's side has a more masculine, modern edge, though Anaïs's touch can be found in the details. Dark woods and blacks and grays, a glass desk instead of a heavy wood monstrosity, and rather than animal heads mounted on the walls, great white trillium flowers and eastern white pine branches are pressed into hand-carved frames.

Maybe it's the knowledge that her accent is fake. Or that Butch hasn't spoken to his elderly parents in years, but the entire room feels fake. Like I could pull down the curtain and I'd find a sad girl from Richmond Hill pulling the strings, accompanied by her insecure Texan husband and a buttload of money.

The money, at the very least, is real.

At first glance, they ooze perfection, the kind I strive for. Maybe I don't want a fake accent, but I do want the love they have for each other. Though, as I sit across from where Anaïs has settled and smooth my hair, my back straight, clasping my hands to keep them from trembling, I question. I doubt. Is their love even real?

Butch pours coffee into short espresso cups with matching gold-accented saucers and sets them in front of us. He settles on the couch beside his wife, his arm thrown across the back of the gray leather. A king secure in his throne. Anaïs settles a perfectly manicured hand on his thigh and turns her gaze to me.

"How have you been?" she asks with the kind of emphasis that makes it clear this is not a casual hi-how-are-you; it's about the breakup. It's about the silence that fell over my colleagues when I entered the building, cheeks flushed, and cupcake icing smudged against the translucent walls of their carrier.

Maybe they're not firing me?

Even so, my stomach twists painfully. "Is this about Mitchell?"

Butch shifts, avoiding eye contact, and Anaïs purses her lips in a way her dermatologist would encourage her to avoid.

Great, now they think I'm a resentful ex.

I gaze into the depths of my espresso. "Sorry, I thought you were… firing me?"

Butch slaps his thigh and throws his head back, laughing. "Of course not." He can't speak, he can only boom.

I work hard not to wince at the volume.

"Darling, never. No." Anaïs shakes her head, but the way she's looking at me—like she's secondhand embarrassed—makes me itch. She's remembering the week I took off after he dumped me. I never wanted to be *that* woman, but it was just so mortifying. "We love you, and your relationship with Mitchell will never change that."

"Plus, that's illegal, sweetheart," Butch says. I think he's going for fatherly, but he comes off mansplainy instead.

That doesn't assuage my fears the way it should. I know it's illegal to fire me without cause, just like they know I don't have the funds or the time to take legal action against them.

"I was worried, I guess," I say. "That it had something to do with him."

An expression that looks an awful lot like pity flickers over Anaïs's face. My sweat glands renew their efforts.

I pick up my espresso to give myself something to do with my hands and bring it to my lips.

"Speaking of Mitchell..." she starts.

"He's engaged," Butch booms, too loud and too fast, as if he believes this news is the kind best delivered like a swift punch to the gut.

I choke on the espresso, instantly flipping through a mental calendar to figure out exactly how many days it's been since he dumped me. Because at this point, days are still a reasonable metric of measurement. *Days.*

"How is that possible?" I wheeze.

This is why all those advice columns warn against dating co-workers. Because, inevitably, you will be locked in a mortifying tableau with your bosses whom you'd once hoped would also be your in-laws.

Our history sits between the three of us, an awkward, sore pimple. Is it possible to simply curl into myself continually until I implode? Ceasing to exist would be lovely right now.

Butch picks up a donut, *my* donut, and sticks his finger in the gooey melted marshmallow on top.

"It was a whirlwind." Anaïs laughs, throwing her hands in the air like *what can you do?*

"Thirty days is pretty fast, even for a whirlwind." My shrill tone echoes back at me in the sudden quiet of their office.

Her smile fades and she looks to Butch for help, but Butch has lost himself completely to the second donut. I wish I were lost in a donut right now.

Mitchell was cheating on me. If the news that he's engaged felt like a punch to the gut, this is like being trampled by a horse. He replaced me. Like I was nothing. Like he'd been waiting for the better version to come along. I was exemplary, the exact kind of woman he should want; ambitious, talented, poised. I made myself perfect. Yet not even that was good enough.

"Why..." My voice cracks and I take a deep breath before I start again. "Why are you telling me this?"

"We're hosting his engagement party in a couple weeks," Butch says.

Wearing an apologetic smile, Anaïs slides a four by six piece of thick, textured paper across the coffee table.

"We're inviting the whole office, but we wanted to let you know first because..." Butch trails off, staring wistfully at the donut crumbs on his plate.

My already trampled-on heart crumbles further as I scowl at the engagement party invitation, the high-quality cotton blend paper, the looping calligraphy, their names, *Mitchell and Catherine.*

Of course, her name is Catherine. A woman with a name like that is poised and gracious, smart and successful. Catherine has a master's degree and her PhD. Catherine never had to drop out of school. Catherine can afford designer clothes and to send her sister to school. Scratch that—Catherine doesn't need to pay for her sister's education because Catherine's father isn't an asshole who started a newer, better family without her.

"We didn't want you to feel like you had to come," Anaïs says.

"I'm invited?" My stomach sinks like waterlogged trash to the bottom of Lake Ontario. Nothing could make me go to that party.

"You know Mitchell. He wants everyone to be friends and get along," she says, which is a laughably charitable view of him, even for his mother. Mitchell is insensitive, sometimes by accident but also on purpose.

This is bordering on cruel. Would he really be this unkind? When I walk out of this office, will I find him watching me, wearing a smug look?

"But you don't have to come," she says again, more firmly this time.

Turns out there is one thing that could make me go to this party.

"But I *am* invited, right?"

They look at each other again, brows furrowed, another silent conversation between married people.

"Yes," Butch says slowly.

I swallow the taste of bile, straighten my already straight back, and clasp my hands tighter, the pale pink of my at-home manicure an unintentional color match to my mid-length charcoal gray skirt.

"Then I wouldn't miss it for the world. I'm so excited to meet Mitchell's new partner."

My smile—saccharine and innocent—is one I've practiced so many times, it feels real. It feels like a trophy compared to the shock that crosses over Anaïs's face.

"No, no. We don't want you to feel uncomfor—"

I stand abruptly, cutting her off. "It's not uncomfortable," I say, despite the way the word acts like a noose around my neck. "I just want everyone to get along as well. Especially now that I can introduce Mitchell to *my* new partner."

I'm still wearing that smile as I leave their office a few moments later and jog down the breakneck spiral stairs. The expression is a Band-Aid to the sharp pain in the balls of my feet and the numbness creeping into my pinky toes. The smile doesn't falter until after I've locked myself in a bathroom stall and leaned against the door, my palms sweaty and my stomach churning.

"Fuck," I whisper. The only response in the blessedly empty bathroom is the rhythmic drip of a tap. Why couldn't they have just fired me? It would be preferable to this. Because now, on top of being a laughingstock, I've turned myself into a liar. I most certainly, definitely, do not have a boyfriend.

I KICK the cursed booties off, flinging them into a pile of my sister's shoes. My throbbing feet are so relieved to be bootieless I can't even bring myself to grumble about her mess or line my boots up with the other shoes on the mat. "Jade?"

The TV is too loud. The hall light, the kitchen light, and I'd bet the bathroom, and her bedroom lights are on. I could choke on the artificial scent of Provencal lavender fields, Jade's favorite candle.

But at least I'm home.

The century-old floorboards creak as my little sister stomps around the corner from the living room. When she stops in the hallway, she glares pointedly at my hands.

"What?" I ask, dipping my chin. Only then does the realization hit me. "The donuts." A frustrated huff escapes me. I left them on my desk.

Jade resembles a potato sack in her baggie blue sweats. Her short hair is pulled back from her face in chunky barrettes as she grows it out from her latest experiment with a pixie cut. A crease appears between her brows as she growls, "Where are they?"

Her attempts at intimidation are lost on me though. The little girl she once was sits just below the surface, complete with button nose and freckles that don't fade in winter.

"Hello, sister," I say in an attempt to distract her. "How are you?"

Her nostrils flare. "Don't change the subject. You promised you were bringing me donuts."

My stomach sinks. "I know. I'm sorry. I had a terrible day. I forgot them at work." I hang up my coat and hers—which was draped over the small bench at the front door—then gather her school and gym bags along with my work bag and hang them all on the hooks above the bench. I'll deal with her shoe pile later.

With a harrumph, Jade shuffles back into the living room, where another documentary about cheetahs—her most recent hyperfixation—plays and a cornucopia of snack foods sit on the coffee table. The couch sags in the middle as I sit next to her.

Despite her disappointment, she leans into me. "What kind of donuts did you get?"

"All your favorites." I snuggle into her in return and pet her hair.

"It was Butch, wasn't it?"

Once, I ordered an overpriced gift box of four hand-stuffed gourmet chocolate chip cookies for Jade's birthday and had them delivered to the office to surprise her with that night. Butch interrupted my business call to ask me if he could try them. Not actually listening to him, I whispered furiously with my hand over the phone, *I'm on a call, yes, yes, whatever*, and he *took the whole box* like the villain from an absurd children's movie.

She's never forgiven him.

Neither have I, honestly.

Either way, I omit that Butch did in fact enjoy two of our donuts today.

"I have news." Aptly timed music from her nature program accompanies my announcement. From the tone, a baby gazelle or injured wildebeest is about to be eaten alive. That's how I felt today, like the weakest member of the herd. Easy pickings for Anaïs's plastic smiles and Butch's hushed whispers.

Jade grunts.

My heart pounds once again, but I force the words out. "Mitchell is getting married."

"*What*?" She lurches with such force that a half-eaten bag of chips falls to the ground. "To who? You just broke up like a month ago. Oh my word." She presses her hand to her chest. "Was he cheating?" she whisper-hisses.

"I don't know," I say around a mouthful of floor chips. The news is still sinking in, like waves of realization from deeper and deeper depths. The shock, the betrayal, the humiliation. Emphasis on shock and humiliation. And let's not forget my foolishness.

"But that's not the news." I grab her by the front of her U of T sweatshirt. "I told Anaïs and Butch that I have a boyfriend."

Jade slowly chews a carrot stick, unperturbed by our sudden

closeness. "Jasmine Rosemary Palmer," she says sternly. "That was a lie."

"I know."

"Also, why?"

With a defeated sigh, I dive into how pride and shame, in equal parts, got me into this mess.

She passes me a new bag of ketchup chips, unsullied by floor. "It's going to be okay," she says firmly. "We're going to fix this."

We're not. We're absolutely not. There's no way I'll find a man I want to date in just a couple weeks and convince him to be my boyfriend. Oh, and also get him to lie about how long we've been together.

"I have to quit my job," I say into the bag of chips. There's chip dust on my fingers and the bag is lighter than when Jade set it in my hand, but I don't even remember eating them.

That's a lie. I can't quit my job. I can't run away from this hole I've dug for myself. If I could up and quit like that, then I'd have never walked into work on Mitchell's birthday. I would have saved myself the embarrassment. Even though there's no solution to this, it feels better just being here, telling my sister everything. With her, the incessant need for perfection doesn't drag me around by the teeth.

"*Noooooo*. We'll find someone. Let's comb through Instagram and see who's lookin' good." She shimmies on the couch, snapping her fingers to some beat in her head.

I'd rather pull out my eyelashes one by one than use social media to find a boyfriend. I only go on Instagram to periodically update my sewing account. My timeline is a singular reminder of everyone else's personal and professional success—PhDs and MBAs, entrepreneurships, first homes, renovations, even secondary properties, travel, weddings, promotions—and a stark contrast to the lack of my own.

The last vacation I went on was to Disney World before our father left our mother to start a new family with a younger woman. And the idea of purchasing a home in Toronto's astronomical market is more tragedy than comedy, even though I've been good with my money. I've stayed in this tiny Annex apartment far longer than I should. I'd planned to leave once Jade graduated and I was married, but who knows if that will ever happen.

Whether it does or not, I don't need a front row seat to all my high school friends' achievements in the meantime.

Besides, I sank all my finances into Jade's education, and I don't regret a cent of it.

The only thing that doesn't bother me about social media is the babies. I've done my best work raising Jade. Plus, who needs kids when you're attracted to men.

"No way. Then I'd be no different than those creeps who slide into women's DMs with dick pics and sugar daddy propositions. Don't you know someone you could set me up with?" Anxiety swelling, I crumple the chip bag.

She makes a sound of protest, lifting the bag gingerly from my hands and flattening it back out. "My psychology professor is very sweet."

For a moment I'm hopeful. I met one of her profs last year and he made tweed look like a truly luxury fabric.

"But he's like sixty. And married. And he tucks his shirts into his underpants so you can always see his Jockeys."

I glare. She winces.

"The Jockeys are old, too."

With a huff, I drop my head into my hands. I don't want to do all this again, the *this* of meeting someone new, learning about them, what makes them happy and what doesn't. It's exhausting figuring out a person, what they need and what I need to do to be enough for them.

"Is it still cool to say FML?" I whine.

She pats my back. "It was never cool." Her smile is bright. "But I've been thinking about the men you date."

I groan into my hands. Not this again. The men I date are never good enough for her, regardless of how charming or successful they are. That's easy for her to say when she barely dates, and when she does it's definitely not cis men.

"Just listen, okay? You give all of yourself to your partners. You give too much, and you never get anything back."

"What does this have to do with lying to my bosses about having a boyfriend?" I ask, gathering up empty snack plates and chip bags and *three* cans of pop because apparently people don't experience gut rot until their thirties.

Jade follows me to the kitchen, her socked feet sliding along the floor. "You deserve a partner who will be good to you, who's just as serious and invested as you are. Even if it's just for a date to an engagement party."

I sort trash and recyclables and stack dishes next to the already full sink. Through the window above the sink, a family of raccoons peers at me from the balcony across the alley, their eyes glowing in the dark night. The dishes need to be done, and the front hall needs to be tidied up. I'll have to check Anaïs's emails at least twice before bed and schedule reminders for her appointments tomorrow morning.

I may not be sure of what I deserve, but I know for a fact that the kind of relationship Jade envisions isn't real. It isn't real for me, and it wasn't real for our parents.

"You should sign up for this matchmaker," she says, shoving her phone in front of my face. On the screen are happy smiling couples of every age, race, and body type. Same-sex and straight-passing, they snuggle like whatever they're feeling is real and they haven't been paid for the use of their likenesses.

"They do one-on-one interviews and have an algorithm with a ninety-nine percent success rate," she says when she sees my dour expression.

Normally, the words *near perfect algorithm* would be all the argument she'd need to make. Taking the emotion out of it, the feelings, the misconceptions, and the preconceived notions, makes dating crisp, clean. Sterile. Things I love. But I'm immediately defensive at the idea of a computer telling me what to do.

I take the phone from her to navigate to the services page. When I see their pricing, I drop the sponge into the sink.

"I can't afford this," I screech.

"We have the money to spare."

"In our savings."

"Exactly," she says. "*To spare.*"

I make a mental note to create a slide deck about personal finances. I've clearly failed her on this subject. "That's not how savings work."

"Jazz, please. First of all, they're not *our* savings. They're *your* savings. You've invested so much of your time and money into me. Rent, food, *school*. And I've seen your bank balance. You definitely have the money to spare."

"You shouldn't be snooping," I say tightly.

"You deserve this," she says, ignoring my chide. "I want this for you."

Jade has always had the ability to channel a big-eyed woodland creature in times of her highest need and she employs that talent now. Terribly unfair. She knows I can barely deny her when she's *not* using these tactics.

"It's a lot of money…" I say. In our family, that amount of money is the kind our mom stole from our college funds to buy into another pyramid scheme.

But she's right. I can afford it. I'm thrifty. My budget could be a case study for the spreadsheet Olympics, but if there's one thing I learned from my father, it's that I can never be too prepared for my entire life to blow up in my face. There's no such thing as too much of a rainy-day fund. While using some of it now wouldn't hurt my bottom line, the idea of parting with it is painful.

In a perfect world, one where I have no worries about stability, security, or the future, I'd invest in a business. I'm already contributing to a retirement fund, and I have a small, medium-risk investment portfolio, but neither gives me the freedom and flexibility of a silent partnership or the enjoyment of working for myself. For a while, I thought I could make an offer for a small share of Haüs, but that was a plan for the distant future, and it was reliant on me being married to Mitchell.

And yet, an ache forms under my breastbone. I ache to be desirable, to Mitchell—or to men like him—his parents, the people I work with. To be *seen*, appreciated, loved.

I'm tired of being so easily cast aside.

Those five pairs of reflective eyes blink at me through the window and when I turn to Jade, she's somehow managed to make the same pouty, wide-eyed face of our animal neighbors.

"Fine." I sigh. She bounces on the balls of her feet, making excited squeaking sounds. "Let's sign me up for matchmaking."

Blue phone light already illuminates the little V between her eyebrows. "I've already started your application." She smiles, her tongue poking between her front teeth. She shoos me away. "Go get the credit card."

And I do.

2

———

NICK

There's nothing more depressing than a dive bar the morning after. Moonbar glowed last night, bursting at the seams with people, and laughter, and music. As daylight trickles in from King Street through the high-set windows, the graffiti wall looks more like a misdemeanor than art, and every surface looks sticky to the touch.

And that's after I cleaned up.

"Nick, seriously. Thank you so much." On the other end of the line, Bernie sounds exhausted.

I flick off the main lights and push through the Employees Only door. Then I take the stairs in the freezing stairwell two at a time.

"I'm so sorry you had to work on your night off."

"Berns." I close the door behind me and rest my head against the wood. Home sweet home; warm, cozy, never sticky. "I promise it's fine. I did last call after you left and woke up early to finish closing this morning. I hope Adam's feeling better. Let me know if you need anything."

On cue, Bernie's six-year-old son retches in the background.

"Oh shit. I gotta go." She hangs up.

I should shower. And eat. And start the booze order for next week. And finish the schedule for next month.

Instead, I fall onto my unmade bed.

I should sleep first. Sleep is critical for me, a guy no longer in his twenties. I dragged my own ass out of bed after midnight, bartended for two and a half hours, then got up at seven to avoid the inevitable *who the fuck closed last night?* text I'd get from Rocco this afternoon.

Vibrations from my butt pull me from the almost immediate sleep I've drifted into. I fumble for a minute, digging my phone out of my pocket, then answer without even lifting my head from the pillow. "Bernie, I promise everything is fine. Just worry about Adam."

"Who is Bernie?"

Life leaves me in a single slow breath at the sound of my father's voice.

"And who is Adam?"

Chest tight, I roll onto my back and blink up at the bright February sky through the angled skylight above my bed. "Dad. What's up?"

"I am fine, Nicholas. How are you?"

It's Nicholas today. That can't be good.

I clear my throat, tamping down my unease. "Tired."

"That's what a party lifestyle will do to a thirty-year-old man."

God, he is condescending as fuck. Does it come naturally to him or did he take classes in how to sound disdainful? I've always wondered.

"Excuse me," I say with all the huffiness of a twenty-one-year-old girl who thinks I don't know how to make a cosmopolitan. "I'm thirty-one and a half. And I wasn't partying. I was working."

To Dad, they might as well be the same thing. He's the kind of person who is polite to his servers, friendly with his garbage collector, and tips his cab drivers, but can't abide any of his children stooping to such work.

The horror.

"What do you need, Dad?"

"It's our fortieth wedding anniversary in a few weeks. Are you and Carrie coming?"

I throw my arm over my eyes. Instantly, I gag and drop it again. Apparently, I stink. "Carrie and I broke up."

Carrie dumped me. She said I have Peter Pan syndrome and she's honestly not wrong. Not that I'll tell my father that. The breakup wasn't a total surprise; I liked Carrie, maybe even could have loved her, but she wants to be with a guy who works a nine-to-five job. She's ready to move into a house in the suburbs with four bedrooms, three and a half baths, and a two-car garage with a man who'll take her for brunch on weekends. She deserves that. She deserves all the things she wants.

But I work nights and weekends, and I hate brunch on principle alone. I know how difficult the shift can be for service workers. And I was always too tired from working the night before to take her anyway. I'm a guy who lives above a bar in an apartment with one bathroom. I don't even know what half a bath would look like?

Dad's quiet for a long moment. Finally, he says "I'm sorry to hear that" in a tone that makes me think he's about to add something fatherlike.

Instead, he says, "Your mother will be devastated, as you know." Yeah, that's more like it. He's more interested in making a fool of me. "She really liked Carrie."

Well, Old Man, devastating my mother is my favorite pastime. "Do you want me to see if Carrie can make it? I can stay here."

"There's no reason to be snarky." He sounds legitimately surprised by my reaction, because what it really comes down to is this: my father and I don't *get* each other. "We just want you to achieve the same success as your siblings."

"To be clear, in this scenario, I'm only successful if I'm dating someone?" I feel like the child of one of Jane Austen's mother characters.

"Maintaining a long-term relationship would be the first step toward marriage and starting a family, yes."

Joke's on Mom. Being an uncle is more my jam. I can't say that to her, though. Her desire for grandkids comes from a good place. The only thing she loves more than being surrounded by her family is being surrounded by *more* of us.

"By the time he was your age, Alex was already..."

Here we go. Dad launches into an explanation of all of my perfect eldest brother's achievements starting with marriage to his high school sweetheart, Robert, then moving on to their two and half children, if you count the dog—which I do—and Alex's job working at the only truly acceptable company in my father's opinion, his own: Scott & Sons Furniture Solutions.

An airplane works its way across the sky above me as Dad moves down the list of his other successful children.

Miranda, the type A super-mom who has been able to read a lie on my face since I was old enough to deny that I'd supplied it. Not currently employed but married to a guy rich enough for her to be a stay-at-home mom.

Then Claire, a lawyer, also married with a kid. This one's hard for Dad to reconcile. On the one hand she gets points for being a working mom, on the other a mother should be home with her children.

Alex and Rob never get this kind of hypocrisy because Rob is the one who stays home with Tilly and the new baby, and he is neither a woman nor my father's child.

I've got a long day of work ahead, regardless of what my father thinks about my job or relationship status, and I've had enough of this conversation. Like a coyote, I'm willing to chew off my own foot to get out of this trap.

"Dad." I cut him off before he can list the reasons Charlie, my closest sibling in age, is a better son than I'll ever be. Spoiler alert: it's because he's the youngest and he can do whatever he wants. "I got to go, but I'll be in Muskoka for your anniversary weekend."

"Alone," he says with the contempt of a health inspector ticking off multiple health code violations.

Fuck this. "Nope."

"I thought you broke up."

"You'll just have to wait and see."

"What's her name?" His tone is skeptical, and rightfully so. I have no girlfriend or date to speak of.

"So sorry. You're breaking up. I'm going through a tunnel. I ran out of minutes," I yell into the phone.

"Nicholas, I know you're not—"

I hang up and toss my phone across the bed. Then I press the heels of my hands into my eye sockets. Anything to relieve the pressure built from another friendly conversation with Mr. James Scott.

"Shit." I do this every time. Win the battle, lose the war. Maybe Dad is right. Maybe I am a loser, because after a decade of arguments like these, one would think I'd know how to stop having them. But without fail, by the end of another round with him, I've reverted into a seventeen-year-old, begging his dad to let him apprentice as a carpenter or take a gap year or apply to culinary school. Anything but the Bachelor of Commerce from the University of Toronto he expected of me.

Now, I'm a thirty-one-and-a-half-year-old lying to his father about having a girlfriend, just to get the guy off the phone.

THE SHOWER HELPS the smell I'm giving off, and a load of laundry helps the T-shirt.

Working nights for my entire adult life has gifted me the magic power of sleeping at any time of day. After a long nap, I tackle the schedule and the beer and booze orders for next month. Before I go downstairs to start prep, I schedule social media posts for the bar and lie in bed daydreaming about what it would be like to own the place myself one day. The business is probably valued around eight hundred k. Throw in property taxes, bank loans, and insurance, and there's no way it'll happen in the next five years. Though it's a nice ten-year goal.

Maybe fifteen.

I started working here as a barback when I was nineteen, in my first semester at U of T. By summertime, Ed, the owner, promoted me to bartender and I quit school to work full-time. My dad didn't know until he tried to pay my tuition for the upcoming semester and was informed by some poor bastard in the accounts department that they had no record of my enrollment.

He didn't speak to me until Christmas and then it was only to ask me to pass the mashed potatoes. As if the silent treatment was a punishment. Dad thought he could keep me under his sphere of influence if he kept paying for my school, so I made sure I'd never need his money again.

Rocco shows up half an hour before their shift with an early dinner for us and their plans to pitch expanding the cocktail menu to Ed at tomorrow's staff meeting. Their easy company and excellent cooking ease the tension from my shoulders. I can once again pull off Nick, The Man, who's friendly, if not a little apathetic, instead of Nick, The Kid, who really needs to talk to a therapist about his daddy issues.

Despite the modicum of comfort I've found, I still don't know who to bring to my parents' anniversary party.

I sneak a peek at Rocco, who's cutting limes next to me.

"What?" they ask without breaking the rhythm of their chopping.

"I like your nail polish," I say, because Rocco needs buttering.

They pause their work, stretch out their fingers to show off the dark red, glittery paint, and smile at their hands. "The color is called Blood of Beelzebub. It's a good choice for Valentine's Day, don't you think?"

I think it sounds positively occult, but I plaster on a grin. "Yeah. It looks great."

They flip their shoulder-length hair out of their eyes so I can get the full effect of their cocked brow. "I'll ask again, Nick. What?"

"If I needed a date, would you have someone to set me up with?"

They smirk. They've got the kind of smile that draws blood, and I've been left bleeding many times. "Absolutely not."

I laugh. "Rude, but please enlighten me as to why the hell not."

Rocco points their knife at me, abandoning the limes. "I appreciate that you don't date in the industry. Some of these bar managers work their way through the college-aged servers like they're McConaughey in that movie all the straight guys love."

"Not a predator. Good to know."

"But Nick. Nicky. Nico. Do you know what would happen if I set you up with one of my friends?"

I lean against the bar, folding my arms across my chest. They mimic me. If I were a man who "took things more seriously"—thanks, Dad—I'd accuse them of insubordination.

"You'd be helping your best friend out because he really needs to find a woman he can pass off as his date before his parents' wedding anniversary?"

Turning, Rocco rolls their eyes and picks up the knife again. "Though that sounds like a hilarious story I don't actually want to get invested in," they say, going back to cutting, "that is not what would happen. No, I guarantee she'd fall for you instantly because you've got that scruffy *I'm a stray dog and just need some love* look."

I blow out an annoyed breath. Not a huge fan of the dog comparison, but I'll let it slide.

"With your flannel and your band T-shirts and your daddy issues."

I turn around, too, and scoop my limes into the container. "First of all, only I'm allowed to say I have daddy issues. Second, I thought I wanted to hear this, but it turns out, I do not. Thanks, Roc."

"Nick." They place a hand on my shoulder, their green eyes softer than I've ever seen them. "Women love you from the start and I can tell you like them, too. But you leave them hanging."

I flick a piece of lime pulp off my Man Machine Poem tour T-shirt. It's hard to be self-righteous about the band T-shirt comment when I am literally wearing one.

And Rocco's not wrong. I certainly left Carrie hanging.

A couple patrons trickle in, and Rocco heads over to take their orders while I finish up prep.

"I'm taking a smoke break," I call down the bar.

They tuck their hair behind their ear with one hand while shaking a martini shaker with the other. "You don't smoke, baby."

The bar is quiet for now, but that's the thing about King Street West on a Monday. It could be quiet for the rest of the night. Either I'll cut Rocco and maybe even close early, or thirty people will pile in here in the next half hour and we'll be slammed until last call.

Here on this block of King Street, life is always teetering on the edge of a party. The loudest place to be when a Toronto sports team is winning, the worst place to try to sleep after last call. For now, I'll take advantage of the quiet.

"Just pretend." I blow them a kiss as I pull my winter coat around my shoulders.

The alley behind the bar has one light over the door. I stick to that small halo, more for some semblance of warmth than out of a need for safety. It's cold as balls out here. I shove my phone between ear and shoulder and stick my hands in my back pockets.

"Nico." Carrie's voice is the only warm thing out here.

Sinking into the comfort of it, I lean back against the cold bricks. "Hey, Care."

Rocco thinks it's unhealthy that I talk to my ex, but we didn't break up because we weren't fond of each other. We just want different things.

"Aren't you working?" The sound of her television fades from the background. I can picture her moving through her Roncesvalles condo, the three steps it takes to get from her living room to her bedroom door.

"Taking a break. How's work?"

Carrie launches into a description of her kindergarten class's latest art project. For a few minutes, I soak in the easiness of our friendship.

"Nick?"

I blink out of the trance I've fallen into. "Yeah."

"You didn't call to hear about my kindergarteners."

Traffic is picking up on the street, the noise building with it. "I need a favor," I say, my heart suddenly in my throat. "Is there any way you could come with me to my parents' house in a couple weeks?"

She sighs.

"Just as friends…"

"As much as I'd love to see your mom again, I don't think that's a good idea." Her tone is gentle but firm.

"Yeah, no." I rough a hand down my face and swallow back my embarrassment. "I get it. It was a bad idea anyway. I already told Dad we broke up."

"What happened?" she asks.

"Don't worry about it." I open the back door and sneak a quick look down the hall to where Rocco slings drinks behind the bar. "I just ran my mouth with my dad again and screwed myself. It's fine. I'll go alone."

"It's not like you have trouble meeting people, Nick."

Two cabs duke it out with those classic urban orchestral instruments: car horns and asshole-puckering obscenities.

I jam my finger into my ear with a little more force than necessary. "Yeah, I guess."

Rocco wasn't exaggerating about the older industry folks who use their younger staff or clientele like their very own dating app. I've never pursued bar patrons, even if they were closer to me in age. Ed's first rule of working here: don't shit where you eat.

"Dating app?" she suggests.

I grunt a noncommittal response. I've downloaded and deleted plenty of apps. I can't explain it, my disinterest in meeting someone that way.

Fuck. Maybe Dad's priorities are rubbing off on me.

"My sister got engaged last week," she says.

"No shit. That's amazing. Tell her congrats."

She laughs. "She met her fiancé through a matchmaker."

"I remember." Carrie's sister, Mandy, wouldn't shut up about Core Cupid and her matchmaker, Chloe, when she joined. She went on and on about how the company created an algorithm that can predict romantic attraction with a ninety-nine percent success rate.

"Have you ever considered it?"

"Carrie, come on. I cancel my thirty-day trials on the twenty-ninth day."

"So?"

The door flies open, almost taking my nose off. Rocco breathes a harsh cloud into the cold air. "It's getting fucked up in there."

I cover the phone. "I'll be right there."

Without a response, they're gone, the door slamming shut behind them.

"So," I say into the phone. "I'm too cheap to pay for matchmaking." Not to mention I'm not the greatest at planning nights out. Most of my dates with Carrie involved her having a drink at the bar while I worked before she'd slip up to my apartment until my shift was over. Unless the women I match with are willing to sign up for Underground Karaoke or taste test Rocco's newest cocktail recipes, I can't see it working.

If Dad knew what a workaholic I'd turned into, he might actually be proud.

Music from inside vibrates through the door and the brick wall into my bones. There's a scream, and not on the street, but from somewhere inside. "Shit. I've got to go."

Already, my brain is behind the bar. I'm three orders deep with a towel over my shoulder. I love my job, especially early in the night like this, when patrons are still wide-eyed and no one is even thinking of doing bumps off the toilet seat yet. Maybe I'll fire up the karaoke. The people love spontaneous karaoke.

"*Nick*," Carrie says, her urgent tone making it obvious it's not the first time she's had to say my name. "Just think about it, okay?"

"I will, I will." I stop with my hand on the door, the cold creeping into my skin and under my layers. "Carrie." My breath billows in a silver cloud. "I'm really glad you're still friends with me."

Her voice sounds like a smile. "Me too, Nico."

⌇

WE NEVER TURN the heat on in the cramped manager's office. No one spends enough time in here to justify the cost. Over the decades, it's become a storage space for tax documents and lost and found items, as well as a closet for our winter coats. In the summer, it's sweltering back here, but now in winter, I'm surprised I can't see my breath. Despite the frigid temperature in here, I'm sweating. Bernie and Rocco don't look much better.

Ed's rattling breaths are the only sound. He's had a cough for a while now. At first, we thought he'd caught a bad bug and just couldn't shake it. Then, he started losing weight, and he stopped coming in as much as he used to. When he did, he looked more and more haggard. He'd try to hide the pain he was in, wincing through a cough or stopping a fit of laughter short with a grimace. More than once, we've caught him hiding in the back hallway, his hand splayed out on the wall to hold himself up, unable to catch his breath.

The stubborn man refused to go to the doctor until Rocco went on strike a few months ago. They even made a picket sign and marched back and forth in the snow outside of Ed's Cabbagetown row house, chanting, "What do we want? For my uncle to go to the doctor. When do we want it? Yesterday."

Ed went the next day.

He practically raised Rocco after their dad—Ed's brother—died. From the tears brimming in their eyes, I think this is the first time they're hearing Ed's news.

"So, that's about the long and the short of it," Ed says in a wheezy voice that can likely be as attributed to emotion as it can the cancer the doctor found in his lung.

Rocco squeaks and Bernie reaches for their hand, squeezing tightly. I shut my spiral notebook. My scrawled notes about reminding everyone—cough, Rocco—about closing duties and preparing for St. Patrick's Day are insignificant in the face of this news.

If Rocco is the embodiment of flight and I'm freeze, Bernie is all fight. "I'll start prepping frozen meals so you and Rocco don't have to worry about cooking during treatment. Roc will take you to your appointments and Nick will start the hiring process so we can fill the gap when Rocco can't be here."

Ed holds up his hand, and Bernie presses her lips together, like she has to physically restrain herself from more planning.

"That's very sweet of you, Berns." He sounds tired. *So* tired. Was he this tired last week? Has he been this tired for a while now and I just didn't notice? He stands slowly, obviously sore, joints making a snap, crackle, pop sound that is all the louder in this stiff, scared silence. "But I can't do both at once."

"Can't do both...of what?" Rocco asks.

Ed dips his chin and focuses on the desk calendar eternally stuck on May 16, 1999. "I have to sell."

Rocco gasps.

Bernie blinks like Ed just slapped her.

I want to fucking roar. What I've longed for, literally dreamed of, asleep and awake, is to buy this bar, to keep it here, a small piece of Toronto history, a constant on an ever-changing street. To covet all the best parts of Ed's haven and build new traditions. That one day, I'd be the Ed, giving the next generation more and more responsibility until they could practically run it themselves, letting them learn and adapt and grow with my increasingly unnecessary guidance.

I almost do roar *I'll buy Moonbar* at him. The words are a hurricane force battering at my ribs so violently they'd blow this old man over if they escaped.

Until I remember that buying Moonbar is less a realistic goal and more the answer to the job interview question, where do you see yourself in ten years?

Ed outlines the process. Hiring an appraiser, then a broker. He says that these things usually move slowly. He doesn't bother to say what we're all thinking. *Usually* doesn't take into account the many developers in this city who wouldn't turn down the opportunity to commit horrific crimes in order to build condos on our footprint.

I'd rather slather my balls in fish guts and dip them directly into the Amazon River than let that happen.

Rocco hovers around Ed, adjusting the hat on his head, gathering his things and stuffing them into his old canvas backpack, offering him the faded green army jacket that's way too thin for us to let him go outside in. "Do you want my coat, too? What about a scarf? Mittens on or off?"

Ed's mouth works but he says nothing about their meddling. Instead of responding, he turns to me, like he can hear my thoughts. "You don't know anyone who wants to buy this old dump, do you?" His laugh rattles in his chest.

Bernie and Rocco still and zero in on me, their expressions etched with hope. It's no secret, my dream, but I thought I'd have more time. I fucking hate that I can't keep it here for all of them.

"I'll do my best," I say, my voice a harsh rasp. If I have to go into debt up to my hair follicles, I will, to keep Moonbar in the family.

Ed nods, patting my shoulder in a paternal way that makes me feel like a kid, even as he has to reach up to me.

"We'll have the staff meetings in my apartment from now on," I say as he shuffles out of the office, Rocco trailing behind. "It's warmer up there. More comfortable."

He waves me away. "I don't want to fuck with the stairs. Don't worry about it, kid."

Bernie follows them, squeezing my forearm as she passes, her mouth still pressed into a grim line. When it comes down to it, I really only have two options. I could apply for a loan, though it's unlikely I'll be approved. Maybe if I was a restauranteur or corporate entity, I'd have a chance. But just me? A bartender guy with pretty good credit, an abundance of band T-shirts, and no MBA? Fat chance.

Or I could get a personal loan. Like the kind my father has doled out to almost every one of my siblings, used to build an addition to a house or to start a side business. The kind he's never offered to me for obvious reasons. Why would he lend any of his hard-earned generational wealth to the family disappointment?

I have a better shot with the bank.

From the doorway, I watch Bernie and Rocco fuss over Ed as he snoops around behind the bar, grumbling and growling at the way they hover as he goes.

For them, it's a shot I'm willing to take.

3

JASMINE

Never wear a crop top in Toronto in February. There is no event worth this skin-puckering cold. For the entire subway ride, I keep my arms wrapped around my midsection despite the calf-length wool coat I wear overtop. The silk lining brushes against my tummy, creating a strangely illicit sensation. One I'm not interested in experiencing on a first, essentially blind, date.

Core Cupid has strict rules for matches. First names only, to prevent curious Googling. Locations—submitted by matches but ultimately chosen by the maker—must be public, for safety. Highest-ranking matches made first, because that's how confident the organization is that the algorithm works. Ghosting is prohibited; if you miss a date without adequate warning you're removed from the client roster. No sex on the first date—obviously more of a strong recommendation than an enforceable rule. Clients are highly encouraged to look beyond our usual types to "the connection beneath." That's the sticking point for me. How can a computer code tell me what kind of connection I'll have with a stranger?

I take the sticky stairs down to Moonbar on the basement level of the old King Street building. The dive bar is a far cry from the fancy plant-based restaurant I suggested. In an almost comical contrast to the other women in jeans and T-shirts, I'm in winged eyeliner and poppy red lipstick that complements my red hair. Jade wanted me to wear it down, because my red hair is my "best feature," but I reminded her my hair would still be red in a bun and put it up instead. The high-waisted pleated pants are sophisticated and showcase my long legs, the top simple but sexy and a little daring, according to Jade.

Mostly, I vacillate between loving the way it shows off my ample, expensive breasts and worrying the person I'm meeting will judge me for having plastic surgery. Through my teenage years, I was teased mercilessly for my flat chest. Even my mother commented on my lack of development, reminding me constantly that she'd been a C cup by the time she started high school.

I bought every type of padded bra known to the intimates section. Tried push-up bras even though I had nothing to push up. I sprinkled flax seed on my food because I read an article touting the—limited— scientific evidence supporting the claims that flax seeds' phytoestrogens encouraged the growth of breast tissue. I even found a recipe for an at-home massage oil that claimed the combination of ingredients and massage would increase the size of my breasts by at least one cup, but it just made my skin smell like mustard.

On my eighteenth birthday, I knocked on my dad's home office door with my sales pitch already prepared. I had a binder of doctors to choose from, most of them referred by my friends' moms. I wrote a five-page thesis on why I was emotionally mature enough to have the surgery. In the end, I don't think he was convinced by any of it, he just wanted me out of his office. If I'd known that was the last birthday gift I'd ever receive from him, maybe I would have asked for something more expensive. Like his care and attention.

The bar is dark and a little dingy. Graffiti spans the wall across from the long bar top. A few tables are crammed into the space at the front of the room where thin, high windows allow in weak light from the streetlamps outside.

My date's name is Nick. But other than the bartender and a group of patrons who look at least half a decade younger than me gathered around the stage at the back of the bar, there aren't any men who appear to be here alone.

Waffling near the front door in an outfit that no longer leaves me feeling sexy and sophisticated but rather out of place, I'm garnering stares. So, I take a seat at the bar and slip a mini bottle of hand sanitizer out of my purse. There's nothing glaringly viral about this place, but I can't tell if it's just dark in here or if everything is covered in a fine layer of grime.

"What'll it be?" The bartender slides a Labatt Blue coaster in front of me and leans in like my drink order will be our little secret.

"Do you have wine?" I ask, raising my voice above the music pumping from crackling speakers overhead. My chances don't look good. There are enough beer taps to justify a barback whose only job is keg changing, but I don't see a single bottle of wine.

He looks offended that I had to ask.

I perk up. "Cab sauv? French?"

His lips twitch. I can't tell whether he wants to frown or laugh. Neither would be preferable.

"I know what I like," I say before he can make a snide remark.

"Good," he says with a nod. "Most people don't."

As he walks away, presumably to unearth a long-lost bottle of French cab sauv, I open my camera app to check my makeup. Technically, my date doesn't start for a few more minutes, but already I'm nervous; not a single person has walked through the front door since I did.

The bartender stands up from behind the bar with a green bottle in his hand. With a pop, he pulls out the cork from the pre-opened bottle and sniffs it.

Please don't let that be mine. Please don't let that be mine...

Lips turned down, he presents the bottle, his hand wrapped around the neck. "We have a merlot. I think we opened it last week?"

Maybe I should meet Nick outside and suggest another place. There are plenty of bars to choose from on King West.

The bartender watches me, his gaze slow and perusing but not uncomfortable. "Are you meeting someone?"

After a moment of weighing the safety risk of sharing my plans with a stranger, I admit, "Yes."

I feel exposed, waiting here at the whims of an unknown man some computer deemed romantically compatible. As if a computer has any clue about romance.

The bartender angles in again, the move sending a wave of dark brown hair falling over his eyes. He hasn't shaved in a few days. In his Buffalo plaid flannel, he looks like an ad for Northern Ontario tourism. The fabric is well worn. It's not threadbare, but soft, loved. The kind of textile an entire exhibition could be planned around. I'd start with the history of Scottish tartans, the pattern's origin and how it was made iconic through its adoption by the rustic fringes of society. I'd include early examples produced in Scotland, in the North American wool mills. There'd be a room on twenty-first century mass production of the pattern and its proliferation throughout design, its synonymy with masculinity and the queer community.

I blink once, then again, pulling myself back to the present. Sometimes I catch myself dreaming like this. Creating visions that unfurl like flowers, soft and almost alive, like silk held delicately between my fingers. Despite catching myself in the dream, I can never stop the inevitable swoop in my stomach that follows, the reminder that this will always only be a fantasy.

"Pull it together." Berating myself, I then bring my glass to my lips for a fortifying sip of old wine. The last thing I need tonight is to fall into a downward spiral. Actually, considering alcohol is a depressant, maybe I should spit this out.

"Excuse me?" the bartender asks, his brows arched.

I shake my head and wince as I swallow what could arguably be called a cooking wine. "I was talking to myself."

He cocks his head to the side, examining me like I'm a strange bird species. I wish Jade was here. People enjoy talking to her, and more importantly, she wants to talk to them. I'm too in my head. Too worried about my clothes and if my phone has enough battery and whether my fucking date will show up.

"Are you going to sign up for karaoke?" he asks.

I follow the bartender's gaze to the stage at the back of the room and shudder. Wherever this Nick is, I hope he didn't choose this bar for the karaoke. "God, no."

Even the idea of singing in front of strangers turns the wine in my stomach. And that wine was already pretty well turned.

In this bar, a sea of sensory overload, he is a buoy; not still, but moving with the tide. A raft I can cling to. Without saying a word, just a teasing expression that isn't as snide as I originally thought, he makes it easier for me to say more when I'd usually stay silent. Maybe bartenders have the hairdresser effect, enabling people to spill their guts to them.

"The only thing worse than singing in public is singing terribly in public." I straighten the coaster between us. "Which is what would happen if I were to sing."

"It's karaoke. You're not supposed to be *good*." He maintains eye contact as he turns the coaster on a forty-five-degree angle.

Oh my god. *Dick*.

"It's funner when you're not."

"More fun," I say, kind of under my breath but kind of not.

With a grin, he rolls up his sleeves, his forearms thick and peppered with dark hair. When he catches me looking, I glance at the door even though no one new has entered the bar.

Sighing, I pat down my hair for the hundredth time, then check my phone, though I haven't received a single notification since I arrived. Anything to distract myself from the conspicuously empty seat beside me and the thick veins that trace their way from the back of my bartender's hands to the inside of his elbows.

A woman with a halo of tight curls and light brown skin rushes through the back door and slips behind the bar. "Sorry I'm late, Nicky."

"No worries, Berns," my bartender says as he dries a pint glass.

My heart stutters. *Nicky. Nicky? Nick?*

I blink between them as she leans over the bar to take an order. He knocks twice on the wood.

"Be right back," he says before I can confirm. Is he Nick? Is this my date?

He bounds onto the stage and the volume in the bar rises to a cacophony. Under the attention of the rowdy group, he completely transforms, his smile growing, his chest following suit. The curtain on the small stage pulls back to reveal a band—with drums and various other percussion instruments, a keyboard, and a bass and electric guitar—crammed into the space. The words *Underground Karaoke* are projected onto the screen rolled down behind them.

My bartender, Nick, beams, a cheeky man-boy who suddenly looks half his age and clearly loves the attention. It's terribly obnoxious, mostly because of how charmed I am by it. I can't help but smile. Though it *is* a bit unconventional to suggest one's own workplace for a date. Especially, since…is it rude to be *working* during the date? Has he already realized that I'm his date and didn't say anything?

"It is time," he says into the mic.

The room breaks into raucous whistles and cheers.

I've walked past the bar a thousand times. It's never seemed like anything more than a dive. The kind of place that smells like vomit and lets underage girls in without checking their IDs. And it *is* dark and dirty. But it's almost like there's community here. As if these people know him. As if this is a routine they've come to expect.

A giddy laugh bubbles out of me, and I take a sip of the disgusting wine to ground myself again.

"We have a newbie to karaoke tonight." He waves at me.

Like a puppet on his string, I find myself waving back. Until the group of karaoke-ers turn to wave, too. Face flaming, I drop my arm and force a smile.

Okay, double *dick*. Maybe that's why he scheduled this date while he was clocked in, that way it would be hard for me to hide the body of this well-forearmed lumberjack cosplayer after I murdered him for inviting me to my own personal hell. Because he has to be my date, "my" Nick. He's just so…familiar.

I busy myself with my phone screen again, letting the flush fade from my face. Hopefully, he gets the point that I will not be obliged into performing.

He introduces the first performer, then the band dives into what sounds like the rock version of a Spice Girls song.

"I'll take the next song, Nick," the other bartender says as he slips behind the bar again. She glances in my direction in a way I assume is meant to be stealthy but isn't, especially when she winks.

His cheeks flush and he mutters something that sounds like "Shut it, Bernie."

Even though he sealed his fate by scheduling our date while he was on shift, watching him get flustered about it is still cute. Incredibly so.

"So, you're Nick," I say when he takes his spot across from me again. "I'm Jasmine."

I hold out my hand. Hopefully, a firm shake will convey how I'd like the rest of this date to go. Because even though he's charming and attractive, the algorithm definitely got this match wrong. It's not *just* that I have to sit here and watch him work for who knows how long; he's just not my type. I can't date a *bartender*. Our schedules would never align. Co-workers and patrons probably flirt with him constantly. The hint of a smile that seems permanently etched onto his face, while hot—hello, dimple—also makes it appear as if he's always joking. Even now, a heartbeat after a flicker of confusion passes over his face when he looks down at my proffered hand, the smile reappears. It's accompanied by a Peter Pan–like twinkle in his eyes that confirms this would never work.

Plus, with the turnover in the industry, there's basically no such thing as stability or security in bartending.

But that doesn't mean the whole date has to be a bust.

Instead of shaking, he gives my hand a gentle squeeze. "It's nice to meet you, Jasmine," he says in a voice that's almost too low, too quiet to be heard over the woman butchering Mel B's lines.

"So, listen." I lean forward and he mirrors me and whoops I didn't actually mean to bring my mouth this close to his.

Backing up a fraction, I say, "I don't want to waste your time or mine."

"Oh. Okay."

"You seem very nice but it's probably not a perfect match."

A crease forms between his brows. "Is that a requirement for you?"

"I mean, it would be ideal, yeah." Especially considering how pricey this service is. "But what are you doing next weekend? Specifically, Saturday night."

He shakes his head, the frown deepening. "I...I...don't know? Working probably?"

"Do you think you could get the night off? I know it's a big ask when all you know about me is my first name and that I'm looking for a match," I say quickly as his face morphs from confused to incredulous. "I have this engagement party I have to go to. It's kind of a long story but I need a date. I think you'd be good for that."

He's handsome and easy to talk to, the perfect person to bring to an event where I'm determined to prove that I'm not the trash my ex-boyfriend so obviously thinks I am.

"Do you have a suit?"

"I do," he says slowly. "But..."

"I can take your shift." Bernie, the other bartender, pops up over his shoulder. "In case you were asking him on a date?" she asks me. Her smile is large and mischievous, her voice almost singsong with delight.

"I guess, technically, I was."

"He looks excellent in a suit." She drops her chin on his shoulder.

Nick brushes her off like a long-suffering older brother, which only endears him, them, all of this to me even more. I know what it's like to be annoyed by while also at the whim of another.

"That's great. So, what do you think?" I ask. "Will you be my date?"

4

NICK

What the hell is going on?

One moment, we're flirting...I think...the next I'm getting turned down, despite not having even asked her out. And she did it in a strangely familiar way, as if we know each other. That's fine, she owes me nothing, but my ego didn't even have time to feel the bruise when she asked me to be her date. A platonic date, if I'm reading this correctly, where I am quite literally filling a blank space.

Also, she's looking for matches? I think we have a few matchbooks somewhere.

Behind me, Bernie's excitement is electric. The hairs on the back of my neck stand up as she practically vibrates. She will have a play-by-play of this entire interaction in the group chat the second she takes her first break. Thankfully, a patron calls for service down the bar and she has to peel herself away from my back.

The bar moves on around us—there's not much that can stop music and legal stimulants—but I'm desperate for a pause button, to rewind. So, I take the chance to step back and read this woman, read the entire interaction, more thoroughly.

The longer I stand here, the greater my confusion grows, the more her expression cracks. It's subtle but it's there, the smile plastered on her face turning more and more rigid.

"You'd like me to be your date to an engagement party?" I ask, mostly to stall for time.

She shifts on the barstool. "Yeah, I... It's kind of a long story."

"I've got time," I say, though I really don't. Underground Karaoke is our busiest non-weekend night. It's our best night. The atmosphere is fun and vibrant and diverse. Our usual patrons, the young influencer types mingling with a handful of boomer regulars who find this place too obnoxious on the weekends. The audience is always supportive, kind, and generous with their cheers and their tips. By some unspoken agreement, all these people come together once a week to sing and be silly and make Moonbar a shit ton of money. I should be with them, hosting, taking orders, and cheering.

Yet I haven't been able to look away from her since she walked in, regal and stiff with her hand sanitizer and her vintage wine order.

"It's my ex's engagement party," she says, staring at the collar of my shirt, her face turning pink. "He dumped me last month. And now he's engaged."

My stomach bottoms out at the confession. As my niece Tilly loves to say, *mess. Big, big mess.*

"And you want to, what? Make him jealous or something?"

Cuz yeah, no thanks.

"Definitely not," she says, shaking her head and waving her hands between us. "Godspeed to whoever has decided to marry that man. It's just...the way he did it. He dumped me over text message." There's real anguish in her voice. "On his birthday, when he knew that I'd made cupcakes for him and that I'd helped plan his party. He told his *mom* he was breaking up with me before he told me. We work together, by the way. His mom is my boss."

I close my eyes as I process all of this information. Her storytelling reminds me of Tilly's. It makes no sense, yet I find myself needing to know what comes next.

"That sounds very cruel," I say slowly. I want to come around this bar and hug her, not for any reason other than she looks like she needs one. But I don't actually know this woman, even if her over-sharing has made me feel like I do. She hugs herself instead, her arms covering the smooth skin of her midriff.

"Anyway, I don't want to be with him. I want…" She sighs, her shoulders slumping. "I can't believe I'm telling you this. We're practically strangers."

Practically is a generous assessment, but I let her have it.

"We dated for two years," she says, her voice shaky, "and then he dumped me in the most casual way possible. Like I was some random hookup and not a person he'd talked about honeymoon destinations with." Her eyes go glassy, but she blinks the tears away. "I just want to show him and his parents, and everyone we work with, really, that I'm more than that, I'm better. And that he didn't hurt me," she adds quietly.

"But he did."

Her green eyes shine. She shrugs. "Yeah," she says, finally. "He did."

One of our regulars, Sam, absolutely butchers the final notes of an 80s ballad, and across from me, Jasmine's expression morphs from humiliated hurt to sheer horror.

"I told you," I say. "You're not supposed to be *good*."

She blinks back to me, schooling her expression into one of neutrality. She fidgets with her glass of wine, the coaster, her sleeves. Usually, I've got good instincts about people; a quality pretty common for my trade, like how most firefighters are brave and most cops are assholes. But she's hard to get a read on, encrypted words in an open book. I can't tell if her fluster is from lingering embarrassment or being caught grimacing at Sam, but either way it makes me want to laugh. Not *at* her. She doesn't seem the type. But, fuck, she's just kind of delightful?

"If you're not supposed to be good, then what's the point?" she asks.

I turn toward the stage as the next patron starts an offbeat version of "Uptown Girl." Also, to avoid having to look her in her big green eyes, at the furrow between her eyebrows, the genuine curiosity on her face that still makes me want to laugh but also bite down hard on my knuckles. An instinctive urge I can't let her see. One I can't quite explain.

We get a lot of peculiar people at Moonbar, but she's my favorite by far. Not because she smells fucking fantastic, like a spice that reminds me of Christmas, sweet like honey, rich both in wealth and abundance, or because she's pretty.

It's because she's intriguing. Not many people can make me want to sit and talk to them for longer than I have time for, and the more she talks the more she comes undone in a way that has nothing to do with the vinegary wine or the music or the flirtatious peek of tummy.

"Yes," I say, turning back to her.

"The point is yes?" Her frown deepens.

"Yes, I'll help you out. With your ex's engagement party."

She sucks in a sharp breath, her shoulders straightening. "You will?"

"Yeah." I shrug, nonchalant. But I am chalant. I am very, very chalant.

The smile that lights her face is the first genuine one she's given me since she walked in, but even that slowly fades. "Why?"

Because you've got guts, I almost say. I don't though, because that feels like revealing too much about me and because of the innate and unknowable instinct inside me that screams she would cringe at the use of the word *guts*.

I'll save it for later.

"If I do this, then you'll owe me a favor, right?"

"What kind of favor?" she asks slowly. She leans away from me like she's finally realizing the implications of spending time alone with a strange man she met in a bar.

I can't help but laugh this time. "Not that kind of favor, you pervert," I say quietly, just to see her blush.

"That's not what I meant." Her nose scrunches in annoyance. I think she might even call me a dick under her breath.

"I know."

She doesn't hear me. She's too busy hopping off her barstool and pulling on her coat.

I give her my phone number and don't bother asking for hers because of the firm look in her eyes when she says she'll contact me "when she's ready."

She's walking away when the childish part of me, the immature teen boy that exists like the devil on the shoulder of every straight man, pipes up just so she'll turn around and look at me one more time.

"Cause it makes you happy."

She spins on her heel. "Pardon me?"

I don't actually think she means to come off quite so bitchy. But when she stands there in her expensive clothes, with her eyebrow arched and her perfect manicure already tapping away at her phone screen while she frowns at me, she embodies the archetype. She's Cruella de Vil meeting a puppy, or Miranda Priestly interrupted by an intern.

I should probably interrogate my feelings about villainous heroines from older films at some point.

"You asked what the point of doing karaoke is if you're not good at it. You should do it because it makes you happy. That's the point."

"Oh. Well, okay. Bye?"

A hold up my hand in goodbye, then throw a clean bar towel over my shoulder and turn my back to her. In the grand scheme of first dates and easy letdowns I've witnessed in this bar, that was nothing. It was nothing enough that no one even noticed.

"Oh, Nicky," Bernie singsongs.

I wince. Almost no one noticed. She keeps pouring a beer while she grins at me over her shoulder.

I'm never going to hear the end of this.

5

NICK

Bernie was right. I look fucking spectacular in a suit. But I only have one. And tonight, I don't feel spectacular at all. It's not this suit's fault. The sales associate assured me the navy blue, modern fit, single-breasted Italian wool was the kind of design that would never go out of style, which was perfect for me since I don't have a lot of reasons to wear a suit. I pull it out of my closet once a year, tops. I'm about to set a new record, though; this is my second time wearing it this week.

I forwent the tie and opted for a light-blue collared shirt tonight, instead of the white shirt and gray tie I wore to my meeting with my bank's business loans advisor on Tuesday. Like a few small changes would ensure tonight went better than that meeting did.

Still, the bad vibes cling to the wool like the lingering scent of a nut-and-lentil loaf from the vegetarian, gluten-free bakery and café run by the crunchy granola mom in my hometown.

The only thing with stronger lingering power was the collective look of disappointment Bernie and Rocco gave me when I told them my bank loan to buy the bar wasn't going to happen.

Despite my surprisingly good credit, I don't have the assets or collateral needed to be a good candidate for the loan, not with Moonbar's annual revenue, cash flow, and financials. And while the advisor assured me those factors aren't insurmountable, the loan amount is. It all comes down to location and Moonbar's is prime, skyrocketing the valuation from a mid-six figures to an easy seven.

No amount of charm or offer of free drinks is enough to make a bank write me a check with that many zeroes.

Which is fair. If we all have to opt in to this capitalist hellscape, then the least the authors of our current economic construct can do is not bury me in debt.

"Nick?" Jasmine asks from a few feet away. I offered to pick her up, treat this like the real thing, but she was cagey about giving me her address and insisted we meet "somewhere neutral," which turned out to be the benches across from the big clock in the Great Hall at Union Station. She wants to finalize the pages' worth of details she texted me this week before we head to the engagement party across the street.

"Hey." I lean in for a hug but stop myself before I can make contact. Shit. That's probably weird. She shook my hand when we met but that was probably weirder. I wave instead. Unfortunately, that's weirdest.

She inspects me, blatantly so, her mouth a squiggly line of disapproval.

"Do you have a specific grievance?" I ask, stuffing my hand in my pants' pocket. "Or has the whole package turned you off?"

The disapproval frown deepens. "You said you'd wear a suit." Her voice is higher than I remember, maybe from nerves.

I make a point of checking my clothing, plucking at the pant leg, opening the jacket to reveal the hot-pink paisley silk lining. "Oh, I'm sorry. What do you call these in your culture?"

That almost does it. She almost breaks. But at the last second, she slams down the hint of a smile making her lips wobble and rolls her eyes instead. "I just meant you're not wearing a tie."

"You didn't say I had to." I even checked and double-checked the list she sent in her fake dating information package.

Then I showed it to Rocco in the hopes of sharing a laugh about her level of organization. They glanced at it with an arched, well-groomed brow and told me she was probably too good for me.

Technically, they're not wrong.

"I didn't think I had to," she says through gritted teeth. She brushes off my dandruffless shoulders and straightens my straight collar, her fingers grazing my collarbone and the dip at the base of my throat where my shirt is open and unbuttoned.

I pull away when she reaches for my hair, my skin prickling in anticipation of her nails against my scalp.

"Can you chill, please?"

She freezes with her hand still in the air. "I am chill," she says in the least chill voice I have ever heard.

Gently grasping her wrist, I bring her hand back down to her side. Her skin is warm despite the cold she just came from. She's wrapped up so tight in the same long coat she wore to the bar that I can't see what she's wearing beneath, other than the deep emerald green pants where the coat ends at her calves.

Union Station is both loud and hushed around us. It's filled with the familiar noise of people running for commuter trains, announcements for departures, and families reuniting, echoing off the vaulted ceiling high above us. When I came to Toronto on my eighth-grade class trip, we arrived through this very station, our underpaid and overtired teachers trying to wrangle three classrooms' worth of feral preteens with the kind of energy that only comes from a three-hour train ride. Even then, as I'd looked up at the arched iron-and-glass roof, I'd known I would do anything to live in a place like this. A city whose train stations look like a place of worship rather than a transient space.

I step in closer, telling myself it's so I can hear her better and not because I want to catch that honey-rich scent again. "Jazz," I say. "Can I call you Jazz?"

She lifts her chin, imperious. "You may not."

"Yeah, you sent me a twenty-point bulleted list on what I may or may not wear tonight, so I'm going to call you whatever I want."

In heels, she's almost as tall as me. When she huffs out an exasperated breath, it blows across my lips and chin. I turn my face away, just an inch, because she suddenly feels too close.

"Smell me," I say.

"Excuse me?" She rears back, sounding horrified.

"Smell me." I open my jacket, lift my arm. "Since you're so worried about my personal care practices. You can check to make sure I've showered."

"No." She bats me away, scrunching her nose in disgust. "I believe you. You showered."

"Damn right, I showered. My hygiene is impeccable." I even got my hair cut for this.

"I'm sorry, okay," she says, sounding not very sorry at all. "I'm a little nervous."

"Wow. I never would have guessed," I retort, deadpan. "It's almost as if passing off a complete stranger as your boyfriend to make your ex-boyfriend jealous isn't such an airtight idea."

It's meant to be a joke, the kind of sarcasm I'd drop into conversation with Rocco or Bernie or my siblings. Light teasing that people who are comfortable with each other can do, but when her face falls, I remember. She's not Rocco or Bernie or my siblings and she's certainly not comfortable with me.

She presses her glossy pink lips together. "I'm not."

"Not what?"

"Trying to make my ex jealous."

"Sure. Right." I've spent much of my life pretending I don't care; being unserious even about serious situations is its own sort of therapy. But I can't be anything but serious about this, or maybe I just can't pretend. Not tonight. Not this week, with the loss of Moonbar and my trip home looming over me.

"Please don't," she says, her tone quiet, her head lowered.

"Don't what?"

"Make fun of me."

Fuck.

"Hey." Chest tightening, I squeeze her wrist between my fingers.

Regardless of how I feel right now, I made a promise to this woman. This equal part fearless and shy, strange, beautiful woman.

"I'm sorry. I think I'm just...nervous, too. Had a shitty week."

She pulls her hand from mine. "What happened?" she asks as a family of three plus grandparent runs through the Great Hall and down the ramp to the Concourse Hall to catch their train.

I hesitate, shifting in my Chelsea boots. My job has made me good at listening to other people's problems, but I'm still incapable of sharing my own.

For a long moment, she's silent, giving me time. When I don't respond, she shrugs. "We should know stuff about each other. How our weeks went. That kind of thing. Since we're supposed to be dating."

She's right. And yet, that doesn't make it any easier to share such a big personal and professional failure.

"Okay," I say, nodding toward the Front Street exit and the Royal York Hotel across the street where the engagement party is about to begin. "I'll tell you on the walk."

It's a short one, so I won't have to get into too much detail. Unfortunately, it's also colder than Kris Kringle's asshole. Jasmine's teeth are chattering before we can even cross the street; her coat is long, but she isn't wearing gloves or a hat. I pull off my gloves—an old leather pair I stole from my parents' front closet years ago and have somehow managed to hang on to all this time—and hand them to her. She takes them slowly, like she expects she'll have to trade something for them, but when I simply continue to tell her my tale of woe, she slips them on.

"Do you have any savings? Investments?" she asks, curious more than judgmental.

That doesn't stop the defensiveness in my voice. "I have some savings."

"*Some?*"

"I was thinking of starting a retirement plan...?" Not that it's any of her business.

"Most financial advisors suggest contributing to an RRSP as soon as you begin earning a full-time salary."

"You wanna see my tax returns next?"

She stops at the bottom of the steps to the hotel, shuts her eyes tight.

"Sorry," she says. She opens her mouth like she's about to say more, but shakes her head and trots up the steps instead.

"What are you going to do, then?" she asks after we finally push through the revolving doors at the front of the Royal York. I don't even take the door for an extra spin, which feels like personal growth.

I sigh. My only option for a loan—and it's a long shot—is my dad. "Hope for some help from generational wealth, I guess? Though, that's unlikely."

"How come?"

I catalog the opulent details of the lobby, the dark wood ceiling and crystal-and-gold chandeliers. I listen carefully to the muted rhythm of our steps as we cross from the marble tiled floor to the carpeted sitting area, anything to facilitate disassociation while I explain my father and his expectations of what "success" looks like. To Dad, professional success is informed, improved, by family. Both building one's own and listening to the one already in existence.

The party is hosted in an event space off the main lobby that is inexplicably still called the Imperial Room.

Classy.

In the room sponsored by white supremacy, a live band plays the kind of instrumental music best described as pleasant, in that it's the perfect volume to exchange pleasantries. The lights have a soft purple glow that reaches through the open doors to reflect into the marble foyer.

I turn back to Jasmine and find her watching me, her eyes bright and her lips turned up. While not an unwelcome sight, it is surprising.

"Have you reached a new level of nervous where you're just going to smile like that the whole time?"

She skips the step between us and flattens my lapel, then tugs on my cuffs. When she reaches for my hair, I suppress my natural instinct to needle her and let her run her fingers through it. I *do not* close my eyes. But I want to.

"That's how I'll repay you," she says, her tone bright.

Confusion clouds my thoughts. "Huh?" What were we even talking about?

"I need you to…" She steps closer, looking for eavesdroppers even though there's no one around. "Be my boyfriend," she whispers. "And you need me to be your girlfriend."

Oh. My heart rate picks up at the thought. "You'd do that for me?" Where did this girl come from?

She opens her clutch and rummages through it. Though she never actually pulls anything out of it, she smiles the whole time like she has a dirty little secret. "Of course. You're doing it for me. It's the least I can do."

"Let's wait and see how I perform before you commit to a road trip to the Muskokas with me."

She snaps her clutch closed, then pulls at the belt on her coat, revealing a crushed velvet jumpsuit, the emerald green color making her matching eyes sparkle and complementing her red hair and the pink blush in her skin.

"Just as long as you don't completely embarrass me"—she slips her coat from her shoulders and *good fucking god* there's no back on this thing; the straps tie around her neck and dangle down the soft curve of her spine—"or mention that we met through a matchmaker, I think we'll be good."

"Uh-huh." I tear my eyes from her body. Clearly, I can't listen and look at her at the same time. "What matchmaker?"

She points her finger gun at me and winks. "Exactly."

My stomach lurches. "Wait. No. What?"

She spins on her heels and heads into the ballroom. I have no choice but to follow. I reach for her, my fingertips brushing a strap gently bouncing along the base of her spine. She giggles as I make contact with her skin. Fucking giggles, sweet and soft and terribly cute.

She's on fire tonight. I wouldn't mind getting burned.

JASMINE WAS LYING. She had to be. Before we arrived, I was expecting...well, I don't know what I was expecting, but it wasn't this. After what she told me at the bar and the information she sent in her pre-date package entitled "Org Chart"—I wish I was making this up —I thought we'd be walking into a pit of vipers.

Instead, everyone is *nice*.

Her co-workers are friendly and welcoming and seem genuinely happy to see her. Even her bosses, who the Org Chart identified as "nice to your face but would not hesitate to stab you in the back," were polite. Anaïs double kissed my cheeks and Butch shook my hand like I was his own personal Shake Weight. Jasmine hasn't exactly ditched me, but I'm not really sure why I'm here. I'm basically arm candy, which is a compliment, I guess.

When a new band set up on stage and launched into a set that included danceable music, she eyed me tentatively. Then and there I told her, with much conviction, that I don't dance. Now, she and a few co-workers sway and bounce to the beat but mostly chat with each other.

"You're Nick, right?" A petite woman with light brown skin, a tentative smile, and a pink and tan turban-style hijab slides next to me against the bar. "I'm Zara."

"Yeah. Hi. Nice to meet you."

She nods toward Jasmine, making her gold hoop earrings glinting in the ballroom lights. "She told me how you met."

I pause, stomach twisting. Is this a trap? Or maybe it's a test. Was the matchmaker thing some sort of inside joke?

I stall. "Interesting."

"The matchmaker? I think that's really cool."

Okay. What the hell is going on? A nervous laugh escapes me. "Yeah. So, what matchmaker are you talking about?"

She laughs, but the sound is drowned out by a group at the other end of the bar, the center of which is Jasmine's ex, Mitchell. Around him, his bros raise shot glasses and toast him with a series of intricate gestures and call-and-response phrases fitting of his douchebag culture. I've served enough guys like him over the last decade to instantly recognize the type.

Am I being unfair to him? Probably. I don't know the guy, other than shaking his hand when he approached Jasmine and me and thanked us for coming, then introduced us—Jasmine, really—to his fiancée, Catherine.

"It's okay." Zara leans in closer, dropping her voice to almost a whisper. "She told me about it in the bathroom. And about how you guys are keeping it on the DL."

I survey Jasmine on the glossy wood dance floor, then eye Zara next to me again before scanning the space, searching for the hidden cameras. Maybe Carrie will pop out and tell me that she signed me up for Core Cupid behind my back, because with every mention of this matchmaker I have to remind myself that I did in fact say *no* when Carrie suggested I join.

"Is this a joke?" I ask.

"Why would I joke about that?" Zara asks, a line forming between her brows.

I close my eyes, shake my head to clear it. "Tell me exactly what she told you in the bathroom?"

Zara shifts her weight, avoiding eye contact and fuck, she's gonna tell Jasmine I'm a creep. "Just that she signed up for Core Cupid and that you guys were a ninety-nine percent match according to their algorithm or whatever and…" She shrugs. "Now she's going to meet your family?"

"Right," I say as a muted ringing fills my ears. "Right." I nod in her general direction, though I can no longer see Zara, or Mitchell and his bros down the bar.

Instead, I'm replaying the night we met. Jasmine, nervous and shy as she stepped into the bar, like she was waiting for someone. The way she spoke to me like I was supposed to *know* her.

"And she said *I* was her match?"

Zara blinks at me like she's worried I'm having a medical emergency. "Yes. She read me the email. *Jasmine and Nick are a match*," she says in what I suppose is her fake Jasmine voice. "She was so nervous because they don't include photos of your match, which to be honest is not something I could handle, but it worked out well. Didn't she tell you this?"

Realization washes over me in a frigid wave, like I've just stepped confidently into a slushy puddle in waterproof boots with a hidden hole.

Jasmine thinks I'm Nick.

Not this Nick. Not me Nick.

A different Nick.

A matched Nick.

She thinks an algorithm took all her complexities and nuances and broke them down into data points that fit like puzzle pieces with *my* data points. Shit. I don't know her, not really, but I know enough that I can envision exactly how she'll react.

Jasmine is going to flip the fuck out.

And so help me, I try to be a good guy. I do. I strive to be generous and kind, to tap into the well of empathy buried deep inside me without the help of psychedelics. To not be the kind of guy who would dump a woman over text message. If I'm not, then may the memory of Carrie Fisher strike me fucking dead. But in this moment, I'm not a good guy, not generous or kind and certainly not thinking about anyone but myself, because my first thought is not for her, the embarrassment she'll feel, the anger. My first thought is that if she finds out, there's no way she'll laugh this off, and there's no way she'll come with me to my parents' next weekend.

When she finds out I'm not the Nick she thought I was, I'll never see her again.

That is untenable. Not just because she won't help me, but because I fucking *like* her. I'm plagued by this unquenchable thirst to tease her, to wind her up and pull her apart piece by piece. She is charming and shy, sweet and vengeful.

She offered to help me, and she hadn't questioned whether

purchasing the bar was a good idea or suggested I give it up. She saw that my dream was out of reach and offered me a ladder.

"Well, anyways. It was nice to meet you," Zara says, though from her awkward tone and frown, she very obviously doesn't mean it.

"Yeah. Yeah. Sorry." I'm a fucking mess, but she's already gone.

The music changes again, the easily bopable tune transitioning into a slower, more romantic sound. The band has changed again. Damn. By the number of bands here alone, cost is clearly not an issue for these people. The song is about falling in love, which isn't a surprise; most songs are. What is surprising is the way their cymbals collide in my head and their bass beats from the inside out, how everything inside me shifts out of position with a few strokes of the piano keys.

Especially when I see her. On the dance floor. With him.

That douche canoe is dancing with his ex-girlfriend at his own engagement party. His fiancée stands with his parents, chatting amicably, but Jasmine's shoulders are hunched. He swings her around the dance floor with her back to me. I don't know her, have no claim to her, and even if I did, I'm not the kind of man who would stop a grown woman from doing whatever the fuck she wants.

But I've gotten really good at picking up subtle cues a lot of men can't or refuse to see. Cues that mean a woman doesn't want a man to keep fucking touching her.

I owe her a conversation. I owe her the truth. I am not the Nick she thinks I am. But I'll tell myself, her, anyone who asks, that the music made me do it. The music made me stride across this mostly empty dance floor and stop a little too close to them.

I'm not supposed to want her. But it's the music. It's rearranging what I want, shifting my needs and desires out of place with each incremental beat. It's the music's fault. It's not the soft glow of her bare shoulders or the way light glints off her fiery red hair. The music makes me do it. Not the memory of her smile, lips stained blush pink and tilted up at me.

They stop dancing mid-turn. He smiles. She doesn't.

"Mitch." I grip his shoulder. Not too tight. I'm a nice guy, after all.

And even if I did, it wasn't *me*, it was the music. "Thanks for keeping her company."

Mitchell's smile goes rigid, and he drops his hands from her lower back.

I'm going to wipe his touch off the surface of her skin.

"Jasmine." I hold out my hand to her. The music slows, stops. None of us move, Mitch and I dangled on the edge of her line. "Dance with me?"

6

JASMINE

When we first matched, I thought maybe the algorithm was a dud. Or maybe I was unmatchable. While cute and funny, Nick was nothing like I'd expected, and he was not the kind of guy I'd ever consider for myself. Forget the fact that I'd never have a compatible schedule with a bartender. The man had me meet him for our first date *at* his bar, *while* he was working. He's too unserious, too fun. Good for a good time, not a long time. I'm still not convinced about the algorithm, but out of all the people in this huge room, most of who know me better than he does—which isn't difficult since he barely knows me at all—he's the only person who bothered to save me. I don't have anything against being saved, I'm just not sure it's ever happened to me before.

Usually, I have to be my own hero.

I put my hand, still warm from Mitchell's skin, into Nick's palm.

Then, it's like Mitchell doesn't exist, never existed. Nick pulls me into him. His hand spans my shoulder blades, crushing the bow holding my jumpsuit up. He interlocks our fingers and sways as the band plays a new song with a more upbeat tempo. Nick's movements don't quicken, though. We move in a slow circle, out of time with the music. He fits his cheek against my temple, like it was meant to be there. Every breath brushes my ear, sending the piece of hair I can never keep tucked behind my ear floating. His breathing alone sends shivers down my spine.

"Nick," I whisper, hit with the urge to explain myself. How I said no when Mitchell asked me to dance. How he then raised his voice into a petulant, drunken whine. How I didn't want to be a part of whatever scene he was ready to make so I danced with him, hoping at once that no one would see us, and that anyone would. "It wasn't…"

He squeezes my hand and shakes his head. I'm choosing to read that as *whatever you're about to say, don't.*

"What are you doing?" I ask instead.

"Dancing with you." His deep tone vibrates through me, drowning out the lead singer's crooning.

We're a music-box couple.

"Not really," I say. "We're barely moving."

He sighs, like I've just made the most egregious error of my life, then he spins me. Once, twice. The room becomes a blur, of the fractals from the mirror ball, of the dark shadows cast by the band, their instruments, the other guests. He reels me back in, my back pressed to his chest, his arms crossed in front of me, still holding my hands against my hips, setting his chin on my bare shoulder.

We dance. Nick *dances.*

His hips, his shoulders, sway mine. He hums along with the singer. A fire ignites in my chest, burning low and sweet.

"You can't dance," I say, breathless. My colleagues' stares are heavy on my bare skin. Who wouldn't stare at two people moving like this, plastered together from shoulder to knee, moving in a way that makes them look far more intimately acquainted than Nick and I are. I keep my eyes on the place where our fingers intertwine against the soft velvet of my jumpsuit.

He spins me again, back around to face him, and notches me back into the place against his cheek. We slow, dancing against the music. My limbs don't fight so hard to keep the beat anymore. My muscles follow his lead, the music in his head.

"I *can* dance," he says, his voice low. "I just *don't.*"

I lower my chin, surveying the space between us. The shine of his shoes catches a glint of light as he leads me through another gentle turn. Pressed this close to the open collar of his button-down, I'm enveloped in the scent of the cologne I asked him to use. Suddenly, I regret not doing it earlier when he demanded I smell him.

"I hate to tell you this." I press my nose to his throat.

Nick doesn't flinch but he does make a sound, so low I can't hear it but can feel it rumble through his throat.

"You're dancing."

The drummer hits his cymbals *again again again* on the outro. Nick's hand is a kite line, the only thing keeping me from floating into the bunting draped above us.

"Like I said, I *can* dance. I just don't." He pulls back and studies me. His brown eyes hold none of the sarcasm or snark that feels natural to him.

"So, why are you dancing with me?"

He slips one hand up my bare arm, leaving heat in its wake like the burn of bourbon. Cupping the side of my neck, he brushes his thumb along my jawline. He presses at the corner of my lips. He'll smudge my lipstick.

I lean into his hand.

He shrugs. "Just seemed right."

We're standing in the middle of the dance floor, unmoving. "Is everyone looking at us?"

"If they were, would that bother you?"

Yes. Usually. Not right now. "Maybe we should..." I lick my lips, my mouth suddenly dry. "Maybe they think we're fighting." A silly, stupid lie.

Nick knows it. His thumb brushes my lower lip.

My words are breathy. "We should look more like a happy couple."

He nods. The lead singer's voice lingers on a haunting final note.

"I want to kiss you."

"Okay," I say, my voice strangled.

He pulls me closer, his arm around my waist. He keeps his eyes open, only letting them fall closed as his lips, fruity and spicy with the taste of red wine, meet mine. I can't look away from the fan of his lashes against the delicate skin below his eyes or the diamonds reflected onto his features from the glittering lights.

He opens my mouth with his, grips me everywhere, his palm against my upper back, my shoulders, his other hand pressed flat to my collar bone.

I explore the width of his shoulders, the expanse of his back, the soft hair at his nape that curls around my fingers like it wants to keep me there. He smiles against me, following the curve of my mouth.

An ache blooms in my chest. Each time his lips brush mine, the ache grows deeper, until it's pulsing inside me. Already my muscles remember where he touched me. My body knows what's next even if my head is fully aware that we're standing in the middle of a dance floor, surrounded by my co-workers.

We could get a room upstairs. He'd hold my hand in the elevator. At the click of the hotel room door closing behind us, he'd pull at the tie on my jumpsuit and let the top come loose, peel the garment down my legs. He'd press his mouth between my thighs. Slide his fingers up the inside of my leg. He'd find me wet, and he'd make me come like that, with the gentle touch of his hand, the soft suck of his lips.

This wasn't part of the deal. Suddenly, though, I can't remember why. Maybe our plans could change, just for tonight, for right now. It won't mean anything if I press him down on the bed. If his stubble leaves marks across my thighs and chest. We can go back to the plan tomorrow, after he rolls me over and slides into me, just this one time, tonight.

"Jasmine," he says against my lips.

I can't stop exploring, the heat at the base of his spine, the place where his jaw meets his earlobe.

"Jasmine." He breathes my name. I could live like this, off these little gasps of air.

He pulls away, grimacing, like it hurts him to stop. My hands are fisted in the lapels of his blue suit jacket, my hair looser in its pins, my lips likely bare of any color I added before I left my apartment.

The music has stopped. The room is brighter and suddenly cold. I close my eyes, if only to avoid the bewilderment on his face.

He kisses my forehead, eliciting a shiver.

This is not the plan. This is not how I stop the stares and the whispers.

"Nick?"

He nods against me.

"I think I'm going to go home," I say. "Alone."

7

———

JASMINE

"**D**arling." Jade pats my head. "You seem distraught."

"I am not—" I huff, my biceps burning, my hands aching. "Distraught."

Finally, the food she let stick, calcify, and fossilize onto the stockpot detaches from the stainless steel.

"Honey, you've really got to remember to let these soak," I say gently but not for the first time. Holy fuck, do I hate doing dishes.

I fill the pot with an abundance of dish soap and warm water; a late soak is better than never soaking at all.

Jade hums a ponderous sound that means something along the lines of *yes, yes, shut up so I can talk about what I want now*. "You don't usually get *this* distraught about dirty dishes."

I throw the sponge into the sink where it lands with a wet splat. "I told you I am not distraught."

Jade laughs, loud and artificial. "You're such a joker, Jazz."

I flush. Stupid Nick ruining that stupid nickname. *Gah!* Even the word *nick*name is ruined.

"What happened at the engagement party?" she asks for the thousandth time since Saturday.

"Nothing." The word is anything but believable, yet I stand by it.

"Sounds like something a distraught person would say," she singsongs, following me from the kitchen to the living room. Jade has always been my shadow. Mom called her my little duckling because of the way she'd waddle around behind me as a toddler.

For the first time maybe ever, I wish she would just go away.

"It was fine. I swear." I ignore the pang in my chest and begin the never-ending task of cleaning up my little sister's mess. First, her LEGOs—her newest hyperfixation—go in their bin. Then I collect her dishes from the coffee table and check the couch cushions for garbage, phones, keys, bank cards, money, jewelry, trinkets, and treasures. She went through a rock collecting phase that I only found out about after I pulled a handful of unwashed rocks from the couch that she insisted were opals.

They were not.

"Mitchell asked me to dance. He was pretty drunk so that was kind of weird. But fine."

"And this Nick boy was respectful, was he?" she asks in her old granny voice. She pulls the collection of throws she made a nest with earlier from my hands and wads them up one by one.

Even though I'll have to refold them later, I let her do her part. It's not her fault I'm a control freak. I really should stop doing this kind of stuff for her. She's an adult, even if she still seems like that little duckling at times.

"Nick was respectful." Nick was fine. Jasmine was *not*.

His eyes had gone wide and his lips had parted in bafflement when I told him I was leaving, but he was a perfect gentleman. He walked me to the porte cochere and called me a car. Later, he texted me to tell me he'd gotten home okay, asking if I had, too.

I sent him a thumbs up for the trouble.

All of those reasons I thought we weren't compatible seem so flimsy now. Because he's a bartender? Because he scheduled our date at his work? I never even gave him a chance to explain. I'm a snob. I'm exactly like the people at work that I complain about.

To make matters worse, I threw myself at him, then promptly left.

The poor man probably has whiplash; meanwhile, I can't stop thinking about him, the way he kisses.

"So, matchmaking was a success?" Jade asks.

I blink myself out of the dissociative episode I've fallen into, a state where my mind is filled with nothing but horny thoughts about Nick. Again. "Yeah. Yeah, I guess it was."

Maybe the algorithm was right? Maybe I needed to stop being such a fucking control freak and let someone else take the lead for once. Clearly, we're far more compatible than I thought possible. But at this point, he probably wants nothing to do with me.

"Are you going to be okay if I leave?" she asks, true concern wrinkling her brow.

Frowning, I assess her. "Where are you going?"

"To the movies."

Unbidden, worry seeps over me. Like it always does where my sister is concerned. "With whom?"

"My friends," she says, like *duh*. "Is that okay with you?"

"Yes, sorry..." I wave her away and swallow back my trepidation. "Just make sure you—"

"Text. Yes, I will. I *know*," she says in a firm tone, reminding me that she is an adult woman working toward her degree.

I fuss over her as she leaves. Does she have a warm enough coat? Maybe she should take a different hat. Does she want her own snacks? The movie theater overcharges for popcorn.

She lets me, even though it annoys her. It makes me feel better knowing that I can dote on her now. After Dad checked out when she was little and Mom gave up parenting her once she turned eleven, it's become imperative for me to make up for them. It's illogical, yes, but impossible to suppress.

I close the door behind her and sag against it in relief. A heartbeat later, my nerves are frayed again by the sound of my phone chiming from the kitchen. I rush for it so fast my downstairs neighbors will probably complain.

Nick Scott: still good to drop by tonight?

He texted last night. I'd spent the whole day fielding questions and comments from co-workers about Nick and how we'd met and what he does and where he grew up. The plan worked; everyone was so focused on Nick they all but forgot that Mitchell and I broke up just a month ago. But I can't even celebrate our success. I feel too terrible about lying. To them, to him. To myself, too.

> Me: Yes. See you soon.

He said he wanted to *talk about something important*. The word *important* had arrived separately. That alone emphasized its significance, making it seem more than just important. Scary important. My fake boyfriend is breaking up with me important. At least I'm not getting dumped over text message this time.

With all that in mind, I asked him to come here. It's easier to perform my righteous indignation in my own home.

I'm pacing by 7:07 p.m. He said he'd be here between 7:00 and 7:30, so he isn't late. But if I were the one who'd said I'd be somewhere within a half-hour time span, I'd be waiting outside their house five minutes before the clock even started.

But as Jade often tells me, that sounds like a you problem.

So, I pace for my own anxious energy rather than out of impatience or resentment.

I should journal about this. I believe this is called growth.

There's a knock on the door. I freeze, my heart picking up its pace. It's probably Enzo, the downstairs neighbor who hates when we make noise but has no problem verbally abusing his girlfriend for all of us to hear. He's probably here to threaten a noise complaint because I step too loudly.

"Listen," I say before the door is even fully open. "I have a guest coming and—"

"Hey, Jazz."

My mouth slams shut.

Nick leans against the doorframe, his hair messy like he's had his hands in it, a canvas tote bag slung over his shoulder. And the man is wearing round, wire-rimmed glasses.

"How did you get in?" I ask. "Since when do you wear glasses?"

"A beefy white guy with a really thick neck." He juts out his jaw, imitating Enzo's familiar underbite. "And since I had trouble seeing the blackboard in seventh grade." He straightens, his large frame crowding the doorway. "Can I come in?"

"Sorry. Right." Mind still reeling, I step aside and survey him as he toes off his boots and hangs his coat up on one of the hooks. "Enzo shouldn't have let you in. We're supposed to open the door for our own guests only."

One side of his mouth ticks up. "I'm pretty sure you're the only person who follows those rules."

Well, that's unsafe.

"Here." Nick hands the tote bag to me. It's printed with a floral graphic and the words *Be a slut do whatever you want*, so I absolutely do not take it.

"Am I the slut?"

"Huh? Oh." The grin that's always tugging his lips grows wider. "I got it at a market last Pride. The bag is mine. The wine is for you."

"Oh. Thank you." He doesn't strike me as a hostess gift–bringing type of person, but I appreciate the gesture.

"It's your fave," he says.

Frowning, I assess him, working to decode his meaning.

He laughs at my confusion. "Cab sauv. French. Ordered a couple cases straight from the winery."

"That's...surprisingly thoughtful," I say, managing to make my gratitude sound particularly ungrateful.

He sighs, and I take the bottle to the kitchen to avoid any further foot in mouth situations.

"Do you want to open it now?" I don't usually drink wine on a work night.

Nick follows me down the hall. I try not to look over my shoulder. He's not calculating my net worth based on the thrifted and IKEA furniture or the water damage on the ceiling the landlord ignores.

Normal people don't do that. *Nice* people don't do that. Just the guys I've dated in the past.

Perhaps that's even more of a reason to trust this process. Clearly, an algorithm can pick a better man than I ever could.

"Only if you feel like it," he says, sliding into the seat of our teeny two-person dining table in the kitchen corner. "But don't open it on my account. It's probably too fancy for my palate."

That might be a dig at me but I'm choosing to ignore it. "I usually like to have warm water with lemon slices in the evening." Why I say that is beyond me. It feels strangely vulnerable and intimate, telling him what I like to drink as I wind down.

"Sure."

He plucks a lemon from our overflowing fruit bowl and joins me at the counter as I fill the kettle with water. He cuts large wedges and I drop them into mugs. We wait for the water to boil in a silence that stretches louder as each second ticks away. The longer we wait, the more crowded my head gets, filling with one potential comment after another. All things he could say about my behavior, which has ranged from weird to rude for no reason.

"I'd still really like to come to Muskoka with you," I blurt as the switch on the kettle pops.

He props himself up against the counter and crosses his arms. "Still?"

I blow on the hot water and drop my attention to the stained Formica countertop. "I think I've been unfair to you. I'm sorry. I want to make it up to you."

"Jasmine," he says, his tone so serious I can't help but turn to him. His dark eyes are sincere. "It's very nice of you to say that, but you have nothing to make up for."

"No. I do. You helped me when you didn't even know me, and I know how I come across."

"I'm sure I have no idea what you're talking about." He picks up a mug and gulps the hot liquid. He winces, like he ate an entire lemon wedge. "I don't know what I was expecting. Lemon water really is just *lemon water.*"

I take my own sip. It tastes fine to me. "I was being a snob, Nick."

He chokes, laughs, coughs up lemon water. I pat his back, but he waves me away.

He replaces his mug with my hands, turning to face me fully. "I promise I have never thought that about you."

"It's fine. I was. I am."

"You're not."

"Whatever, I don't want to argue with you about it. I feel like I was being snobby. And also sending a lot of mixed signals after..." My face heats. The thought of that kiss still makes me disproportionately aroused. "What are they like? Your family?" I ask, because if discussing his family can't calm my overactive libido, nothing will.

He leans against the kitchen counter with the same ease as when we met, comfortable, assured. I imagine Nick is comfortable just about anywhere.

"As you know, my dad is... We have trouble communicating." He puts his words in air quotes. "Mom did the whole stay-at-home thing." From there, he ticks his siblings off his fingers. "My brother Alex is my father's golden child. He works for my dad's company, and he'll try to sell you office furniture within five minutes of meeting you. Miranda is my eldest sister, she's like a second mother to me. We used to be really close but..." He gives a defeated shrug. "Claire is cool. Way too competitive, but she likes to argue with my dad so she's a good ally. I'm two years younger than her. And then there's Charlie. He's the baby."

I smile. "Say no more."

"You have one, too?"

"My little sister. Raised her myself," I say proudly.

"Charlie works for my dad, too," he says with the kind of fatigue that makes me think there have been a lot of conversations about the family business in his past.

"And you don't."

He takes another sip of his lemon water, this time fighting back a wince. "I do not."

I want to ask why he and Miranda aren't close anymore and how much Charlie gets away with and why it's so important that his siblings—maybe just the boys?—work for the family business. But those questions seem too probing, especially when I haven't shared very much about myself.

"My dad thinks I'm a disappointment," I say, then clamp my mouth shut. That was stupid.

"Okay," he says slowly, cupping his mug with both hands.

"Sorry, I don't mean to imply you're a disappointment, too." *Shut up, you loser.* "He left when I was in my first year of university and he cut off contact with us soon after." He preferred his other family to ours, but that's too much to share. "But not before he told Jade that I was pathetic for dropping out of school."

He whistles his shock.

"Ironic, since I only dropped out because our mom couldn't deal after he left." My tone is flippant, but if I let myself feel even an ounce of the pain he inflicted on us, then my voice will break. "And Jade needed stability. I got a job, and she moved in with me and..."

And that was that.

"You did a good thing," he says.

I shrug. I did what had to be done, but his words ignite an ember of pride deep inside me, an affirmation I didn't know I needed until I heard it.

"Is there anything else you need me to know about your family before we leave?" I ask.

"There is." He stops there, finishing the dregs of his lemon water and hooking his finger into the handle of my empty mug. "Well, technically it's not about my family."

He turns toward the sink, where the stockpot still sits filled with soapy water.

"I can do that," I say in a rush.

"It's fine." He waves me away. "Washing dishes is sort of my specialty."

He means it as a joke. I'm pretty sure most of the things that come out of his mouth are meant to be jokes. But my next move is more a compulsion than a choice. I don't let other people do dishes for me. I do the dishes for me and for them. Even if I really fucking hate dishes.

Besides, shouldn't he get a break from dishes if washing dishes is part of his job description?

"No." I put my hands over his, where he's lifting the soapy stockpot filled with cold, stagnant sink water and the crusty detritus left over. "I got it." I pull the pot toward me.

He resists me. "I said, it's fine." His voice is strung just the slightest bit tighter.

I pull harder. Because excuse me, this is *my* stockpot, and my dishes, and maybe I let him save me at the party, but I don't need saving in this. I don't let other people take care of me; I take care of them.

"Nick," I say through gritted teeth.

The water sloshes in the pot.

"Jasmine," he replies with a stubbornness I haven't seen from him before. His jaw is clenched hard like mine, and he's wearing that stupid fucking smirk. The same smirk I've wanted to wipe off his face numerous times since we met. Now, though, I don't want to get rid of it with a slap. Now, I have the distinct urge to kiss it off his face, to smother it against my throat.

The way the curl of his lips tints the sound of my name alone is enough to make me dizzy. If he asks, I'll tell him it was that unsteady, faint feeling that makes me do what I do next. Because I don't just let go of the stockpot. I shove it back at him, with the kind of impulsivity I haven't felt since before my prefrontal cortex was developed.

Nick stumbles back, his hip slamming into the counter and the water in the stockpot rising in a bubbly, orange-tinged wave. I shut my eyes before I have to witness the rest of the carnage.

Nick screams, not like a horror film's final girl, but certainly an octave higher than I thought he was capable of. His torso is soaked with a combination of water, soap, and...other stuff that looks like it was once spaghetti sauce. Or maybe chili?

"My Chumbawamba T-shirt," he says, his eyes bulging and his neck straining.

"Your what?" I whisper, bringing a hand to my chest.

He points at his graphic tee. "It's '*Tubthumping*,'" he says with barely contained outrage. Though with easygoing Nick, I suppose it's more like a tame amount of outrage.

"I don't know what that means," I cry.

He holds the fabric away from his body. The gray T-shirt is worn so thin that with the water, it's starting to have a wet T-shirt effect. The image on the front of the shirt, a flexed bicep with a boxing glove encircled by the words *TUBTHUMPING* and *CHUMBAWAMBA*, is absolutely soaked. There's a dark stain in the most embarrassing spot possible on the front of his jeans.

"It's vintage."

"I can fix this," I say with a confidence I actually feel for once. If there's one thing I know, it's fabric. This time when I grasp the pot, he gives it up without a fight. I drop it into the sink with a clatter. Dirty water soaks into my socks as I yank on the hem of his shirt and lift.

"What are you doing?" He grasps my wrists and pushes them down, bringing his shirt with them, and we're stuck in another strange tug-of-war.

"I'm washing your shirt." I cringe. Now that the water is no longer stagnant, it's a bit stinky. "And you should probably let me wash the pants, too."

"You can't," he says with a sharp intake of breath, his cheeks pink, his eyes a little wild.

"Why"—I try to lift his shirt again, but he keeps his arms pinned to his sides—"not?"

"Because you'll see my...my..." He drops his focus to where I'm still gripping the wet fabric. "Belly," he says, defeated. Finally, his shoulders droop. He gives in and lets me pull it over his head.

"I'll just..." I hold the crumpled fabric in the air and turn away, hiding my smile. There are a lot of features in this crummy, old apartment I hate, but the in-unit washer and dryer in the small "mudroom" off the kitchen that leads to the fire escape isn't one of them. "Give me your pants," I say over my shoulder.

"They're fine," he says, but there's no fight in his tone this time.

The room goes quiet, the only sound the shuffle of denim, and then the denim lands in a heap on the floor next to my feet.

I spray the shirt and the jeans with a stain remover I made using dish detergent, hydrogen peroxide, and baking soda. It's gentler on fabric, especially the flimsy stuff fast fashion uses, than the store-bought stuff.

"Normally, I'd let this soak a while." The explanation is unnecessary, but he's behind me, in my kitchen, with barely any clothes on, and I'm putting off turning around.

Eventually, I don't have a choice. He stands in the middle of the kitchen, his hands gathered in front of him, covering up any suggestion of the body parts beneath the thin black fabric of his boxer briefs.

"You don't happen to have a T-shirt I can borrow? Maybe some sweats?"

Every version of Nick I've met so far has been self-assured; even at the engagement party, surrounded by people he didn't know, performing a role, his energy and poise invited everyone to take him or leave him without much concern for their choice. But Nick is so clearly out of his element now, and I don't want that for him. He's lean but not muscular. His body hair is dark, thicker on his chest than his stomach...or rather his belly. His nipples are pebbled and pinker than I expected.

I read in a fashion magazine that the lip color most flattering to a person's skin tone should be a color match to their nipples. In practice, the lipstick I found didn't wow me.

His, though, would make his mouth look kissable; more kissable than it already is.

I'd love to wear his nipples on my mouth.

"What are you staring at?" he asks. He glances at his chest because despite his question, it's very obvious where I'm looking.

I'm not sure what possesses me, maybe the tendency to please men I can't shake. The need rooted, according to Jade and her first-year psych textbook, in deep-seated abandonment issues.

The floor creaks beneath my feet as I approach him. I hold out my hand, my palm flat, and he stills. When he doesn't back away, I place it gently on the soft curve of his belly. He hisses, trembling beneath my hand.

"Cold," he says, though he still doesn't move away.

The washing machine hums and clicks its way through the quick wash cycle, a soundtrack to the moment.

His skin is warm, soft. This close, I can see a collection of freckles at his hip, a dark tuft of armpit hair.

"I like your belly."

He frowns, puts his hand over mine, but doesn't remove it.

Dipping my chin, I clear my throat. "I know I was...weird...after the engagement party."

He shakes his head, clasps my shoulder with his other hand, locking us in an awkward sort of waltz. "You were fine. You were perfect. I should have—"

"I haven't stopped thinking about it." The words are pulled from me, except I don't know who did the pulling.

He falters, his response fizzling out like a sparkler on the Victoria Day long weekend. "I... You? Honestly, me neither."

"No one has ever kissed me like that before."

I close the space between us and press my mouth to his. In comparison, this kiss is flat, almost clinical. An experiment to see whether the last time was as incredible as I remember. Or maybe it's a restraint, because if we kiss this way, it won't get out of control, like the last one had the potential for.

"Kissed you like how?" he whispers against my flesh, his warm breath sending a bolt of need down my spine.

"Like kissing was the point." I brush my lips against the corner of his mouth, shivering at the sensation of lip balm softness against rough stubble. "No one's ever kissed me like I should enjoy it."

He clutches my hand tighter against his stomach, our fingers intertwined. The position is a little awkward, but I couldn't imagine letting go right now. His grip on my shoulder tightens too.

"Jesus." His voice is harsh, almost angry; whether it's at me or the people who've kissed me before, I can't tell. "How the fuck were they kissing you then?"

His eyes are closed. A deep line mars the skin between his brows. He licks his lower lip, and his chest expands in bigger and bigger breaths. Without his hands as a guard between us, he's hard against my hip, straining against the fabric of his underwear. If I looked down right now, would the tip be wet? Leaking through cotton-Lycra blend?

"Like it's a box to be checked? A means to an end."

He opens his eyes, his dark irises swimming with outrage, and walks me back until my lower back hits the kitchen counter. "Absolutely the fuck not."

Nick kisses me. This time it's nothing like the experimental contact I tried before. He cups my jaw, and with his thumb, he tugs gently at my chin to open my mouth. He kisses me bodily, his arms and hands holding, his legs bracketing mine, his hips a gentle force against mine.

"You know this," he says between breaths, "is what you deserve, right?"

I try to nod but am stopped by a hand at my jaw, his teeth as he mouths at the side of my throat.

"I know." I gasp.

"You ask for this from now on." He kisses me like a command. "You demand only the kisses you want, okay?"

"I will." I feel chastened for not demanding better in the past, even though I didn't know I could or even what it was I should ask for.

Nick lowers his hands. The click of the washing machine, the signal that the cycle is done, the load ready to be flipped, cracks like a gunshot through the house. He's barely moved away and though he's the one without any clothes, a chill creeps over me like he's left me alone and exposed in the middle of a blizzard. I loop my arms around his neck and pull him close. I nuzzle my face into the space between his neck and shoulder. He lets me. He doesn't resist. But rather than touch me in return, he grips the counter on either side of my hips.

"Do it now," he says, softer. "Demand what you want."

My instinct is to defer to him, to take my best guess at what he wants me to say. In the past, that would have been what I wanted: to please him. But with Nick, it's clear that molding and shaping myself to make him happy wouldn't make him happy at all. The only way to make him happy is to put my happiness first. Which is actually kind of confusing.

"Jasmine," he whispers, like he can feel me thinking too hard about it. "Please."

"I want..." I say, unsure of what to ask for.

He kisses me again, soft, like a reward, and I'm overwhelmed by the sudden, concrete knowledge of what I want.

I open my eyes. "I want you to kiss my pussy the way you kiss my mouth."

8

NICK

I don't know how I got here. I came to tell her that I think she made a mistake, that I am not the Nick she thought I was. Instead, I'm on my knees in her kitchen, pulse thrumming, dragging her black athleisure pants down her legs.

It wasn't supposed to happen like this, but I can't stop. Not now. Not when she told me what she wanted. She said pussy for fuck's sakes. French cab sauv drinking, hand sanitized, bullet listed wardrobe requirements Jasmine said the word pussy and told me to eat hers.

Her underwear is black, cotton, a little faded. A few short, dark hairs are visible against the fair skin of her upper thigh. I don't know how I got here. I shouldn't be here. But look at her. God, look at her.

The heat she ignited in me when her lips touched mine is burning hot now. I rub my thumb along the hairs at her panty line, relishing the prickle against the pad of my thumb.

That's all it takes for the horny haze she's floating in to burn off. With a gasp, she clamps her legs together, and her body goes stiff. Jasmine strikes me as the kind of woman who keeps a regular bikini or Brazilian waxing appointment, and apparently I must strike her—wrongfully—as the kind of man who fucking cares about body hair.

I should put a stop to this. I *need* to, but if I do, then there's a good chance that she'll assume my reluctance has something to do with her body.

With my hands splayed on her thighs, I hold her gaze and lean in, pressing my nose, my mouth, against her body. I don't close my eyes until I'm enveloped by her, her scent, her warmth. I take a deep breath, just to make a point.

"Sorry," she says, a little breathless. "I didn't think we'd be..."

"I like it." Though I'm unsure of whether she's apologizing for the not-traditionally sexy lingerie, the pubic hair, or something else entirely. "And please don't ever apologize for letting me anywhere close to your pussy."

Her legs relax beneath my hands, and she lets me spread her apart, even though I shouldn't.

"Hold on to the counter," I tell her, my body clearly unwilling to listen to my brain's warnings.

"Okay," she says, her fingernails disappearing underneath the lip of the laminate.

I angle in, eyes closed again. I should not be fucking doing this.

Like she can read minds, she closes her legs once more. "Do you need a cushion?"

I growl, pulling her legs apart. "No."

"But the floor is hard."

"So am I, Jasmine." I grip my dick in my Jockeys for emphasis. "I'm on the hard ground and I'm still hard for you."

I squeeze myself enough to hurt, because it feels good in that weird way that painful things sometimes do and because I'm mad. I'm fucking livid at the men she's been with. The men who have clearly made her feel like she has to apologize for these things. Even if they didn't explicitly make her feel that way, they still, clearly, never cared enough to consider her pleasure.

I'm mad at myself for letting it get this far.

I breathe deep again, to collect myself, to get my anger under control. Because it's not her I'm mad at. None of this is her fault.

When I open my mouth next, I'm still not sure what I'll say, if I'll ask her to give me more or if I'll finally be the man I hope I am.

"Do you want this?" I ask.

Fuck.

She bites her lip, plump and pink. Her eyes are blasted, black eating up all the color. Her hair falls in long tendrils around her temples and in front of her ears. She looks messy and messed up and fucking beautiful.

My heart stumbles at the sight. Fuck. How did I get here?

"Do you remember," she asks, "what our compatibility percentage was?"

I blink slowly. Like I'm drunk. Maybe high. When I'm this close to her, so close I can almost taste her, there's absolutely no way I can process her words and make responsible choices.

"Remind me," I say, my mouth dry.

"99.338%," she says with a little thrill in her words. Like she's proud of the percentage.

Of course she would be. She would think that getting an A+ in compatibility is something that is both achievable and normal to want.

She runs her hands through my hair, not pulling but not gentle either. I close my eyes and let my head fall wherever she wants, lean into her as she scrapes her French tips along my scalp.

"I didn't trust this process before," she admits, her voice a whisper. "I didn't think there was any way some computer code could find the One for me, but I'm willing to admit when I'm wrong."

My heart hits my ribs like a hammer. The words *stop* and *never fucking stop* are fighting a war in my head.

She grips my hair tighter and tips my head back. "I want you to eat my pussy, Nick."

It's my name that sends the blood in my body back to my brain and away from my dick. I can't do this with her. Not when there's some other Nick out there. Not when she thinks I'm him.

Maybe he ghosted her that night. Maybe he's fucking dead. It doesn't matter what the reason. If I do this with any kind of secret between us, I'll never see her again. We just met, yeah, but I've learned enough about her to know that.

I sit back on my heels. The lust and anticipation on her face fade slowly to confusion.

"I can't do this," I force out around the lump that's lodged itself in my throat.

She opens her mouth. Closes it. The flush in her cheeks transforms, pink to tomato red. Fuck fuck fuck.

"I'm sorry, Jasmine. I—"

"Well, well, well." The voice behind me is high-pitched and smug.

Above me, Jasmine's face drains of all color.

I peer over my shoulder and find a tiny young woman.

It's obvious she's Jasmine's sister, both in appearance and in the shit-eating *I'm never going to let you live this down* grin on her face that can only be produced by a person who has caught their sibling with their literal pants down.

"Looks like pussy is back on the menu, boys," the little sister says with a forced growl.

"Is that supposed to be Lord of the Rings?" I ask. Despite the awkward moment, I can't help but chuckle.

She points a finger gun my way. "*The Two Towers.*"

I nod my approval. "Nice."

She steps into the kitchen, her hand lifted for a high five.

"*Stop.*" Jasmine uses a tone that is pure older sister and sends a shiver down my spine.

"Jade, *get out,*" she screeches. She turns her wrath on me next. "And *you.*" She pokes my chest. "Get your clothes and *go.*" Then, despite having exiled both of us from this kitchen, Jasmine pulls up her pants and runs from the room. A few moments later, a door slams.

I wince. "I'm Nick." Now that I'm not about to have a mouthful of pussy, this floor is actually really uncomfortable. I stand, grab the tea towel folded neatly over the oven door handle, and hold it in front of the engorged parts.

"Jade." She waves. "Where are your clothes?" she asks, clearly unconcerned about finding a nearly naked man in her kitchen.

"In the wash."

"Ahhh." She crosses the kitchen, giving me a wide berth, which makes me feel better about her survival instincts. "I'll flip those for you and then..." She turns in the laundry room doorway. "I think you better make like a fucking tree, dude."

Fuckkkkkkkk.

BY THE TIME I get home, my clothes are stiff and chafing. They were practically sopping when I yanked them from the dryer. I considered going to find Jasmine, to apologize, to explain, but when Jade saw me waffling at the door, she shook her head.

"She's probably too embarrassed to be capable of speech right now. Give her some time."

It felt wrong, but I did.

I slip through the back door, successfully fighting the urge to check in on the bar; it sounds like things are quiet, even for a weeknight. After peeling the wet clothes off, I drop them in a pile on the bathroom floor. Though I have a washer and dryer here in the apartment, I forgo laundry for now and immediately get in the shower. I don't bother waiting for the water to warm up. It's already warmer than my core body temperature. The one benefit of waiting for public transportation in wet clothes is that it completely and totally killed any lingering effect Jasmine's pussy and my proximity to it had on my body's ability to pop and maintain a boner.

Once my balls have thawed, I force myself out of the hot shower. I dig out my warmest fleece sweatshirt and a pair of flannel pj pants Mom buys all of us—in matching sets—for Christmas every year. My teeth are still chattering when I get into bed with my laptop. I have one thousand things to do before I drive to Muskoka on Friday. Bar prep things so Rocco and Bernie won't be left floundering in an emergency. Business proposal things, the only way I can convince my dad to help me. He probably thinks I don't even know what a business proposal is. Though, without Jasmine, there might not be a point in pitching this scheme anyway.

And there definitely won't be a Jasmine there. Because I *have* to tell her. I can't put it off anymore. I don't care how much I like her. Once I tell her, she'll go off to find the real Nick, not this generic version.

"Stop feeling sorry for yourself," I say to the furniture in my bachelor apartment. I flick off the bedside lamp; with the light pollution from the city around me, there's not much need for it anyway. The hum from downstairs, conversation punctuated by laughter, the bass from music that doesn't invite dancing but makes you feel good, has become so normal it can lull me to sleep almost as easily as my sound machine and the three milligrams of melatonin in the bottle sitting on my bedside table.

I roll toward it, arm outstretched, ready to take my dose even though it's early. Early for me at least. All the things I need to do can be done tomorrow, the first of which will be talking to Jasmine.

Next to the bottle of melatonin, my phone lights up and beeps. My stomach sinks, and I consider ignoring it. But that little red notification bubble glares at me, shouting the existence of One New Email, and I am nothing if not a millennial, helpless when confronted with the tyrannical reign of my smartphone.

The glare of the blue light is so harsh that at first I'm sure I'm misreading the name of the sender. I blink and rub at my eyes, but when I open them again, it hasn't changed: Dad.

I don't want to deal with whatever he has to say and normally wouldn't. But the subject line catches my attention before I can put the phone down:

Re: Your visit this weekend.

Fuck. I jab angrily at the screen. Fine. This better be good.

He starts it with *Nicholas,* and I almost throw my phone. Taking a deep breath, I start again.

NICHOLAS,

    I hope you and your partner will consider
bringing your ice skates.

WHO WRITES AN EMAIL LIKE THIS? To their son? At this point, I have to assume the man I believe to be my father is AI.

THE LAKE HAS FROZEN over and your mother is looking
forward to a family hockey game. Does your
partner skate? I'm sorry, I don't believe you
shared her name.
    Regards,
    Your Father

I FLOP BACK on the bed and laugh even though there's nothing funny about this email. Except for the *regards*, I guess. Normally, I'd take a screen shot and send it to the family group chat. Miranda would ignore it, Mom would respond with something like *Oh, Nicky,* and Alex would call me ungrateful. Dad would see it and say nothing, but he'd fume. Claire and Charlie would think it's funny.

Tonight, though, the urge to stir up shit feels empty. At this point, my father probably expects it and despite the total awkwardness of this email it does kind of feel like he might be...trying?

We haven't had a family hockey game since I was a teenager, but Dad would always pick me to be on his team. It was the one time I could see myself in him. When he gets his skates on, he's surprisingly chirpy for a sixty-year-old asshole. And if he's trying, maybe I should too? Try to make him happy, to impress him. To show him, finally show him, that even if I didn't follow the path he wanted, I can be successful. To show him that I still need him.

I sigh and pick up my phone, open my chat with Jasmine.

> Me: Do you skate?

I'll apologize, and I'll tell her. After this weekend.

9

———

JASMINE

y gloves are missing.

I'm so nervous I could puke. I have to leave work in fifteen minutes, but Anaïs hasn't stopped sending me emails all morning. I can't remember if I packed the right bathing suit. I have two missed calls from Chloe, the matchmaker, even though I checked the *prefers to be contacted by email* box on the online form. The guy who was on his knees for me in my kitchen told me he "couldn't do this" and yet I'm a fool and responded to his text about ice skating that very same night. And how did I respond? With a simple "no" instead any of the far more acceptable answers. Answers like, fuck off, go fuck yourself, I hate you, or, my personal favorite, COME BACK HERE RIGHT NOW AND FINISH WHAT YOU STARTED.

I push the thoughts out of my mind and go back to looking for my gloves. My beautiful black leather driving gloves with eyelet details along the cuffs. I found them in a vintage shop in the height of summer, and after a good scrubbing with saddle soap they looked like new again. They're impractical for anything other than scurrying from my door to the TTC but I love them anyway. And now they're gone. Not in my purse, the overnight bag, the insulated soft-shell cooler, my pockets, my sleeves. They weren't kicked to the side on the office floor, and they didn't fall into a dark corner in the communal closet. They're just gone. Somewhere between the subway and my desk, I lost them and this, more than anything else, might be the thing that absolutely destroys me.

"What are you doing?"

The voice startles me and I jump, banging my head on the underside of my desk. Mortified, I crawl out from beneath it on my hands and knees, and there, above me, Mitchell looms, his face caught between humor and concern. Shit. Now I want nothing more than to crawl right back underneath the desk.

"I'm looking for my gloves," I say, head tilted back.

He holds his hand out to help me up, but I use the edge of my desk instead.

"I lost them." To avoid eye contact, I take great interest in removing floor debris from my wool slacks.

"That sucks," is all he says.

My heart clenches at the lame response. "Yeah."

I don't think I ever noticed before how very dull the sound of his voice is. It's not that he sounds *bored*, like he's never been entertained by anything in his life. He sounds *boring*. Because he is. When we were together, I made it my mission to get to know his interests, and in that time, I learned more about golf than I ever cared to know but...that was it. The man has exactly one interest and it's one that he shares with grandparents and old white guys. I feel a yawn coming just thinking about it.

"Can I talk to you for a second?"

"I have to leave in four minutes," I say. Besides, aren't we talking right now?

"I'll walk you to your car," he says quickly. Except he knows I don't have one.

"I'm good, thanks." I collect the bags I brought with me. I'd wanted to take the morning off to finish packing for this great deception against Nick's family, but Anaïs insisted I was needed, then acted surprised when I showed up.

"Where are you going?" He follows me from the open-concept office floor to the coatroom without offering to help me with my bags. As a feminist, I try not to hold it against him.

Nick assumed that I was trying to make Mitchell jealous when I pitched him this plan, and I understand why he'd think that. But as potential answers flip through my head like a train station split-flap display, making my ex jealous is truly the furthest thing from my mind. I'd prefer if he never knew another thing about my life, true or not, so I don't want to say *I'm going to my boyfriend's parents' house in Muskoka.* I don't even want to tell him I'm going out of town. If I do, he'll inevitably ask where and with whom.

"To the subway." It isn't a lie. Nick keeps his car parked at his boss's house and it didn't make sense for him to drive back into the city to pick me up, so I said I'd meet him there.

"When are you coming back?" Mitchell asks, his voice slightly strained, almost whiny, like Jade's used to sound when I'd tell her she couldn't watch TV while we ate dinner. For years, I did all I could to make our family like other families. Jade, who at that age didn't understand why Mom and Dad were rarely around but that when they were, they'd let her do whatever she wanted so they wouldn't have to parent her, would stomp her little foot and ask *Why not?* in the whiniest voice she could muster.

I hide my sigh behind the swish of my coat as I pull it on. "Not until Monday, Mitchell. What do you need?"

"We're still friends? Right?" A genuine frown cuts between his brows as he regards me.

The answer is no, though I'm ready to end this conversation, so I say, "Yes."

His shoulders relax. "Good," he says, blowing out a relieved breath. "Cuz I wanted to talk to you about that guy you brought to my engagement party."

Unease claws its way up my throat, but I swallow it back. "Oh?" I pat my pockets, looking for my gloves before I remember. They're gone.

"Just like, how well do you know him?" he asks, shifting from one foot to the other. "You guys started dating pretty quickly."

For a second all I can do is gape. He thinks *I* jumped into a relationship too quickly?

I almost let this get the better of me until I remember: I'm not actually dating Nick.

Mitchell doesn't bother waiting for an answer. "You ever just get like..." He pulls a face, like *yuck*. "A bad feeling?"

The expression mirrors the one he made when we went to Canada's Wonderland and I asked him if he wanted to share a funnel cake. With a sneer, he mansplained calories to me and reminded me that funnel cakes aren't keto. He always said he was "on keto," but I looked up the protocols—because that's what I do, learn about my partner's interests—and I was almost positive it would have been scientifically impossible for him to put his body into the metabolic state of ketosis based on the amount of beer he consumed while he golfed.

I have to remind myself that Nick is my *fake* boyfriend, that he pulled away from me the other night. Like there's something wrong with me. That I hate how he hasn't even brought it up, not once. Not to apologize or explain. He'd rather act like it never happened. I wish I could say the same. I have to remind myself of all of this. If I don't, I might scream at my ex-boyfriend in a coat closet about how that bad feeling he's getting is probably his instincts telling him that Nick could get me off better than he ever did. Nick's kisses have made me more wet than Mitchell's best try.

"A bad feeling about Nick? No." I gather my bags. Hopefully, the subway won't be too busy and I'll get a seat, though there's a good chance I'll hit an early lunch rush.

"I don't want to overstep," Mitchell says.

There's no stopping the snort that escapes me.

Unfortunately, this does not deter him. "But I'm a pretty good judge of character and... I don't know." He sighs, his shoulders heaving with feigned concern. "It was like he was pretending to like me?" His brow is furrowed in genuine concern, like he can't grasp the concept. Maybe I'm a better actor than Nick, because I'm also pretending to like Mitchell right now. "But people always like me," he says, mostly to himself.

With a sigh, I shuffle past him. "I'm sorry, Mitchell. I really have to go now."

He stops me, his finger hooked through the strap of one of my bags, jolting me backward and making me totter on my high-heeled booties.

"What the—" I clamp my mouth closed before I let an obscenity fly at work.

He grimaces. Mitchell has never been great at meaningful apologies. "Don't you think that's a little…"

I yank the bag from his grasp. "A little what?"

"Fake." The word lands like a slap.

Fake. Nick is fake. My Nick.

I giggle. How absurd. How absolutely comical that my ex-boyfriend, who is more obtuse than a triangle, thinks my fake boyfriend is *fake*. But when he dated me, he never noticed how fucking fake I was. Fake rich, to impress our co-workers, his family and friends. Fake breasts. Fake interests, fake needs, fake perfection. Fake fucking orgasms.

My giggles stop abruptly, and I swallow to keep the sting of tears at bay. I have spent so long faking it in the hopes that if I try hard enough, I'll be worthy. I'll be safe. I'll be enough.

"Nick Scott is the realest man I've ever met," I say with only the slightest tremor in my voice, before I walk away.

Whatever empowerment I gained from that deflates as I step outside and am hit with a blast of frigid air. I still have to walk to the subway with all these bags. I'm halfway down the block when a man shouts behind me.

"Hey, wait up."

I hunch my shoulders and move faster. Rule number one of walking in Toronto: never acknowledge street harassers.

"Jasmine, wait," the man says, closer, huffing and out of breath.

I turn, my bags swinging, and suck in a sharp breath. "Nick?"

His cheeks are pink from the cold or maybe exertion. The snap buttons of his jacket—hip length, fleece-lined, plaid flannel, because of course he only wears plaid flannel—are open and his chest and stomach heave against the white T-shirt underneath.

"What are you doing here?" I ask, my stomach twisting. "I thought I was supposed to meet you at your boss's house. Am I late?" I can't possibly be late. I set three reminders.

He reaches for me and on instinct I take a step back.

He smirks. "You want to carry all those?"

Oh. I pass him a bag. "Thanks," I say quietly.

"You're not late." He takes another off my shoulder, then nods in the direction I was heading. As we walk to the station side by side, he says, "I assumed you were going to overpack and figured you'd need help carrying your bags." His tone is teasing and his eyes dance. Before I have time to scoff—even though he is clearly correct—he adds, "Plus, I felt bad for not picking you up."

An altercation between two cab drivers catches his attention as we wait at the intersection, so he doesn't notice how I can't look away from him. Even when I psychically beg him to look at me, he doesn't turn his chin. It's probably for the best. In this moment, I think he might be the most beautiful thing I've ever seen, and that thought is probably written all over my face. His throat bobs as he swallows, the move so sexy I try to shove my bare hands into my pockets, bag straps and all, to ensure I will not act on the urge to trace the skin there, close my eyes as the stubble he can never seem to keep off his face roughens the pads of my fingers.

He pulls his gloves off and hands them to me. He must assume my hands are cold. The stairs to the subway station are across the street, but I let him assume and take the gloves, body-warm, leather-soft.

"Thanks."

"What?" he asks as we descend the stairs, the screech of the train already audible.

"Huh?" Wow. Eloquent.

"You're staring."

Shit. I panic. "Don't you think the subway smells like mothballs?"

Nick shoots me a funny look over his shoulder as he scans his pass and the gate swings open. I do the same, carefully sliding the card back into its easily accessible place in my bag. Hopefully, he'll forget I said that.

"Generally, it smells like piss and garbage," he says as we descend another set of stairs, baggage banging against our legs.

We pick up the pace halfway down when we see the train is already in the station, the doors open.

"Yeah. It does."

He makes it to the door first and stands in it, holding it for me.

"Thank you," I say, then frown. How many times have I expressed gratitude in the last five minutes? "That's what I thought as a kid. That it smelled like mothball," I explain. "The trains especially. I really liked the smell."

I flush when I'm finished. I'm not sure I've ever told a man I was attracted to that before. Why would I? It's silly and ridiculous and inconsequential. I take a seat on one of the red upholstered benches and Nick stands in front of me, his arm stretched overhead as he holds the railing above us. The hem of his T-shirt lifts, revealing a sliver of skin and dark hair on his stomach. For the rest of the ride, I forget to be nervous, forget to be mad at Mitchell. I even forget about my gloves. We sway and rock with the rhythm of the subway, and I pretend that we could be as real as Nick is.

10

NICK

Jasmine winces as I throw her slightly worn brown leather overnight bag into the trunk of my rust bucket Buick.

"You know we're not moving there, right?" I stuffed everything I needed for the weekend into the same canvas backpack I used in high school.

Jasmine has four bags.

"It's not all clothes," she mutters.

I take off my coat and shove it in the trunk along with the luggage. I motion to her outerwear. "You're going to want to take that off. This old beauty has one heat setting once she gets going and it's tropical."

In all fairness, that could be a lie. I bought the car off Ed years ago, but don't have a place to park it at the bar. He lets me keep it in his driveway, and that means I don't use it very much. Great for saving on gas, terrible for preparing for a long drive in the dead of winter with a car as old as I am.

Carefully, she folds her coat and places it on top of mine. I turn away to hide my scowl. She looks lovely. Her long cardigan is the structured kind that looks businesslike but up close is mega soft. Her white turtleneck stretches over her breasts and her pants are black and slim and show a peek of her ankles between the hem and her heeled boots.

I never knew I was an ankle guy until I realized Jasmine had a pair.

Her cheeks and nose are pink from the cold, and when she adjusts her emerald ear warmers, it reveals a pair of pearl earrings. Her red hair is collected in a bun at the top of her head, the color as shocking as it is every time I'm in her presence. Maybe it strikes me that way because it's winter, and it gets dark so early, and everything is dull and gray. Hopefully, it's that and not something else, something stupid like the attraction I'm supposed to be suppressing.

"Is there any chance we could stop somewhere soon?" she asks as we slip into our seats.

I twist around, the seat beneath me creaking, and assess her. "We haven't even left yet." The words come out more harshly than I mean, so I clamp my lips shut to ensure I don't accidentally snap at her.

She fidgets with her fingers, not quite meeting my eyes. "I know, but..."

Ah. "Here." I unclip a set of keys from my ring and hand them to her. "You can use Ed's bathroom."

"I'll be quick." Keeping her gaze down, she snatches the keys. Then she's hurrying up Ed's porch steps. "He's not home, is he?" she asks, spinning at the top, a look of sheer panic on her face.

I shake my head as I get in an arm workout cranking the window open. "No," I shout. He's with Rocco at a doctor's appointment. "But he wouldn't stand on the other side of the door listening to your stream if he was."

She makes a strangled, annoyed sound, then whips around and unlocks the door with jerky movements and slams it behind her.

I settle in the driver's seat again and start the car to let it heat up. Once I've fiddled with the heat settings, I press my forehead against the steering wheel and close my eyes. This was a mistake, this lie. This lie on top of another lie, on top of more lies. Every time I think I'm going to come clean, all I can picture is the devastated looks on my friends' faces when I tell them I can't save Moonbar.

Does she have to be so goddamn pretty, though? And nervous. She's clearly very anxious, and of course she is. Jasmine is a *serious* woman who takes things *seriously*. So, when someone asks her to pretend to be their girlfriend for a weekend, she fucking *does* it.

Finally, hot air pumps from my car's vents. I'm in the perfect spot in Ed's driveway for the midday sun to slice right through the windshield and warm the polyester upholstery. While I wait, I let the inexplicable smell of leather cleaner that I can't get rid of, despite multiple air fresheners, wash over me.

I take out my phone and flip to the playlist I made for this ride, songs I love and songs I hope she'll like too. A belt in the motor squeals even though the car hasn't moved, so that's pretty ominous for the journey ahead.

When the front door of Ed's house opens, I pretend to adjust my mirrors while I watch her lock up before stepping carefully down the stairs. When she settles into the passenger seat, her back is so straight it has to be uncomfortable. She adjusts two of her bags, ones she insisted had to stay with her in the car, searching for nonexistent foot room.

"What's that?" I nod at the insulated bag.

She pulls it to her lap and unzips it, frowning into its depths. "I made snacks for the trip so we wouldn't have to spend too much money at the rest stops."

"Jasmine." Her name is a frustrated sigh. "I'm happy to buy you lunch."

She shrugs. "Now you don't have to. Also, I made a Bakewell tart for your mother for a hostess gift." She holds up a pie-shaped good with white and pink feathering drawn perfectly across the top.

"You made that?" I say, the question more skeptical than shocked.

"Yes," she says, pulling it to her chest with a scowl. "Also..." She puts the tart away and gathers the other large canvas bag on her lap. "Do you think she'd prefer a scented candle or a succulent?"

She pulls both from the bag and shoves them at me. The candle smells divine, like her home. Instantly, blood rushes to my dick, my knees ache, and my mouth waters like I am in her kitchen again, on my knees for her.

"The candle." My voice is gravel. I turn away, put the car into drive, inhale the synthetic scent of my pine air freshener. "You didn't have to bring anything." I slow-roll out of Ed's driveway, creep down the middle of the narrow road lined with dirty snowbanks. Gritting my teeth, I silently curse myself. Her thoughtfulness is another reminder of how little I deserve this kindness from her.

Jasmine has no clue how very much my mother will appreciate the gesture or how much it will please my father to see my mother happy.

"Of course I did," she says, packing things away. "Although, I wasn't sure if you had any allergies. Which is why I made..." Turning awkwardly in her seat, she sets the food bag on the floorboard behind us. Then she lugs a binder out of the canvas bag that I'm beginning to think has Mary Poppins powers. The sucker is at least six inches thick and lands with a *thwack* on her thighs. "We need to know the things that boyfriends and girlfriends would know about each other. Like allergies."

"What the fuck is that?" Again, my voice is sharper than is warranted. It's not her fault I'm a faker to the power of two.

Before I merge onto the highway, I sneak a peek at the binder. There are color-coordinated tabs. Holy shit. Why do I find this so hot?

"It's our relationship. We can study it on the way up."

The car is too warm, and now with her in it, too small. I thought the hardest part of this drive would be the constant gnawing guilt; and that is really hard, but honestly, I deserve it.

In reality, the hardest part is trying not to stare at the sharp edge of her jaw or the long fan of her lashes. It's not pulling to the side of the road and telling her everything but begging her to forgive me anyway. Not because I need her to impress my dad, but because she's so damn lovely.

Slowly, her smile fades, like she's misinterpreting my expression.

"What?" she asks, her voice tinged with wariness. She closes the binder.

"Nothing." I keep my eyes on the semitruck in front of us. It's easier that way. Forcing myself to focus solely on the road takes my mind off how badly I want this to be real. Because if this was real, if I was real enough for her, I might pull over on this 400-series highway and kiss her senseless.

"Nothing," I say again. "I had no idea my fake girlfriend was such a nerd."

A FEW HOURS LATER, just as the footbridge they built over the highway comes into view, we whizz past the black and white sign for the best goddamn burger joint north of Highway 401. The exit is a few hundred meters away and I've got to get into the right lane if we're going to stop.

And I really want to stop.

With every kilometer we get closer to home, my skin feels tighter. Baker's Burgers is the only good thing about this drive. I look forward to it every time I make the trip. It's probably a placebo effect, but I like to think I land a few more zingers on Dad when I have Baker's Burgers in my belly.

"You hungry?"

Jasmine stops midway through reading aloud from The Binder, looking confused. "For what?"

Case in point: she's taking this so seriously she seems to have forgotten that hunger is a thing. I check my side mirror to hide my smile. "For food."

This perks her up. "Would you like your muffin now?" she asks, pulling the Tupperware from the insulated bag behind my seat.

A Baker's Burger has an impossible to recreate flavor. They use the processed cheese that melts and congeals in a way you know will clog your arteries, but the flavor is so damn good, it's hard to care.

They're always liberal with their barbecue sauce and grilled onions. A Baker's Burger burger is a heaven I only get once or twice a year.

She looks so hopeful, though.

"Sure," I say. "Thanks."

The sun, which had tucked behind a cloud about an hour ago, breaks through at the exact moment we pass Baker's Burgers, giving it a heavenly quality, taunting me.

She holds the muffin daintily with her pastel-pink-tipped fingers. She's even peeled the wrapper off for me. As I alternate between keeping an eye on the road and inspecting the muffin, she lowers her head like she's studying The Binder, but she's quiet, like maybe she's waiting for me to take my first bite. So, I do.

"*Oh my goddddd,*" I mumble around a mouthful of muffin. It's not a greasy cheeseburger, but it's buttery and a little bit spicy. It's good.

Her answering smile rivals the sunbeam we just passed. Dimples bracket her wide mouth. I'm so used to seeing it pinched in a frown, I can't help but be blown away by the way it changes her, loosens her.

"You like it?" she asks, her tone full of so much hope.

"It's amazing," I say through another mouthful.

"So." She unfolds a napkin and drops it on my lap. "How we met." The words escape her quickly, like I didn't notice she dropped the napkin from half a foot above me rather than touch my thighs. "I was thinking we'd say we met at the grocery store. Something classic but easily forgettable, like we were both reaching for the last bag of cake and pastry flour."

"Why not the last bottle of AXE body spray?"

"Why would I buy AXE body spray?"

"Why would I buy cake and pastry flour?"

She nods, making a note in her binder. "Fair. We'll circle back to that."

"You didn't make a binder for the engagement party."

"So?" She bites the tip of her pen.

"So, why do we need one now? Why don't we just tell the—" I stop myself. I can't suggest that we tell the truth, because "the truth" isn't true.

"This is different," she says. "At the engagement party, we had a few hours to kill with people who were too drunk to remember much. Now we're spending an entire weekend with the people who know you best."

Questionable, but I'll let it slide.

"You wouldn't..." I speak slow, searching for words that won't make me feel like I'm blatantly lying even though I am. "Would you not tell your family about matchmaking? If we were going to see them."

Instantly, she looks away, flipping the binder closed. Tracing her finger along the plastic edge, she says, "Probably not." That simple response is barely audible over the sound of the tires on the road, the wind whistling between the rust and duct tape holding this thing together. "It's not something we'd talk about, and if we did, they'd likely see it as a personal failing on my part."

With a sigh, she turns to the passenger side window, very clearly ending this conversation. Except I don't want it to end.

"I'm sorry," I say, almost as quietly. "We don't need hard and fast facts though."

Her shoulders sink. "I thought working together to create a favorable narrative about our relationship could be a good way to get to know each other."

"Sure, but do I really need to know that your second-grade teacher was Mr. Knight and he wore space-themed ties?"

Finally, she turns back to me. "So, you were listening?" she asks, like *gotcha!*

I ignore that. Of course I was listening. "You know what we need? A song." I tap out a beat on the steering wheel as a new track comes on my playlist. "You like The Cure? Should this be our song?"

She shrugs. "They're okay."

I jab at my phone screen to skip to the next track. A Bob Seger song. Fucking classic. I need to remember to add this to the Underground Karaoke library.

"Come on. Bob Seger. You have to love Bob Seger."

Another shrug.

I screech out the next few lines. The wince on her face says one thing, but the way her knee bounces with the beat tells a different story.

"Yeah, this is it. This is our song, babe."

She makes a face at the pet name and I laugh.

"Sing with me."

Jasmine settles back in the seat, somehow managing to make a car that's probably responsible for most of Canada's CO_2 emissions look regal. "I told you I don't sing in public."

"This isn't public. This is my shitbox."

"I'm not going to sing." Her voice cuts cold through the music.

I turn the phone off. Poor Bob Seger.

Other than the whine of a motor belt and constant hum of the road on my winter tires, the car is quiet again.

"I'm sorry," she says.

"It's fine."

Ducking, she gives her head a shake. "I don't like doing things unless I can do them well."

"I know," I say. "I remember." And then, because I can't help myself, "You don't do things unless you can do them perfectly, right? If I lived my life that way, I'd never do anything."

Her stare feels hard against my face, her voice cold. "You're judging me."

"No," I say quickly. Fuck. How is it that I go from frustrating her on purpose to annoying her by accident, yet I can't ever land anywhere in between? "Yeah. Maybe a little. I take a more casual approach to life, I guess."

She snorts.

"Now who's judging?"

Her only response is a noncommittal hum.

"Why do you feel like you have to be perfect?" I ask.

Huffing, Jasmine puts The Binder back into her bag. She picks a muffin from the lunch bag and pulls at the wrapper but doesn't eat it. Instead, she stares at the baked good like it has all the answers.

"I think we've gotten to know each other enough for now," she says. With that, she turns again and watches the scenery pass by her window.

Fuck. I wish I had a cheeseburger right now.

11

———————

JASMINE

Between the hip-high snowbanks and the grayish-brown slush, the dead of winter can make even Canadian cottage country look dull. Though Nick's hometown manages to keep some of its shine with century-old façades on the storefronts down the main street and hand-painted signs even on the nationwide chain restaurant.

He drives slower than the speed limit, but I doubt it's for my benefit. He's gotten surlier since we got off the highway, and fidgety. He keeps scrubbing at his chest. Either he's anxious or his T-shirt—which I discovered is a Taylor Swift Reputation tour tee when I stole furtive glances at him through the windows when we stopped to get gas—is itchy.

When we stop at a light, I pull out my phone.

Me: Arriving in Muskoka.

Jade: fire

Me: What are you doing?

Jade: I'll tell you what I'm not doing…

Jade: I'm not avoiding conversation with my fake boyfriend.

Me: I'm just checking in!

Jade: I'll be fine.

Me: <3

Jade: do me a favor ok?

Me: Ok…

SHE'LL EITHER ASK me to buy her something like I'm our dad bringing gifts for his new family after a business trip, or she'll tell me to do something physically impossible. Like "unclench."

Jade: since Nick is technically your boyfriend for the next however many days can you P L E A S E at the very least let that man dick you down??????

I make a strangled sound and half-drop, half-toss my phone back into the open bag.

"What's wrong?" Nick doesn't look at me, but there's genuine concern in his voice.

Mentally, I shake myself. I breathe deeply, willing the heat in my cheeks to dissipate. I need to get back in the right mindset and that does not include Nick's dick. We've tried that already. It ended poorly.

Except now I can't get the image of him kneeling at my feet and gripping himself through his boxer briefs telling me he's hard for me out of my head.

"Jazz. Are you experiencing a medical emergency?"

"No." The single word escapes me far too quickly. My pulse beats at my throat so hard that I'm sure if Nick didn't have to focus on the road, he'd see. I'm hot. And honestly, a little dizzy. And oh my god I'm wet. The thought of Nick touching himself has made me wet. This has never happened before. I didn't think it was even possible to be this aroused by a thought, a memory.

"Jasmine?" The car slows, and a click-click-click sound pulls me back to the present. Nick is side-eyeing me, his hand still on the indicator as if he's actually preparing to pull over.

Pull. Yourself. Together.

If I could slap myself in the face without making him consider a forty-eight-hour hold, I would.

"Sorry." I clear my throat. I've never sounded less like myself. "Can you remind me again of your siblings' names?" I flip open the binder again and click my pen, the tip hovering over blank lined paper.

We turn off the main road and wind through residential streets. Some houses still have their Christmas lights up and almost every driveway has a hockey net against the garage.

"Alex is married to Robert," he says. "Miranda to Jake. Claire is married to Philip. Charlie is marrying Rashida next summer."

"And this is in birth order?"

"Yeah." By his tone, it's obvious he's smirking. I've learned that much about him already. Still, I peek over at him to confirm what I already knew: for some reason, that question amuses him.

"And Charlie is younger than you, right?"

Nodding, he fiddles with the knob on the radio.

"Their children's names?" I ask, my pen poised over the paper again.

The houses are fewer and farther between now, set back from the road with miniature streetlamps flanking the long driveways. Nick turns onto a gravel road reduced to single track with car-high snowbanks on each side. Between the trees, I catch glimpses of a lake, the snow cover blindingly bright then disappearing in irregular intervals.

"The only kid you need to know about is Tilly." For the first time in at least an hour, he sounds relaxed. It's oddly comforting, but I'll take that to the grave.

"Is Tilly the only one?"

"Tilly is the only one that matters," he says definitively, one hand on the steering wheel.

"Are you saying that Tilly is—"

"My favorite? Absolutely, I am." He grins over at me. "Listen, I love all my nieces and nephews. Every one of them is wonderful and sweet. But Tilly—Alex's daughter—she *loves* me, and I love her. She's my goddaughter. She made me an uncle. It's nothing personal." He shrugs, his cheeks turning pink maybe from his enthusiasm, or maybe because he's embarrassed by that enthusiasm.

Jade and I have half-siblings we've only stalked on social media, but even if I did know them, I don't think there's anyone in this world I could love more than I love her.

"I get it."

"I used to sing Beatles songs to her when she was a baby. She'd fall asleep to 'Maxwell's Silver Hammer.'"

My heart squeezes, making it momentarily hard to breathe. That's cute. And a bit homicidal.

His levity slowly fades, his expression dulling. I grasp for something I can say to bring his good mood back. We can't both be freaking out at the same time and right now I have reserved all of the freaking out energy for myself. Because, for the life of me, I can't figure out what it is about this man that turns me on so fucking much.

It keeps coming back to one explanation: the matchmaker, and her miracle algorithm, was right.

"We're here," he says, like a doctor might say *time of death*.

My butt, which has fallen asleep, is relieved. Otherwise, this announcement ratchets up my nerves even more.

"Here" is a long, winding driveway lined with more of those miniature lampposts that disappears behind a hillock and a copse of ice-covered trees. The snow is even deeper here, but the paved driveway is professionally cleared by Jim's Snow Removal at the turn off. Finally, as we crest the hill and slowly navigate through the pines, Nick's parents' house comes into view.

When he mentioned he'd grown up in Muskoka, I was expecting a suburban home. When he said he grew up playing hockey, I assumed he meant at a public arena. And the pool he mentioned? Perhaps a local community center. Anaïs and Butch have a cottage that's about an hour from here. It's nicer than any home I've ever lived in, with an attached garage, shiny wood paneling, and a fire pit on the waterfront. Some of the neighbors have pools despite the lake access.

But even those cottages are nothing like this.

The three-story home is lined with windows with clear views all the way through to the lake on the other side. A two-car garage stands open with luxury vehicles in the bays and I'll eat my secondhand booties if there isn't a boathouse on the water. Nick's family's home has a bigger footprint than most McMansions.

I look from Nick to the house and back. "Are you related to any NHL players?"

A laugh bursts from him, but he quickly schools his expression, like he's surprised it got the better of him. "No, but I drove the Zamboni in tenth and eleventh grade."

"It seems like a beautiful place to grow up."

Nick's smile dims, turns wistful. He squeezes the steering wheel. "It could be," he says quietly.

The argumentative side of me that only seems to come out around Nick wants to point out that growing up with NHL players and Hollywood actors as his seasonal neighbors could not possibly be as terrible as he's implying, but "money doesn't buy happiness" is a cliché for a reason.

"Shall we?" he asks, his voice like a sigh.

I flip the visor down and pull out my travel makeup bag. Using the visor's mirror, I touch up my lips and smooth down my hair. "You said the candle for the hostess gift, right?"

He's already gotten out of the car, his legs and torso all I can see. As he stretches, the black elastic waistband of his CK underwear peeks out from his jeans.

I can't help but peruse the peek of soft skin of his stomach and follow the dark hair that disappears beneath his clothes.

"Hey." He leans back into the car. "My eyes are up here, Jazz."

"I...no...." I splutter, my cheeks heating. I do not care about Nick's underwear. Of all the underwear in the world, his is the least concerning to my life. Fake girlfriends don't imagine what's beneath their fake boyfriend's undergarments. They don't wonder what his skin might taste like. Whether he'd laugh if she trailed her tongue along the path his hair takes.

He chuckles. Ass.

"Yeah. The candle."

The hostess gift. Right. Okay. Closing my eyes, I take in a long, centering breath, getting my mind and body under control.

He gives me more time to gather myself, or maybe he's trying to tease me, as he stretches again. I pull out the tart and pull the plastic wrap off for maximum effect at presentation. Thankfully, it traveled well. It only takes a moment to settle the candle into the brown paper gift bag I brought for the occasion and tie a twine bow. I really did overpack, though I'll never admit that to Nick, so I shove everything I don't need into the footwell. I'll come back for the rest later.

Every other vehicle in the circular driveway shines. They're all SUVs, making Nick's dingy boat of a Buick look ancient by comparison, but the velvety soft upholstery in Nick's car, the tinny, faraway quality to the voices that came from the radio when he checked the weather, the smell, like Nick and leather cleaner, all of it combines to make me irrationally protective of his self-proclaimed shitbox. I wipe at a spot of dirt on the door handle as if the car is somehow sentient and concerned with its appearance as much as I would be.

"I'm sorry for earlier," he says quickly, his voice a little too loud in the quiet afternoon.

"For what?"

He grabs our bags from the trunk and closes the lid with a thud. "I was short with you," he says, his dark eyes apologetic. "Terse. I don't know. I'm just nervous, and I took it out on you."

Heart thumping against my breastbone, I examine the

perfect feathering on my tart. It's in the top three of the best baked goods I've ever made. I've always preferred fabrics to food when it comes to creating. Probably because fabric lasts, while even the most beautiful tarts have to be consumed eventually.

"What are you thinking?" he asks in almost a whisper. He isn't wearing his coat and goose bumps cover his bare arms, while his knuckles, nose, and ears are pink.

"That I wish I didn't have to eat this tart," I say. "And you don't have to apologize." No matter how hard I try, I can't seem to get him out of my system. Maybe I should just let myself be consumed.

Or as Jade puts it, get dicked down.

He steps closer, his lips twisting. "There's something I need to tell you."

"Nicky, put on a coat," a woman calls from behind us.

Nicky? I mouth, elation instantly coursing through me.

Fuck off, he mouths back, then he lifts his chin and, over my shoulder, he calls, "Hey, Ma."

Ma. His mother. This is it. It's happening. There's no turning back now. I plaster a smile on my face, then spin to greet her.

Wrapped in an overly large Mr. Rogers-style cardigan and men's work boots, Mrs. Scott clomps across the driveway. "Let me see you," she says, her voice high and excited. "I can't believe he's kept you from us."

"Hello, Mrs. Scott." It takes effort to keep my voice steady. "Thank you so much for inviting me to your home. It's such a pleasure to meet you."

My hostess gifts aren't just good manners, they serve as a barrier between me and strangers looking for hugs and handshakes. Except apparently, they don't deter Mrs. Scott.

"Call me Mindy." She cups my face in her hands, undaunted by the tart and bag between us or the blush heating my skin. "Look at you. Nicky, look at her, isn't she beautiful?"

She stares pointedly over my shoulder until Nick sighs and says, infinitely softer than I thought possible, "She's beautiful."

My heart pangs at the words, but I swallow back the reaction. What else would he say in response to that question?

Nick doesn't resemble his mother much, his hair dark to her silver and his dark eyes in contrast to her blue, but they share the same mischievous tilt to their smiles.

Already, Mindy has complimented me more than Anaïs did during my entire relationship with her son, and I've only just met this woman.

"Thank you." I shove the tart pan between us. "I made you a Bakewell tart and here's a small gift. To say thank you for inviting me."

"You're thanking me?" She peeks into the bag. "This is the first time Nick has brought one of his girlfriends home. I should be thanking *you*."

Nick puts his arm around my shoulder, gently pulling me out of his mother's orbit.

"Slander. You met Allison."

She frowns. "Who's Allison?"

"We dated in middle school. She came over to take photos before the seventh-grade dance."

Mindy throws her head back, grabbing my forearm like she needs me to help hold her up, and roars with laughter like Nick is the funniest person she's ever met.

Maybe it's a mom thing.

She lets go of me to squeeze her son. He's a head taller than her, so when he hugs her back, he tucks her under his chin and kisses the top of her head. Whatever trauma haunts him when he's here can't possibly have been caused by this woman. She's lovely.

"Technically"—Nick winks at me over her head—"we never broke up."

Mindy pulls away with a teasing huff, then, squeezing my hand, leads me toward the open front door.

"So, I'm the other woman? Thanks a lot."

Beside me, Mindy laughs again until she's almost breathless. "You'll give us Scotts a run for our money. I can just feel it." She wraps an arm around my hip and pulls me into her. "Welcome to the family, Jasmine."

Her smile makes warmth bloom in my chest, but on the heels of that sensation, a wave of nausea hits me. If I were a better person, one who wasn't spiteful and petty, who needed to lie to her bosses to feel better about herself, I'd run right out of this town. All this time, I've been obsessing over how to pull off this deception. Not once have I given any thought to the feelings of the people we're lying to. Nick's mother is kinder than my own. I want her to keep holding my face, telling me I'm beautiful.

The second I step through this door, there's no going back. We're not playing a silly game, faking it. We're lying.

If I weren't such a selfish person, I'd make Nick take me home, but Mindy's warm presence alone will keep me here this whole weekend. Maybe even longer.

WHILE I'VE ALWAYS LAMENTED our small family, Jade revels in it. She says she likes having me all to herself. As Nick closes the door behind us, I see her point.

There are too many people in this house. Children scream with glee, their shrieks melding together, making it impossible to discern how many there are, just that there are more children than seems safe for an enclosed space. Deep male laughter comes from the open living room, where a group of men stand near the floor-to-ceiling windows overlooking the snow-covered lake, holding steaming mugs or pint glasses. Tweed tartan blankets are folded over the back of the dark leather couches, and the whole space is bathed in a warm glow from the afternoon sun.

"Uncle Nicky!" one of the children screams, running on stubby kid legs toward him, arms flailing.

He drops to his knees, holding his arms open. "Hey, Tills."

Several women gathered around one elderly lady who is stationed on a kitchen stool turn to us and gaze adoringly as uncle and nibling reunite. He squeezes her tight, digging his stubbly chin into her neck, tickling her until she squeals. Mindy watches them with all the joy and pride of a mother and grandmother who lives for her family.

Then she turns that smile on me and winks like we're in on a secret.

Oh, no.

"Nick loves kids," Mindy says.

I nod woodenly. It's bad enough sidestepping awkward conversations with in-laws about family planning, but it's downright confusing to be hit with a pang of true regret at disappointing one's *fake* boyfriend's mom. Not only do I not want kids; I'm not really dating the man.

"Look what Jasmine brought," Mindy says, genuine enthusiasm shining through. She presents the tart and the candle and me to the group. The women all smile, except for the small white-haired family matriarch. She tilts her head, her glasses perched on the end of her nose, and peers at me. They all turn to her like they're awaiting her judgment.

She scowls.

My stomach sinks. That can't be good.

I don't really know how to connect with grandmas. Mine's interests revolved around Filet-O-Fish and menthol cigarettes, so we were doomed from the start.

Eager for backup, I turn to Nick, but he's focused on Tilly, who glares when she notices me. Great. Clearly, Nick isn't the only Scott family member who plays favorites.

"Go on," he says gruffly, giving her a gentle tap on her butt.

Tilly continues her intimidation techniques with intense eye contact and doesn't relent until a smaller child with light brown skin and big curls like Tilly bodychecks her to the floor. With a huff, Tilly scrambles up, then runs after the diapered kid, both screaming.

When I turn back to Nick's relatives, they're still watching me. The intensity of the attention makes me think Mindy might be the only person in the family who likes me so far.

"Hi. I'm Jasmine," I squeak.

"I'm Nick," he says, mimicking the nervous, high tone in my voice.

I elbow him before I think better of it, but I find myself shifting closer to him nonetheless. He's a flotation device in a sea full of sharks and I don't know yet whether they're the people-eating kind.

He makes an *oof* sound in response to my well-placed elbow to his side, and that seems to break their scrutiny.

"Hi, Nico." A woman with dark, wavy hair like his wraps him in a hug. She turns to me, graceful and warm, looking like she's stepped straight out of a Ralph Lauren ad in dark, straight leg blue jeans and a cream cable-knit sweater.

The entire family has leaned heavily into the preppy country-club look. Even the kids are in polos and the baby version of chinos; there's a baby in a cable-knit bear onesie that I know for a fact costs a cool two hundo.

In contrast, Nick is dressed in a well-loved T-shirt that fits perfectly across his shoulders and strains against his biceps, and his fast fashion denim looks soft enough for me to rub my face against. Not that I ever would, of course.

The woman turns to me. "I'm Claire. A sister."

Without my hostess gifts, I have nothing to protect myself from another inevitable hug, though if Claire is anything like her mother, the gifts wouldn't have stopped her.

"Welcome to the family, Jasmine," she whispers into our hug.

I don't choke on my tongue, but only barely.

"Claire, take it easy," Nick hisses.

"We're just excited," she says teasingly as she pulls back, clutching my upper arms. "He's so secretive. My parents had to travel to Toronto to meet his last girlfriend."

Clearly, everyone in Nick's family is obsessed with his dating life. If I was his real girlfriend, I'd be worried. As his tenuous...friend? I'm still a little concerned. Either Nick has serious commitment issues, or he was born into a family of traditionalist busybodies.

Before I can come up with a response for Claire, we're ushered further into the home, which smells of newly cut wood, sharp and sweet. Despite his claim that he favors Tilly, Nick takes several babies from their parents' arms and picks toddlers off the floor as they meander past, planting smacking kisses on their cheeks and sneaking beard tickles into their necks.

In the span of a few minutes, I am hugged by another sister, a sister-in-law, an auntie or two, and offered warm or alcoholic beverages, then warm *and* alcoholic beverages. Before I can choose from the long list rattled off for me, Nick presses a mug of hot lemon water into my hand.

My heart squeezes with gratitude.

"Good?" he asks, quietly, ducking in close.

"Do I look as overwhelmed as I feel?"

He tips his head, brow furrowing, and studies me. "You look like you did the first time you walked into Moonbar."

"That good?"

He huffs out a quiet laugh, stretching and rolling his shoulders.

"I can drive a bit on the way home," I offer, pointing to his shoulders. I hate driving, but I could handle it for a few hours if that's what he needs. "You look a little sore."

A girlfriend would massage them for him, but I don't know whether he'd want me to. Seeming to read my hesitation, he wipes the grimace from his face. "Nah. Just not used to sitting for so long."

"That's one good thing about your job. At least it keeps you moving," says an older man with silver hair and a strong jaw. It's obvious he's Nick's father, because he is Nick, only well aged. If Nick wore slacks and cardigans over Oxford shirts. But his father's jaw is tight, the lines around his mouth dragging his lips down. Where Nick is teasing, forever young, this man looks like he's made of plywood.

"You did it, Dad. You found the one good thing about my job," Nick says, his tone dry as a desert. "This is Jasmine, by the way."

"It's nice to meet you, sir." I hold out my hand.

He looks me up and down before taking it. He doesn't leer so much as catalog, assess. This guy definitely judges books by their covers.

The first time Mitchell introduced me to Anaïs and Butch, Anaïs gave me this same thorough review. I hate myself a little for how eager I am to be considered good enough. Clearly, I haven't grown much since that last introduction.

Nick is stiff, his posture rigid as his father shakes my hand, his grip firm.

"The elusive Jasmine," Mr. Scott says, his chin lifted. "It's nice to finally meet you. What do you do?"

This feels like a test. "I work for an interior design firm," I say, though the statement sounds more like a question, as if I don't actually know where I work. "Haüs Interiors?"

His face lights up. "I've heard of them. They do good work."

A breath of relief escapes me. "Right." Finally, a chance to put The Binder to good use. "I'm sure there's some professional overlap between interior design and office furniture supply."

Mr. Scott's smile grows. "I've met Butch once or twice when I was in the city for meetings. Maybe you can get Nicholas a job at Haüs since he refuses to come sell for me."

Nick leans forward, his chest a furious presence behind me, his body heat soaking into me. As I shift out of his way, I catch a glimpse of his expression. It's tighter, angrier, than any look I've ever seen from him, his eyes narrowed and his mouth a thin, sharp line. He looks like he's about to say something he's going to regret.

"Listen, old man."

Part of me wants to hiss *drag him, Nick*, but I grab his arm and hope to god the pressure I place on his forearm, my nails digging into the delicate skin of his wrist, conveys something along the lines of *I don't like my dad either, but this is not the time, Nicholas.*

"Old man?" Mr. Scott spits.

Before he can muster a response, Mindy is there, slinking beneath her husband's arm, wrapping both of hers around his waist. Her presence softens him, turning him from hard-ass businessman moonlighting as a father to slightly squishy grandpa in a cardigan.

"You know, Jasmine." Her eye contact borders on maniacal. She's clearly had experience distracting these two from tense moments.

The rest of Nick's family continues on around us. This must be normal for them, their father and their second-youngest brother butting heads. Rather than come to Nick's defense, they let it happen. At the very least, Jade has always had my back when I needed it.

"Nick never told us how you two met."

"How we met?" Panic builds in my chest, making it hard to breathe, because all my brain can come up with now is the silly, convoluted truth. If I ask them to please hold while I run out to the car, they'll find that suspicious. I can't help my frown, until the memory comes to me. In The Binder, Section 2.3: Backstory: Met at grocery store.

Except Nick hated that and we never came up with an alternative.

It's been an interminably long amount of time now since Mindy asked. At least it feels that way, but if I open my mouth, it won't form the right words. With my luck, I'll blurt out, *It's all a lie. Forgive me, Mindy!*

"I never told you because you'd never believe it," Nick says.

He mimics his parents' pose, putting his arm around my shoulders and giving me a squeeze that probably looks gentle but feels a lot like *calm the fuck down, Jasmine, Jesus.*

"We met at the grocery store."

As I look up at him, I don't have to feign the adoration on my face.

He's using The Binder. Instantly, the pressure in my chest loosens, and air fills my burning lungs.

"We were both reaching for the last bag of flour."

Mindy laughs, but James scowls. "What were you going to do with flour?"

Nick's grip tightens on me. I squeeze back.

"Just had a hankering for cake, Dad."

"He let me have the bag," I say to Mindy.

"And now she makes me cake." He kisses my temple. It's the briefest touch, the kind of cursory kiss a person would give someone they know they'll kiss again and again and again for a long time. But it makes my heart pound for no reason at all.

"I'll go grab the bags," he says, leaving me to smile and nod at Mindy as she runs through an itinerary of the weekend: a dinner tonight, the party tomorrow, lamenting the fact that we likely won't be able to get out on the lake for a skate. "But you'll just have to come back before the ice thaws," she says excitedly.

Nick returns with *all* of the bags. He smells like the cold and his face is flushed from exertion,

"I put you in your old room, sweetie," Mindy says, giving James a pat on his stomach before hurrying after a grandchild running by with a—thankfully clean—diaper on their head.

His dad is called away by one of Nick's brothers, Robert, I think.

"You?" I ask, my heart pounding for an entirely new reason. "You as in you, right? You will be in your room and I will be...elsewhere?"

"Both of us," he says, one corner of his lips quirking up.

I follow him as he hefts the bags toward a mudroom off the kitchen rather than the staircase that bisects the main room.

"But we can't *sleep* together," I hiss. "Why didn't you tell me?"

He shrugs in this way he has, like he's beleaguered by my annoying questions.

My fingers twitch in response, that's how badly I want to strangle him.

"I thought you'd assume that two adults pretending..." He stops at the foot of the stairs in the mudroom. "Two adults who are *dating* would be sleeping together." With that, he turns and stomps up the stairs.

Of course, the possibility crossed my mind, but it wasn't such a big deal before. Now, after that moment in my kitchen, the idea of being alone with him, behind a closed door, under the same bed linens, *horizontal*? I don't trust myself.

This is all Jade's fault. She planted the seed and now it's all I can think about.

Getting dicked down by Nick Scott.

12

――――――

NICK

Before I open the door of the ensuite bathroom, I take a deep, centering breath and work to convince myself not to do this. I shouldn't do this. But I can hear her moving around on the other side of the door, snooping. She went silent as she crossed the threshold into my room, because it doesn't look like my room. There aren't any old NHL players or pop rock band posters plastered on the wood-paneled walls. No awards, trophies, artwork, pictures from my youth. Just a large flat-screen TV mounted on the wall across from a double bed covered in a crisp navy blue comforter. There's no personality left at all.

Mom kept all our rooms as we left them, I think in the hopes that we'd be more likely to come back, but home isn't really a place; it's a feeling. I took home with me when I left.

On the other side of the door a drawer opens and shuts quietly, too slowly not to be intentional. I shouldn't do this, but I'm gonna.

Tightening the towel around my hips, I step into my bedroom. Jasmine spins from where she was bent over my old desk. When she sees me, she plasters herself against the wall, her clothes folded neatly in her arms and pressed against her chest. Her green eyes make *holy shit* holes in her head.

"You...that..." She blushes, clutching her clothes tighter. "Your *body*," she whisper-hisses, not quite meeting my gaze.

I tell myself that I'm doing this to make her hate me. As if the more I tease her, the easier it will be to have a clean break when I tell her the truth. But honestly, I just love making her flustered. I revel in how easy it is to make her blush and how prim and proper she tries to be. Key word, tries.

I press my hand to my bare chest. "Dear god, not my body again."

She slinks along the wall, keeping a wide berth, then slips into the bathroom and shuts the door harder than necessary.

"It's my bedroom, Jazz," I call.

She doesn't respond, and then the shower comes on.

To my reflection in the mirror above my dresser, I say, "Are you proud of yourself?"

I don't dignify myself with a response. Instead, I flop on the bed to get my heart under control. Each new wave of attraction to her is a surprise, though it shouldn't be. It's as if the more I tell myself I can't have her, the more I recount the reasons I shouldn't be doing this at all—that I am, actually, a huge fucking asshole—the more my body is tuned to her. The Binder, the blush on her cheeks when I frustrate her or when she's scandalized, the way she bravely faced my family, how the sun catches the blazing red and fiery gold in her hair.

I end up air-drying on the edge of my bed thinking about ways I can make her pinch her lips in frustration. When the shower shuts off, I bolt up and hop around the room, pulling on clothes so when she comes out, she isn't confronted with *my body* once again.

I get my shirt on before she opens the door, but just barely. She walks out looking so hot I might have a stroke and die right here on my childhood bedroom floor. Brow furrowed in apprehension, she smooths her hands down the front of her high-waisted skirt and loose knit sweater. The lingering humidity from our showers curls the hair around her temples and at the back of her neck. Her makeup is sparse. If I smoothed my thumb over her lips, I doubt a trace of pigment would rub off.

"You're wearing that?" she asks.

I pluck at my favorite Tragically Hip T-shirt, the one I've owned since the first time I saw them live when I was twelve. "You're nailing this girlfriend thing."

"Sorry." She worries her bottom lip. "I just mean...am I over-dressed?"

"You look perfect," I say, but my voice cracks. Great; loving my reversion to preteen. Anticipate wet dreams next. "It's just family dinner," I assure her. "Tomorrow night is the official anniversary party."

She nods and sits beside me on the bed, leaving a hand's width of space between us. A completely normal amount of space. Except that it feels too close and too fucking far at the same time. A *pop* comes from downstairs, probably Alex opening a bottle of champagne that, while expensive, isn't necessarily good.

"When are you going to talk to your dad?"

Embracing the opportunity to put distance between us, I hop up and grab the business proposal I put together for him. I splurged and had it printed and bound at an office supply store. Keeping it hidden behind my back, I turn to her.

"Don't get too excited, but..." I pull it out and present it to her like I'm a game show hostess. "I'm going to talk to him tomorrow. Probably. I'm gonna give him this."

"Can I see it?" Without waiting for my answer, she snatches the bound package with both hands.

"No." I give an experimental pull.

"Why not?" She yanks back.

"Because I said so?" I am not about to let the perfectionist browse my business proposal so she can point out everything that's wrong with it when there's no way I can make changes before I talk to my dad.

"I just want to see," she hisses.

She's always hissing at me. Why don't I hate it more? I hate that I don't hate it more, the way her lip curls and her eyes squint.

"Why do you care so much?"

She huffs and lets go, the move causing me to stumble back into the desk.

"I'm not going to point out all your spelling mistakes or anything." She pats at her hair, takes a few deep breaths, like she's putting herself back together, making sure she's public-facing Jasmine once again. Sometimes she's so well put together it's almost impossible to find a thread I can pull to unravel her.

"Thanks for assuming there'll be spelling mistakes."

She winces at my shitty response.

Dammit. Before her wince can turn into hurt, I sit beside her again and place the proposal on her lap. "Sorry." I let my shoulders deflate. "I'm a little stressed out. Still. And I'm taking it out on you. Still."

With a sigh, she draws her fingers along the edges of the bound pages, like she's making sure each piece of paper is still in place. "I don't need to read it." She returns it to my lap and I'm imagining things, but it feels like her touch lingers a breath longer than necessary. "Why don't you go find your dad now? Get it out of the way?"

"He's probably in the workshop." He holes up in there when the house gets full.

"You have a workshop?"

"It's attached to the indoor pool."

Her body goes rigid beside me. "You have an indoor pool?" she asks, her voice hitting a totally new octave. "Next to a lake?"

I bite back a laugh at her shock. "Why do you think I told you to pack a bathing suit?"

Head lowered, she peers up at me through thick lashes. "I thought you were going to make me do a polar bear swim."

"And you were going to do it?" I ask, my voice now battling hers for octave supremacy.

She shrugs. "I kind of enjoy them."

"We're going to put a pin in that, weirdo." Mostly because the image of Jasmine pulling herself out of the freezing cold lake, in a bathing suit, her skin pink, her nipples undoubtedly hard, makes me light-headed and I don't trust her not to panic in an emergency situation.

Laughing, she slaps her hands to my chest and gives me a good shove. "We're putting a pin in nothing. You grew up with an indoor pool?" she asks, her eyes wide.

I grimace because yes, I am aware of how that looks. "Yes, but it wasn't installed until I was in high school."

That only makes her laugh harder. "Yeah, completely normal. I had one, too. I shared it with everyone else in my apartment building. There were always used Band-Aids at the bottom and the change rooms smelled like dirty diapers."

I find myself chuckling along with her, not only because she's funny, but because her laughter is contagious. And that's how Mom and Miranda find us when they open my bedroom door.

"Knock, knock," Mom announces herself in lieu of actually knocking.

With a gasp, Jasmine jumps away from me like we're sixteen and just got caught with my hand down her pants. "Hi, Mrs. Scott."

Mom offers her arm, and after a moment of hesitation and a peek back at me, Jasmine takes it. Mom leads her away, chatting about god knows what while Miranda hands me a flute of champagne, and we follow them downstairs. These stairs creak like the ones behind the bar at home and as we descend into the circus that is my family, it hits me. The chaos sounds a bit like the bar, too, on a Saturday night when we're not at capacity yet and the air is already buzzing with excitement.

Mom points out her interior designer's most recent changes. She might be under the impression that Jasmine gives a shit about that kind of stuff because of where she works, but I don't think she does.

"Mom's planning your wedding," Miranda says.

I shush her, which makes her violent. She punches my shoulder. *Ow.*

"Look at you," she teases. Her cheeks are already red and blotchy. After having kids, Miranda could no longer drink a hockey bro under the table, and that hasn't changed in the months since I saw her last, but clearly that doesn't stop her. "You're half in love with her already."

My throat closes at the accusation, enough that I wouldn't mind an EpiPen. "Am not."

"Are too."

"*Shut. Up. Miranda.*" Great. Now I'm hissing.

She frowns in that suspicious way big sisters have, like she can smell the bullshit. "Relax, serial killer."

"We haven't said stuff like that yet," I say quickly. "Lay off." With a huff, I take a sip of champagne to keep my mouth busy. A trickle of cold sweat rolls down my back.

Once, without proof of any kind other than a *I could tell by the look on your face, Nicky*, Miranda clocked that I'd failed a math test and forged Mom's signature. I'd even fooled my teachers. Of all the people capable of detecting our lie, or my lies upon lies, I expected Miranda to. Maybe the lack of sleep she's suffered from since becoming a mother is getting to her. Or maybe I'm a better liar that I used to be.

"But you are, aren't you?" She winks. "Don't worry, little brother. I won't tell."

I don't want to be a better liar, though. I want to be able to come home and feel like I can be myself without judgment.

"She's not your usual type." Miranda narrows her eyes on Jasmine, who's trying to speak to Grandma and getting scowled at for her efforts. "Seems a little...cold. Impersonal."

Hackles instantly rising, I shoot a glare at my sister. Excellent. The criticism portion of the evening has started, and earlier than usual. "Not at all. She's actually...really fucking kind. And she's always worrying about other people. She basically adopted her little sister. And she brought Mom two hostess gifts."

Miranda hums, like this evidence is circumstantial at best.

"Cut her some slack," I plead. "She comes from a small family. She's not used to all this. It's like being the newest member of the Kardashians, without the cameras."

"Thank god," Miranda mutters, dribbling champagne from her glass as she wanders off, finished with her interrogation of me.

"Ready?" Jasmine asks, appearing beside me. Somehow, she's in stealth mode despite wearing a pair of heels that could pass as the weapon she'll use to happily murder me once I come clean. She leans against the back of the sectional couch, surveying my family like they're chess pieces as they begin to take their seats at a dining table so long, my mom must have stolen it from the set of the villain's hideout from the most recent superhero movie.

I tip my glass toward her empty hands. "Liquid courage?"

She shakes her head, her attention never leaving the rest of the Scotts. "Need to stay focused," she says with absolute, endearing seriousness.

One second. I give myself one second to laugh, internally, at this earnest, beautiful, strange woman who asked a complete stranger to fake it with her on a whim. She deserves better than me.

My second is up. "Smart." I set down my glass. "Let's do this."

My mother calls Jasmine's name and she brightens, like how I imagine she did when her teachers called on her to answer a question in class. She's got teacher's pet written all over her.

Mom pats the chair beside her, near the head of the table. The seat usually reserved for Alex.

Alex's eyes widen as we pass him, his brows shooting into his hairline.

"Are we both sitting up here?" I ask, pulling out Jasmine's chair for her to sit.

My mom sits primly, her chin lifted. My dad, surprisingly, looks impressed. I don't look at Jasmine because I can feel her staring at the side of my face.

"Or am I at the kids' table again?"

"You know we don't have a kids' table, Nicholas," Dad says dryly.

"Thanks," Jasmine murmurs as I take the seat next to her, the one Robert usually sits in. I bump my shoulder to hers in acknowledgment, though I'd prefer to have a word with all the guys who never held her seat for her, instead.

My parents hired caterers for dinner tonight and the party tomorrow. Mom stopped trying to cook for all of us once two of my siblings started producing offspring and four siblings had long-term partners. It's expensive, but she's a lot less stressed at Christmas now. She and my dad were the ones who decided to have all these kids anyway.

The volume rises and falls between courses, first a coconut-cream soup, then a salad with goat cheese and cranberries. My siblings get up throughout the night, chasing after errant children, changing diapers or supervising a bathroom break, and putting the littlest ones to bed.

While we wait for the entrées, Tilly wiggles her way between my chair and Jasmine's, icing Jasmine out like the nose-picking Mean Girl she is.

"Dis yours?" she asks, holding a phone up to my face. The screen's background is a photo of Jasmine and Jade sitting on a towel on a Toronto beach on a sunny day. Jasmine wears a wide-brimmed hat, sunglasses, and a flowy beach cover-up over a green one-piece with a swooping neckline, while Jade is hatless, in a neon pink two-piece, and likely no sun protection if the burn developing on her cheeks and nose is any indication. Her hair is longer than when I met her and a vibrant, Smurf blue.

"It's Auntie Jasmine's, honeybuns," Robert prompts, smiling apologetically at my fake girlfriend.

"Oh. It's fine. I mean, I'm not...she doesn't..."

I take the phone from Tills and pass it to Jasmine just to end this spluttering.

"It rang several times while Tilly was helping me put the baby down. We thought you may want to check."

"I'm so sorry," she says quickly, her spine snapping straight and her cheeks flushing. "I hope it wasn't keeping him awake."

"It's fine." Robert rests a gentle hand on her shoulder. "It just seemed like someone really wanted to get in touch with you."

If possible, she tenses further. "It might be Jade." But she doesn't stand or even look at her phone because god forbid she be impolite even while she's probably imagining worst-case scenarios.

"It's fine," I assure her, covering her hand with my own. To play the part, because that's what good boyfriends do. And for no other reason. "Go take the call."

With a tight smile, she excuses herself and hurries to the stairs, her phone clutched tightly in her hand.

13

———

JASMINE

Downstairs, the Scotts talk and laugh, and wine glasses and cutlery clink. But the sounds are muted, filtered, and not just by Nick's closed bedroom door. The moment Chloe answered the phone, it's as though someone popped a fishbowl on top of my head.

The gas fireplace was on when I was down there, the low lighting making the room cozy and warm. Up here? I'm freezing. So frozen I can't even get up to find my sweater, a blanket.

A can of gasoline.

"Jasmine?" Chloe asks, her tone laced with concern.

"Sorry," I say. "I need you to repeat that."

Chloe pauses. I get it. This will be her third time through. "Is everything okay?" she asks.

"Yes. Sorry." People say that Canadians are always apologizing but I've never noticed until now. "The connection here is really bad."

"Okay. Well, um, like I said, Nick was so sorry to miss your date. And I apologize for not checking in with you after the fact. If I had, we would have known that you'd been ghosted. Well, not ghosted, I guess. Since he actually had a good excuse." She laughs, a pretty sound. "But either way, now you know, he didn't actually ghost you."

"Right," I say, my throat so dry I can barely get the word out. "Because he...Nick, my date...or match. Nick didn't show up to our date because..."

"I know. It sounds unbelievable. Like the plot of a nineties rom-com."

A roar of laughter comes from downstairs, and I listen for the cries of one of the babies sleeping on this level. Either their cries aren't sharp enough to break through my fishbowl or their parents have their sound machines on max.

"But I visited him in the hospital," she says. "And I can confirm that yes, that man was hit by a bus on his way to your date."

My brain has somehow become a clunky old machine. I wonder, momentarily, if Chloe is actually speaking French. I pulled As in school but that was over a decade ago.

"Nick was hit by a bus," I repeat. "Then in a coma."

"But only for a few days," she interjects.

Numb, I nod. "Right. But now he's better."

"Apparently, he's a medical miracle."

"Uh-huh. And now he wants to go on the date that we didn't get to have."

"Exactly."

If my Nick isn't *my* Nick, then who the fuck is he?

Chloe must read my silence as disinterest. "Listen, I know it sounds strange. I was skeptical too, at first. But I've checked it all out myself. It's real. And I really do stand by the algorithm. I think you'll be a great match, and just think, if things go well, this will be such a fun story to tell your grandkids."

By some miracle, I'm able to fake a laugh. "I...I..."

"You need some time?" Chloe asks.

"Yes. Please."

"Of course, and listen, if you think it would help—"

The hardwood floor creaks from somewhere nearby. Footsteps in the hall move closer. I've been here a while. Nick is checking on me or Mindy is and I really don't want to see either of them right now.

"—could I share your email address with him?"

The steps stop outside Nick's closed bedroom door.

"Um."

A knock sounds, causing the solid wood to rattle against its frame.

"Sure. Yeah. Whatever you think is best," I say quickly. Without waiting for a response, I hang up, and an instant later, the door opens, and Nick pokes his head in.

The numbness is gone, I'm no longer cold, confused. I'm going to fucking kill this man. Tossing my phone on the bed, I haul myself up and storm across the room before he has time to open his mouth.

"You," I growl. Grabbing him by his lying T-shirt, I pull him into his lying room and slam his lying door behind him.

He stumbles as I push him away, his face a mask of bewilderment.

Rage courses through my veins, humming and heating me from the inside out. My hands shake with anger. I make fists, keep my arms straight at my side. I've never felt this angry before, like I could tear into him with my nails and teeth.

"What the fuck, Jasmine?" he whisper-hisses.

When we arrived, I laid my shoes out so I could survey my options. Now this stable of shoes is an effective armory. I pick up a runner and chuck it at him. He catches it, then uses it to block the high heel. He jumps over the bed to the other side of the room.

"Jasmine." He cuts himself off, and his next words are much quieter. "What the fuck is wrong with you?"

Fury snakes its way up my spine. "What's wrong with me?"

"Keep your voice down."

I've never heard him speak in such a concerned tone. It's almost as if he actually cares about something enough to have an emotional reaction as opposed to his usual amused apathy.

Pulse pounding at my throat, I take a deep breath and focus on getting a handle on this rage. Not because he told me to. But because this isn't like me. I've never been this angry before, never thrown things at my partner.

Except, he's not even my partner. Not in the real way. Not in the way I can't believe I entertained for even a moment and not in the way we faked for his parents downstairs.

"Be honest." I gasp. "Were you ever going to tell me?"

He blinks, frozen, the color draining from his face. "Oh." He slumps onto the edge of the mattress, hunched back to me. "So, you know?" His voice is muffled.

I round the bed to make him face me. Coward. "Yes. Please tell me. What do I know, Nick? If that even is your name?" I suck in a harsh breath and let it out. If I'm not careful, I'll reach screeching levels again soon.

"You heard my entire family call me by my name or some variation of it, of course my name is Nick."

Irritation pricks at me. "Don't."

"Don't what?" He frowns up at me.

"Don't be all...*cute.*"

"I'm not *trying* to be cute," he argues, gesturing to himself, like it just comes naturally.

"Listen, chucklebutt." I wield my index finger at his face like a knife.

"Chucklebutt?" He laughs, but stifles the sound by rubbing his hand over his mouth when he realizes his mistake. He eyes the window above the desk like he's wondering how many bones he'll break if he jumps out of it. "I'm sorry," he says, so quiet I can barely hear it over the blood pounding in my ears.

"Okay. And?"

"Could you sit down?" he asks, dark eyes pleading.

"No." I cross my arms over my chest.

He stalks across the room and pulls out his desk chair. Dropping into it, he holds out a hand, silently offering the bed to me. "I just want to make sure you can't throw anymore shoes at my head."

I am not going to apologize for that, but I sit.

He holds out his hands, a pacifying gesture, like he's animal control and I'm the coyote that's just wandered out of Sunnybrook Park. Now that I'm sitting, the anger, the adrenaline, leaves my body in a whoosh. I'm cold again. A little dizzy.

After a few silent moments, he stands and shuffles into the

adjoining bathroom. He turns on the tap and a few moments later comes back with a glass of water.

At first, feeling spiteful, I don't take it, but my mouth is dry, and maybe the shock of the cold water will calm the way my body is vibrating.

Instead of doing the polite Canadian thing and thanking him, I say, "I want an explanation."

He nods, sits in the chair again. "When you introduced yourself at the bar, I honestly just thought you were...kinda weird?" He grimaces, his gaze full of apology. "But you're..." He throws his hand in my direction, not looking at me. "Beautiful. And you were asking me to hang out with you, and that shit with your ex?"

Tears spring to my eyes, sharp and sudden. Dammit. I divulged those details to a person I thought I "knew." A man who was at least vetted by a business concerned with my personal safety.

I thought I was a fool before. When Mitchell dumped me, when he got engaged a month later. I had to walk around in a world where anyone who knew me knew that I was so inconsequential to Mitchell that he didn't even bother to end things in person. The world knew that I was so meaningless to him that I didn't even deserve his fidelity.

As I gape at Nick, my heart cracks wide open. This is exponentially worse.

"I didn't really understand what was going on, but you said you needed help." He flushes, pressing his lips together so tightly they lose all their color. "I didn't realize what happened until you agreed to help me. At the engagement party? Zara mentioned something about the matchmaker, and you'd said something about it right before. And I realized, *oh fuck*, I think she was supposed to meet a guy named Nick. I think she thinks that's me."

"But you thought you'd keep up the lie for what? So you could get in my pants?"

"I put a stop to that," he says.

"We got caught by my sister."

"I stopped right before." He shakes his head. "I came over that night to tell you the truth, but I also really need to save my bar. I can't let some developer turn it into condos. Ed is like a father to me and he's not doing well. Rocco is my best friend, Bernie, too. She's got a kid. And if I can get the capital," he says, "then I can keep the place going for Ed. For his legacy."

"Fuck you, Nick," I whisper. "You lied for you. Don't try to turn this into some campaign about gentrification or labor. You needed me to pretend to your family." I point to the floor where they sit below us. "Your family who fucking *loves* you. The way your mother looks at you?"

A sob threatens to escape me, so I snap my mouth shut and choke it back. Mindy thinks each of her children is a blessing that she is undeserving of; my mother looked at Jade and me like we were nuisances.

"You made me lie to them so you could get money from your rich daddy."

"You made me lie, too," he shoots back, anger clipping his words. "None of this would have happened if you hadn't wanted to lie to your rich boyfriend and his rich parents so that you could save face."

My stomach twists painfully at the accusation in his tone. "That's different."

"How the fuck is it different?"

Slamming my hands on the mattress on either side of me, I glare. "Because they are assholes."

"Then why'd you date him, Jasmine?"

I look away. I don't owe him explanations.

"You think I'm some loser bartender who doesn't take life seriously."

"I never said that." But he's not inaccurate.

"You didn't have to." He leans back in the desk chair like the boys in my high school used to do, balancing there for a moment before coming back down. "I might be a loser and I might not take things seriously, but I see things. Like how you care so fucking much about what other people think of you that you'll break your back to bend over for them."

"Fuck you." I won't cry. I will not.

My words roll off him like butterflies in the wind—he's unaffected.

"And yeah, I lied. I'm sorry. I should have told you the moment I realized that this was a misunderstanding. I'll take you home. Right now. It doesn't mean much now, but I planned to tell you, after this. I knew you'd be mad." He jerks his chin, a nod to the state of me. "Like you are now. And I didn't tell you because yeah. I am a selfish asshole."

"Piece of shit," I add.

"That, too." He smiles, except none of this is funny. "I didn't tell you because I needed your help. And because…" He stops. His chest rising on deep breaths, he licks his lips, his tongue leaving a sheen of moisture in its wake. His cheeks are flushed, and his eyes are bright.

If I didn't know any better, I might think that Nick is also trying not to cry.

"I didn't tell you because I liked you." His voice cracks and he clears his throat. "Like you. And I'm selfish." He shrugs. "I knew if I did, I'd never see you again. I'm sorry."

I scoff. "Do you actually think this bullshit about feelings will get you out of this?"

"I'm not trying to get out of anything. I'm just telling you the truth."

"How am I supposed to believe that *this* is the truth?" I ask flatly.

"You can't, I guess, but it is."

"You humiliated me." My voice breaks as tears finally fall.

He sighs, nods. "I don't know if it helps," he says. "But I'm really ashamed of myself."

It does not.

I clear my throat. "Can you give me some space?" I ask. "Go downstairs and tell them whatever you want. Say my sister is having a romantic crisis or something."

I'm trapped here; the only place I can truly find peace is the bathroom.

He stands. "I don't have to lie to them. I'll tell them everything and then I'll take you home."

I shake my head. "You've been drinking."

"I had one glass of champagne."

"It doesn't matter. It's late. Maybe I'll just, uh, have a shower?"

I'm numb. Or maybe apathetic is a better word. My anger burned up all my emotion, there's nothing left.

"Are you sure?" he asks, and when I nod, he wanders to the door and grasps the knob, before turning back around. "Do you like baths. It's a soaker tub."

I don't answer him.

Murmurs from downstairs break in as he opens the door. The tone is more subdued, as if they're winding down for the night. Though part of me is fearful they heard us and are trying to listen in. He closes the door with a quiet click, blocking out everything else, leaving me alone.

Which sucks, because I wish I wasn't.

No matter how much hot water I add to the bath, it's not hot enough. While I'm still submerged, Nick returns to the room and goes through what I assume is his bedtime routine, the gentle creak of his bed, his padded steps across the carpet. The door closes again but he comes back a few minutes later. Music plays from his phone, but only one song before he turns it off. It's a song I don't recognize. The bed creaks again, the TV mounted on the wall comes on.

The water gurgles when I pull the plug, drips like rain as I stand and step onto the mat. His bathroom is stocked with bath sheets, the kind big enough to sleep under. They're fluffy and warm and decadent and I spend longer than necessary drying myself, brushing my hair. I go through each step of my skincare routine with purpose and intention, all to prolong the inevitable: opening that door and facing Nick.

The worst part of all this is the disappointment that hit me like a wave when it sank in that Nick—this Nick—is not my match.

My pajamas were a gift from Mitchell's parents; royal green silk with white piping. I wear them like armor, because not only do they feel amazing, but I look amazing in them.

Nick doesn't look up when I open the door. He lounges on the bed, remote control in one hand, the other tucked under the waistband of his underwear peeking out beneath his sweats, his legs crossed at the ankles, feet bare. Not a care in the world.

"I'm not sleeping on the floor," he says, like he's expecting the demand.

"I never asked."

His eyes follow me as I cross the room, putting things away, setting out my clothes for tomorrow.

When I sit on the bed, it's at the very edge, my back to him. "Have you talked to your dad yet?"

He's silent for a long moment, but finally, he responds with a simple "No."

I nod. It's not that I'm going to shrug off what he's done. I don't think I could. But he hurt my already bruised pride and the last thing I want is to leave here owing him anything.

I slide under the covers, pull my eye mask over my forehead, and rub lotion into my hands. Normally, I'd moisturize my feet as well, but Jade's Gen Z sensibilities must be getting to me, because that strikes me as an obscene thing to do in front of him. He flips the channels as the sports highlight reel he was watching ends and lands on a sitcom rerun. The laugh track is obnoxious in the silence between us.

"Do you like this show?" he asks, still homed in on the TV.

"Sure." I shrug. Silk slips against my chest, my stomach. Sitting next to him like this, the sensation is illicit, and it sends goose bumps along my spine.

"So, tomorrow?" he says. "I'll take you home."

I turn to him, pulling in a strengthening breath. "No."

After a moment, he shakes his head. "Why not?" His voice is soft, how I imagine he'd speak to his girlfriend as they lay in bed together.

"Because you still need to talk to your dad," I say, lifting my chin. "And I'm not an asshole."

He reaches across the bed but stops short before he can touch my hand. "I really am sorry, Jasmine."

"Save it." I stare at the TV screen, unseeing, chest still aching and pride still bruised.

"Fine. I'm going to sleep." He flips back the covers. "Do you want to keep the TV on?"

"No." I roll away, clinging to the edge of the mattress. With a few clicks of the remote and the bedside lamp, we're plunged into darkness.

"Goodnight," he says.

Rather than answering him, I pull my mask over my eyes and pretend I have the power of miraculous, immediate sleep. Nick strikes me as the type of person who can sleep anywhere, and that makes me irrationally angry.

He shifts, the sheets stretch, the mattress dips; how am I supposed to sleep with these constant reminders of his existence beside me? Every movement is larger than the last, closer, like he could push me right off the bed or pull me into him.

"Would you quit it?" I yank at the blanket.

"You quit it." He yanks back. "I can feel you over there, festering."

Ew. "I am *not* festering." Festering sounds like an infection. I am not an infection, he's an infection.

"Then relax your body, please. It's like sleeping next to a statue."

Mentally, I do a full body scan. He's right. I'm clenching. I practice a round of the deep breathing exercises I learned about when Jade downloaded meditation apps on my phone.

"Please don't say festering anymore. It sounds like something a witch's cauldron does," I say through barely ungritted teeth.

"That's boil and bubble," he says, like *duh*, because he just has to have the last word.

Don't clench. Don't clench. Don't clench.

I roll onto my back, and he rolls to face me.

Don't look at him. Do not.

My pinky finger is so close to his body, it buzzes from its proximity. If I slid my hand a couple of inches across the sheet, I'd be touching Nick. His leg, his hip maybe.

Jade's deep breathing exercises have never helped. I'm better with lists, like Reasons I Do Not Want to Touch Nick:

I want to strangle him, which is technically touching. Shit.

He lied. He's a lying liar who lied. Though he's right that none of this would have happened if I hadn't asked him to lie for me first.

My heart sinks. Never before has list-making betrayed me in this way.

His gaze is boring into the side of my face. This close, sharing a bed, I'm overwhelmed by his scent. Sharp, sweet, fresh, and citrus. Like if oranges grew from pine trees.

"What?"

Nick shifts onto his back. My heart races.

"Nothing," he says. "Goodnight."

My pinky finger, my hand, my whole arm, tingles. I make list after list in my head. Why I hate Nick, why I don't want to touch him, why I'll never forgive him. But my body doesn't get the memo and I lie awake for a long, long time.

14

———

JASMINE

Hot air blows across my face in time with the telltale wheeze of a mouth breather. I open my eyes, only to be confronted by the owner of the morning breath.

"Where's Nicky?" a small child asks.

I reach behind me, patting the mattress in search of a warm body. "He's right—"

A screaming streak of brown hair interrupts me. "UNCLE NICKY."

The carpet banshee lands on the bed between us, followed by at least three, perhaps five more noise terrorists.

"What the fu—"

A warm hand clamps over my mouth, cutting off my profane tirade. "What the *fluff* is up, chicken nuggets?" Nick yells. In my ear.

I squeeze my eyes shut tight. Is this how I die? Woken too early by a family of yellers? I shove his hand off my mouth and flip over, discovering the bed now overflowing with Nick's niblings. He is absolutely gleeful, smile full and eyes disgustingly bright, surrounded by multiple, impressionable witnesses.

Tilly knees me in the butt as she clambers over me to plop herself down in his lap, all the while glaring at her cousins for infringing on her turf.

"Everyone say good morning to Jasmine." Nick holds out his arms, presenting me like he's a gorgeous bottle blond from a game show.

"Good morning, Jasmine," they all say in creepy unison. One of them, with a flop of straight black hair in their eyes, snuggles against me.

Absolutely not.

I roll out of bed and land on my feet in a move only previously seen in Rambo movies. Nick leans against the headboard, his hands behind his head. Smug bastard.

"I have to call my sister."

He grimaces, almost like he's disappointed.

I rip the charger out of my phone and scurry out the door.

"Bye, Jazz," he calls, and before I can take another step, the children are laughing and squealing again.

"It is an ungodly hour, Jasmine. What the ever-loving fuck."

"Good morning, sissy," I sing, adjusting my earbud. I found an office down the hall from Nick's room. It was empty and has a door that closes so it's as good a place as any to get some peace and quiet. Though, I'm not sure I'm supposed to be in here. From what I can see, it's the junk drawer of rooms; there are mismatched office chairs, a printer covered in dust, a computer tower but no monitor. Three decorative baskets are stacked one on top of the other in the corner, the windows have no treatments, and the computer chair behind the desk squeaks ominously as I settle into it. The room is also exceptionally cold. Already, I regret not grabbing a pair of socks or a sweater in my haste.

"Why are you awake?" The familiar sounds of Jade slapping at her sound machine comes through my earbud.

"Nick has niblings," I say. "And they *love* him." I try not to let my passive-aggression bleed through the phone line. "They woke us up."

Jade yelps, then there's a rustle of sheets. "Wait. What?" I can picture her hair, wild and spiky as she sits up in bed. "Were you in the same room as him? Did you sleep in the same bed?"

She sounds a little too scandalized for a person who requested I get "dicked down" less than twenty-four hours ago.

"It's not a big deal," I mumble. The last thing I want to do is admit what happened to Jade. For years, I was the one getting her to school on time, packing her lunches, making her dinners. I made sure she went to bed at a reasonable time and booked her doctor's appointments and reminded her to floss. Even if our relationship is more sisterly now that she's an adult, and despite how much she loves me and wouldn't judge me, I can't admit to her that Nick is one giant dupe, that I even fail at fake relationships. Not to mention that if I have to admit all that then I also have to admit how disappointed I am that he's not my near perfect match.

The worst part is, I can't even explain the dejection plaguing me. After meeting him, I thought the algorithm had gotten it wrong, so knowing that he's not my match should be a good thing. He's nothing like the men I date, so maybe the real Nick is. I told myself I'd trust in the process, so why can't I do that now?

"Tell me about your night. What do you have planned this weekend?"

Jade chats away as she moves around our apartment, the creak of the hardwood signaling her entrance to the kitchen, the squeak of the springs that she's on the couch. I only hear every other word, though, and she asks me if I'm still there twice.

"Sorry." I curl my toes into the rug to warm them.

"Distracted by your good deep dicking?"

"*Jade Elizabeth.*"

She's cackling in my ear as a knock sounds on the office door. A heartbeat later, Nick opens it, holding a steaming mug in one hand and a pair of socks in the other. With a tentative smile, he tosses the socks to me.

"Jade, I have to go."

"Text me when you're on your way home, okay?"

"I will."

Children's screams of delight—I'm assuming—reach us from downstairs.

"Thanks." I set down my phone and hold up the socks. They're the thick gray work boot kind with white and red trim. They're worn and soft and obviously Nick's.

It feels far too intimate, especially now, to wear his clothes.

"I don't know how you take your coffee." He sets the mug beside me.

"Black is good. Thanks."

He lingers in the doorway. His hair sticks up on one side and his T-shirt has a hole in the shoulder. His facial hair darkens his jaw. "Everything alright?" he asks.

He looks handsome, if not tired.

"Fine." Anger flares in my chest as I regard him with a frown. It doesn't matter if Nick is handsome. He's still a liar.

"Are you hungry?" he asks, ignoring my snark. He rubs his knuckles over his jaw. Maybe I'm imagining the scratch of his stubble as he does it, but real or not, that sound alone sends a shiver down my spine. It takes nothing for my mind to leap from the sound of stubble on his knuckles to what that stubble would sound like against my skin. Against my thighs.

I growl, grunt. An awkward, silly, ridiculous sound. One I would typically save for when I'm alone and mad at myself. As furious as I am at my reaction to him, as warranted as the berating is, I'm not alone.

He cocks his head. "Excuse me?"

My face gets hot and probably turns the color of a nice ripe tomato. I search the room for a weapon. It will be awkward, but I can probably bash my brains in with the old computer tower.

"I was holding in a sneeze," I say in my most prim voice, being sure to hold my chin high.

"Cool. Well," he says slowly. "You've got about a half hour before my mom comes searching for you. Then she's going to feed you, make you wait thirty minutes"—he ticks each item off on his fingers—"and then make you come swimming with us."

"Right. The indoor pool."

He nods. "The indoor pool. Unless..." He checks behind him before stepping further into the room. "Are you sure you don't want me to take you home?"

I stand up from the desk, doing my best to right my pajamas so I can look somewhat proper, even as my heart and stomach ache. "Do you want my help or not, Nicholas?"

Hands held up in surrender, he steps back. "Just checking." He turns to leave, then turns back again, one of his charming grins on his charming face. His stupid, charming face. "Have I told you today that I'm sorry?"

I throw his socks at him.

As promised, a half hour later I am herded downstairs, fed, and kept in my chair until another thirty minutes have passed.

"Nicky can walk you over to the pool once you're changed. You brought your suit, right?"

"I did." A nice green jewel-toned one-piece bathing suit with front zipper closure all the way up to my collarbone and full bum coverage.

Mindy beams. She has this innate ability to make everything a little less terrible. Is this what moms who give a crap about their kids are like? I wouldn't know.

As I climb the stairs in the now quiet house, I find myself surprisingly excited. I've never been in a private indoor pool before. When Nick exits the ensuite, I avert my gaze, worried he's naked again. I let out a relieved breath when I catch sight of him in my periphery. He's already dressed in his bather and a T-shirt. But I'm not looking anyway, so it doesn't matter.

I brush my teeth and put my hair up, wash my face.

Is there a Jacuzzi? God, what I'd do to relax in hot water with jets pointed at my back. Just the thought eases the tension in my muscles. Though as I continue considering the situation, I can't imagine finding peace with children shrieking and screaming in what I assume is a vast tiled space.

When I pull out my bathing suit, my stomach plummets to the floor.

"Shit," I whisper, holding it up in front of me. "Shit, shit, shit."

I rummage through my bag again, pulling out one article of neatly packed clothing after another. But it's not there. My modest, sweet, full coverage bathing suit, best suited for swimming laps, has vanished.

Nick chooses this moment to bang on the door. "Jasmine. Let's go."

Shit.

"Uhhh, just a second." My voice is high and tremulous as I scramble to pull my suit on.

"What's wrong?"

My heart lodges itself in my throat. How can he tell???

"Um. I...I can't..." I rack my brain for a reasonable excuse but come up with nothing. "I packed the wrong bathing suit."

"Oh." He pauses, then laughs, sounding relieved. "I thought you were going to say you were on your period."

Menstruation was right there, you dipshit.

"Why? Is that like, gross or something?"

A loud thump comes from his side of the door. "No, Jasmine. It's not."

"Well, I still can't go swimming." I grab a towel to cover myself. From myself.

"I'm sure it's fine."

"It's really, really not." I'm starting to get shrill.

"Listen, I realize this will make me sound like a dick, but you *need* to calm down," he says, his tone drier than an overbaked sponge cake dry as a desert and muffled like he's speaking right up against the door. "My parents don't care about your bathing suit, Jazz. Pretty sure they love you more than they love me."

I open the towel and peek down at myself. Boobs everywhere. Ninety-nine percent of the time I love my breasts, their size and shape. I even love them in this bathing suit, with its low-cut neck and lower cut back. It shows off the very best of my augmentation. Even so, this suit is best displayed poolside, on vacation, surrounded by strangers. Not in front of Nicholas's parents and siblings. Not in front of *children.*

I can scream about the unfairness of judgment until my boobs fall off, but there will always be people who say particularly nasty things about women who have implants.

"Let me see," Nick says.

"*No.*"

"Open the door," he says in the kind of tone that brooks no argument.

Fine. With a shaky hand, I unlock the door. Then, turning back to the mirror, I grip the towel tighter around my chest. Just in case he tries to snatch it away.

In the mirror, I'm hit with the perfect view of him. His swim shorts are short and red with white piping and his quads are...*wow.* The sight of his leg hair is as overwhelming as my internal panic about this stupid bathing suit. Nick stands behind me, frozen, until I force myself to meet his gaze in the mirror. His faded Arcade Fire T-shirt brushes softly against my shoulder blade, causing goose bumps to skitter down my arms. I close my eyes. What kind of fabric softener has the power to make his clothes so distractingly soft?

"Come on." He jerks his thumb over his shoulder. "Lose the towel. Let's see this thing so we can get down to the pool. I promised Tilly we'd chicken fight."

I've never mentioned my surgery to him, but I'm sure he's noticed considering we've been pressed up against each other more than once. The wise crack he hasn't made is like a third, very loud, naked person shaking their tits at us from the corner. I take a deep breath, close my eyes, and drop the towel.

Nick stays a silent presence behind me. When I open my eyes, he's gripped the marble counter with one hand, his knuckles white with tension. His face is slack and his focus is zeroed in on my chest.

"Told you." I cross my arms and frown at his reflection, wishing the floor would open up and swallow me whole.

"No, no, no, no." Gently, he pulls my arms away. He abandons leering in the mirror for the real thing, moving to the side to see all of me.

Rounding my shoulders, I fight the urge to snatch my towel from the floor and cover myself. "You're being gross."

"You're being..." He drags his hand over his mouth. "What was the question?"

"*Nick*." I punch him in the shoulder.

He grins, unaffected. "You're a rocket, Jasmine. What do you want me to say?"

"I'm starting to feel a little too objectified." I cross my arms over my chest to cover myself again.

"Sorry." He shakes himself. "You're right. If you don't want to go swimming, we don't have to."

"Just go without me."

He arches his eyebrow. "And leave you with Grandma? Nah."

He's got a point. The old bat pretended she couldn't hear me at breakfast but had no problem hearing anyone else.

And Tilly's exuberance for her Uncle Nico this morning tugged at heartstrings I thought were long dormant.

"Maybe I can wear one of your T-shirts. That could hide all..." I circle a hand in front of me, gesturing to my chest. "This."

"Or you could trust me when I say that truly..." He rests a hand on my shoulder, his palm warm, the touch both comforting and electric. "No one will be paying attention to your bathing suit."

I shake my hands out, my worry a knot in my abdomen, pulling tighter and tighter. I want not to care, like Nick does, but the code in his genetic makeup that gives him that ability is one I'm lacking.

"The only person who needs to care about what you think is you," he says, like he can read the thoughts on my face. "Do you like how you look, Jasmine?"

"Yes," I say quietly, heart thudding against my chest. "I do."

The pipes in the wall make a whooshing noise. One of the niblings, a straggler, yells as he runs down the hall outside our room.

"Do you?" I keep my tone casual. I shouldn't care. I wish I didn't. I want to not.

His irises are almost black as he homes in on my face in the mirror. "Since you're asking, I do. I think you could blow our cover. I've never brought a girl home as beautiful as you."

I pick at my cuticles to hide the flush. "You've never brought a girl home at all," I remind him.

"Are you really nervous?" he asks. Not like he's skeptical. Just checking in.

I nod. My hands twitch with the need to fix this, but I'm not sure I can.

"What can I do to make it better?"

It's like when I played that word association game in the high school cafeteria with my friends: What's the first thing you think of when you think of Todd?

Kissing.

What can he do? The first thing that comes to mind is lying beside him last night, how my skin vibrated at his proximity. The way he kisses, like it's the most important thing he'll ever do.

Jade's voice is in my head, entreating me to let him dick me down.

Maybe he sees the flush in my cheeks or how I sneak a glance at his hand, still gripping the marble, because Nick straightens behind me and places his hand gently on my hip. Then he asks again, "What do you need, Jasmine?"

It's not about what I need. Maybe it's about what I deserve. I think of him on his knees, his lie. The way he played me for a fool.

I clear my throat. The hairs too short for my ponytail tickle the back of my neck.

He presses in behind me.

The words are stuck in my throat. For once, I don't want to be the uptight girl, high-strung, in her head. "I need a way to... I need to relax a little."

This bathing suit doesn't leave much to the imagination, but he looks at me like I've hidden secrets beneath my skin.

"How do you want to relax?" He's quiet, yet his voice still echoes in this pristine marble bathroom as he watches me through the mirror.

I should not let this man, the fake Nick, the wrong Nick, touch me. I should ask him for a mug of warm water and lemon. Get my phone. Call Jade. But if I spoke those words aloud, each one would be a lie.

I hate to lie.

The mirror gives the illusion of distance between us when I say, "You could get me off. If you wanted."

Nick is a blanket of heat against my bare back, his T-shirt the kind of soft that girlfriends steal and never give back after breakups.

"Are you sure that's what you want?" he asks, eyes wide.

"Yes," I say, my voice breathy. My pulse hums in my throat and wrists, between my legs.

Nick's jaw is tight, a shallow V forming between his eyes as he brushes his knuckles down my front, over a peaked nipple. He splays his hand over my belly.

"If it's not working," he says into the back of my neck. "Tell me to stop."

I shake my head. "It will work."

It already is. My blood pumps warm and loose through me. I'm using him, that's what this is. Using him, like he's using me, like I used him first. I'm prepared for him to be mechanical about it. Nick makes a joke out of everything; there's no way he'll interpret this for more than it is, more than it needs to be. Nick kisses me, his lips velvet soft on my neck. His mouth open on the side of my throat. A shock of lust and surprise moves down my spine.

"Is this okay?" he asks into my skin.

Eyes closed, I let my head fall back onto his shoulder. The moan that escapes me could only be described as wanton. In any other situation, my desperation would be embarrassing.

He doesn't move until I swallow through my next breath.

"Yes," I say, chest heaving, already struggling to take in air. "You're okay."

He ghosts his fingers those last few inches, then presses softly over my bathing suit against my pussy. There's nothing rote or mechanical about Nick's hands on my body.

He's gentle, passionate.

He slips his other hand between my arm and hip, brushing his fingers over my breast. In the gentlest of rhythms, he presses between my legs. Leaves the lightest kisses along my shoulder. He plays me like a finely tuned instrument; he could make me sing. With one leg, he urges me to spread mine, his leg hair tickling my skin. We look obscene in the mirror. His head bent over my shoulder, his dark hair a mess. His hand moving slowly between my legs. I never want to forget this image.

"Can I?" he asks, slowly slipping his fingers beneath the wide strap over my breast, his other hand hooking into the hip of my bathing suit.

"Yes," I whisper, attention locked on our reflection as he slips the rest of the way under my suit. The fabric of the suit stretches over his hands as his warmth soaks into me. I guide his mouth against my skin as I tilt my head to one side to give him access to more.

I moan as he pushes two fingers into me. I flush with embarrassment at how wet I am.

"Shhhhh," he whispers, sending goose bumps along my skin. "You tensed up. What just happened?"

I shake my head, squeeze my eyes shut. The knot tightens in my stomach.

"You're perfect, you know that?" He kisses me between words, drags his fingers up and down the lips between my legs. "Warm and so fucking wet and soft. You surprised me with this velvet soft pussy. But I should know by now, shouldn't I? You're always going to surprise me."

He slips his fingers inside me again and I gasp his name.

"Perfect," he praises, smiling against my cheek. "You like when I say that don't you? You're perfect now, Jasmine, and you'll be perfect when you come all over my hand."

My knees hit the cabinet beneath the counter. His words alone might be enough to send me hurtling over that cliff. Nick takes his time, moving his fingers in slow circles against me, until I chase his touch with my hips, until the heat in my core hurts and I have to press my lips together to keep from begging him.

I get by on quick glances of us; that's all I can take. But Nick stares at where his hands move over and inside me, his eyes shot black, his cheeks pink. He presses hard into the curve of my ass. I whimper desperate sounds against the rough stubble on his cheek. Try to squeeze my legs closed around him, but his legs on either side of mine keep them apart. I pull at his hair, grip his wrist where his hand disappears between my legs. Anything to pull him closer to me as the pleasure becomes too much.

My orgasm spills like oil down my back, a trickle at first then faster, stronger, more, until I'm coming with a gentle moan against his ear.

"Nick?" his mother calls from the bedroom door as my orgasm melts through me.

I yelp in surprise, but like it's nothing to hear his mother outside his door while his fingers are inside me, Nick slides a rough palm over my mouth, the second time today.

He kisses my cheek once, the scratch of his beard almost pulling another moan from me. "We'll be down in a minute, Ma."

"See you soon, honey," she calls through the door.

My entire body beats with my heart. "Holy," I whisper.

"Perfect," he says with the confidence of knowing he was right. He continues to stroke me lazily until I squeeze his wrist in a silent request. With a smirk he stops. Then he drops three kisses along the curve of my shoulder before he looks at me in the mirror. We're flushed and wild eyed. I'll have to redo my ponytail.

"Good?" he asks.

"I...what?"

Nick pulls his hand out from beneath my bathing suit. My legs tremble, fawn-like. He doesn't take his hands off me until I lean against the counter to hold myself up. Only then does he wash his hands, like he's just stepped behind the bar to start a shift.

"Relaxed?" he asks, inspecting his fingernails.

Words mean things. I can't think of what, but they do. The bulge in the front of his swim shorts looks uncomfortable. The sight of it is all it takes for the logistics of this moment to fully hit me, how usually these kinds of favors are reciprocal.

"Do you need?" I press my hand to my throat, unsure what I'm even asking. I'm doing my best not to dissolve into a puddle on the heated tile floor.

Nick grins down at his cock as he dries his hands and readjusts. "We're good. That's not what this was about."

My heart stumbles at his earnest expression. "What was it about?"

"You," he says simply, one brow arched. "How do you feel?"

The tips of my fingers buzz. Not even the threat of his mother walking in on us could ruin what he just did to me. "Relaxed," I say when I know I won't sound so breathless.

With a kiss on the cheek, he rests his hand on my hip, another casual gesture like he's done it every day for years. "You look beautiful when you come, Jasmine."

My breath stalls, my lungs seizing.

That teasing expression he's so fond of has reappeared. "I'll meet you downstairs. In five minutes, Jazz," he warns, striding out of the bathroom.

"I haven't forgiven you yet," I say, shuffling to the threshold. It feels important to make that distinction.

He nods, a quick jerk of his chin, and leaves.

This changes nothing. Nick's not my match.

15

———

NICK

For the rest of the day, I'm electrified. Jasmine joined me exactly five minutes later at the foot of the stairs, droplets of water still on her shoulders from the shower she must have taken. I'd spent those five minutes going through every Blue Jays loss in recent memory. Nothing kills a boner better than home team heartbreak.

We walked to the pool with a foot of space between us, but the hair on my arms stood on end the entire way. Each strand a lightning rod in the electrical storm that is Jasmine Palmer. At the pool, she kept her beach cover-up on the whole time, sitting on the edge and dangling her feet in the water. In the end, that was probably for the best. There's no way I would have kept it together if she'd taken it off. Alex and Robert would never let me near their children again.

After swimming, Jasmine volunteered to help Mom and my sisters with some last-minute errands in town. She didn't say it, but the way she studied me before she left made it clear she wants me to talk to my dad now.

I take my time climbing the stairs to get my business proposal, telling myself the whole way up that it's so the creaky steps won't wake any of the babies who are down for their naps. I loiter in my bedroom, tidying up my things so they're almost as neat as Jasmine's. I don't bother with the bathroom, though. I'm convinced it will smell like her, and if it smells like her, I may just lock myself inside until she returns.

Dad is in the living room watching a hockey game with Alex and Charlie when I return downstairs. Alex lies across one side of the L-shaped sectional, a beer on the coffee table in front of him, his eyes closed and jaw slack. Charlie takes up the other side of the L, a bowl of chips balanced on his stomach, also fast asleep.

Dad has his feet up in the recliner, no food, no drink, just a man and his big screen. Eventually he notices me skulking behind them.

"Come have a seat," he says. Except there's nowhere to sit, so I perch on the arm of the couch. I have to shove Alex's feet off of it, but he doesn't even flinch. We sit in silence through most of the third period, punctuated only by random snorts and snores from my brothers and grunts from Dad when the Leafs make a bad play, which is pretty often.

I don't know what to do with my hands. Holding the business proposal is making them sweat, but the closest flat surface is the coffee table, and I can't drop it there without standing and taking a step. That will draw Dad's attention and then he'll ask what it is.

Technically, that's what I want, that's what I'm here for. But not in front of my brothers, sleeping or otherwise.

Eventually, the game winds downs, we lose, and the feed switches over to a Western Conference game. The sun dips low over the lake. The caterers will be here soon. Jasmine will be back, and we'll have to get changed. The guests will arrive, and Mom and Dad will be celebrated for their decades of successfully not hating each other. Then, tomorrow, we'll leave. And all of this, the lying, the pretending, faking some things but not others, will have been for nothing.

I'll have hurt Jasmine, for nothing.

"Dad," I say.

He grunts again, gaze locked on the game.

"Can I talk to you?"

He turns slowly in his chair, scowling. Shit. For a moment, I'm sure he'll say no, but he hits the level on his recliner, lowering his feet. He's slow to stand, to stretch, and straighten. "I've got to clean up the woodshop," he says.

Confusion and apprehension swirl in my gut. I guess I'm supposed to follow him.

The path to the pool and shop are lined with large pavers, and when Dad installed a hydronic heating system to the circular driveway a few years ago, he extended it to the path as well. Even on the coldest days, we can get from the house to the pool or the shop without having to put boots on or shovel. He's always retrofitting the house with new technology and features. It's his way of working with his hands even though he has to wear a suit for work most of the time now. Before he was a midsize office furniture and supply company founder and CEO, he handmade custom wood furniture.

When I was a kid, I used to sit out here while he worked. He had very strict rules for children in the woodshop. I had to sit on the bench off to one side; if my butt left the bench, I got one warning. If it left the bench twice, I was gone. Once he knew I could be trusted not to get underfoot or cut my hand off with a circular saw, I was invited to sweep. I had to sweep for a year before I was allowed to touch any of the wood, but finally I graduated to sanding.

As Dad opens the French doors to the shop, the smell of freshly cut wood—better than freshly cut grass one hundred percent of the time—hits me. Instantly, I'm overwhelmed by a sense of safety and warmth. One that makes me feel like I'm eight years old again. I've helped Dad make a lot of cool stuff in here: a stained walnut chair of Scandinavian design, a chest used to store extra blankets and sheets at the foot of my bed, a full-length mirror frame with floral patterns —my first time using a router—and a rocking horse for Tilly that I don't think she ever actually used.

I sit on my bench as Dad moves about the shop. He checks the tools' safeties, inspects for hairline cracks in the saws and blades, and ensures every tool is in its place on the pegboards and in the cabinets. He even built his own tool mounts for the wall instead of using wall mounts and French cleats.

"Jasmine is impressive," he says, frowning into a pair of safety glasses like he's waiting for them to crack.

"Uhhh. Yeah." I duck my head and rub at the back of my neck. It's not that I disagree, it's just a strange adjective to describe her. The Empire State Building? Impressive. The antlers on a moose? Impressive. An adult woman? There are a million other adjectives I'd use first, but I won't harp on this no matter how bad I want to. So, I settle for "She's amazing."

From there, we fall back into silence. I set the business proposal on my lap and survey the crisp paper and ink-jet printing. "Dad, I—" I say, forcing my head up.

At the same time, he says, "Are you going to—"

We both snap our mouths shut and stare at one another.

"Sorry," I say. "You go."

He shakes his head and lifts a hand. "You first."

I take a deep breath, muster all the courage I have. "I wanted to show you something." My butt leaves the bench; I don't get a warning. That's a good sign at least. I set the proposal onto the clean worktable and dive into details about Ed and the bar. When he doesn't make a move to open the bound proposal, I do it for him.

I start with my elevator pitch, set the scene for him in a way I hope he'll relate to. The bar isn't for getting drunk—well, it is, but I don't mention that part—it's for community. I fill him in on the business, how well it's doing and how it generates sufficient cash flow year over year. I lay out why I need the loan and how I'd use it, propose a repayment plan that benefits him. I talk about my experience as an HR, operations, marketing, customer relations, and property manager. I even provide business and personal financial statements so he can see that I'm far more responsible than he gives me credit for.

He's silent throughout, letting me say my piece.

"I know I haven't always made the choices you would make," I say. "But I hope I've demonstrated how serious I am about this business and that you'll consider this loan an investment in a future we can both be proud of."

Forcing my fists to unclench, I drop my shoulders from my ears. Now that I'm not talking, I realize how dry my mouth is, that I'm sweating a little along my brow. Fuck, I hope he sees it for what it is, nerves, rather than a sign that I'm lying or untrustworthy.

"Anyway," I say to break the silence. "I can give you some time to think about it if you need to."

Dad makes a face I've never seen before. His eyes are bright, and a slow smile tips his lips. Holy shit. Is this what pride looks like? I better get Alex in here to verify it, the kiss-ass.

"Wow," he says, regarding the business plan, then focusing on me again. "She's really done a lot of work on you."

"She being…?"

"Jasmine." He slaps my shoulder. "This has to be her influence."

There are moments in every man's life when he realizes his father is an irredeemable dick. This one is mine. Though I'm sure Jasmine could have contributed and even found ways to make it better, she had nothing to do with my proposal. This was mine, all of it, the business, the presentation, the ambition, but god forbid my father see me as anything other than the family fuckup.

Clenching my fists and my molars, I force a slow breath in through my nose. It takes all the restraint I possess not to lose it on him.

He chuckles, clearly unaware of my turmoil. "When you said you wanted to talk, I thought you were going to tell me that you plan to ask her to marry you."

"Whoa." I slap his shoulder the way he slapped mine and resist the urge to squeeze a little too hard. "That's moving a little fast, don't you think?"

He shakes his head. "When you know, you know. I knew with your mom."

Lips pressed together, I nod. Like a fucking automaton.

"I'm just relieved you're finally settling down," he says. "It shows real maturity."

This has to be a dream. I just asked him for a loan so that I could become a business owner, and yet he's steered the conversation to my girlfriend. A girlfriend who's not really my girlfriend. A woman who hates my guts. Not that he knows that.

"Well," I say. *Don't fuck this up. Don't fuck this up.* "Thanks, Dad." My voice is as wooden as the shit in this shop.

"I'll tell you what," he says, flipping through the proposal. "I have to talk to my financial advisor, but we'll move some funds around and get this loan to you both."

"To us both?" My voice is so cheerful, I sound fake. "That's great."

Really, really great.

It takes me about fifteen minutes to shower, shave, get dressed in the navy-blue suit. I forgo the tie, like last time. Though I'm sure my dad will air grievances about it. By comparison, three and half episodes of a syndicated 90s sitcom play before she comes out of the bathroom.

But I can't even pretend to be annoyed, because I think this woman is trying to kill me. Death by boner. Her red hair, pulled into a tight bun—shocking—at her nape, shines. Not a single strand is out of place. It's neat and proper, surely requiring an immeasurable number of bobby pins and hairspray and probably some other hair product I've never heard of. Every detail makes me appreciate her more. The care she takes in all she does, even when she does things for someone else, even someone who betrayed her.

Her makeup is sparse except for her lips, which she's painted with the kind of red that probably comes in a tube labeled Medusa's Kiss or Bad Blood or Revenge. Her dress is simple and black, with a square neckline that shows off her collarbones, sleeves to the wrists, and a skirt to mid-calf. She wears tiny-heeled black shoes with a strap of little diamantes across the top. She stands in front of where I lounge on the bed, fiddling with her pearl earrings, scowling at me.

"Nick?" she asks, waving her hand in front of my face. "Did you hear me?"

Oh shit. "Yes," I lie.

Eyes narrowed in suspicion, she turns, then slips her other earring into her ear.

Good god. All the blood rushes south as I take her in from behind. First, the green jumpsuit, then that fucking bathing suit, now this dress. Another low back. I want to get back down on my knees for her and worship the dimples just above her ass, the subtle dip of her spine, her sharp shoulder blades—

"Are you going to do up the buttons?" She peers over her shoulder, clearly annoyed. Probably because she's already asked me this more than once. But as I inspect the dress, a line of small buttons wrapped in black fabric marching up one side, corresponding elastic hoops on the other, I breathe an internal sigh of relief and devastation. It's not actually another low back.

"Sorry. Yes." I've never felt like I have sausage fingers more than I do right now. The pads of my fingers brush her back as I slowly hide the dimples, then her spine, ending right below her shoulder blades.

"Thanks," she says, stepping away when I'm finished. "Ready?" Though she stands in the doorway of the bathroom, she checks her fit again, adjusting the sleeves, smoothing her hair.

"Yeah." My mouth is so dry, and my pants are suddenly tight.

"Okay." She brushes past me, close enough that the smell of her body lotion or her shampoo or whatever fills my nose.

"Wait." I turn on my socked heels, my shoes still lined up neatly next to all of her unworn ones.

She stands with her back to me, her hand on the doorknob, her shoulders rising and falling, and sighs before she slowly turns back to me.

"Thank you. And I'm s—"

She shakes her head, lowers her attention to the floor between us. "Don't apologize to me again."

That's fair. Words can only go so far. "I won't," I say. "You look lovely."

Slowly, she forces her gaze back to my face, her expression distrustful. I get it. Why she has trouble believing a single word from me.

"That's true," I assure her.

She drops her focus again. "You look lovely, too."

My heart pangs. I've never been called lovely before; it's kind of...
lovely.

"Well," she says, lips twisting, "you will be once you put your
shoes on."

"That is also true."

WE WALK DOWN the stairs to the kitchen together. The second we hit
the bottom step, we're greeted by my mother's *ooohs* and *aaahs*. She's
gone all out for this anniversary party, hiring a photographer to
mingle with the guests to catch candids.

All of my niblings are dressed in what can only be described as
modern von Trapp core, a combination of Oktoberfest-style
suspenders and Navy neckerchiefs. Most of my siblings are already
here, drinks in hand. Alex is outside on the deck with Philip, Claire's
husband, huddled under one of the outdoor propane heaters and
sharing a cigar. Claire and Robert stand inside watching their kids
and glaring at their partners, clearly unimpressed with them. Either
for smoking, or for not helping with the kids who all seem to be
running wilder than normal because of the general excitement of the
evening, or maybe both.

The doorbell rings and Mom makes a high-pitched sound that's
just a few octaves short of only being audible to dogs. Her first guests
have arrived.

"You ready for this?" I ask.

Jasmine's face is pale and her eyes swim with trepidation. She
looks like she'd rather drink week-old cab sauv than be here, but
when she turns to me, she does her best to smile.

My gut twists at her discomfort. "You don't have to do that, you
know."

"Do what?"

"Fake it."

Hands clutched in front of her, she sniffs. "I'm not."

"Jazz, you're allowed to say you're overwhelmed."

"I'm not," she says, the words more defensive this time. "I am not," she says again, evening out her tone. "Besides, between the two of us, you're faker than I am."

Usually, I'm a pro at masking my reactions, but this jab takes me by surprise.

"Well, that's kind of hurtful," I say.

Jasmine falters, her pleased superiority wiped clean, but she gathers herself quickly.

"You're the one who lied," she says. Rather than meet my eyes, she focuses on the gathering group of guests congratulating my parents on their anniversary.

"Yeah. And I apologized for that. So many times that you asked me to stop. And let's not forget that I wouldn't have been in this position if you hadn't asked me to lie first." Now that I've gotten going, I might be madder than I thought I was. "So, it's okay when you do it, but when I do, it's unforgivable?"

"You pretended to be a completely different person," she says through clenched teeth.

"I told you I'd take you home. I said I'd tell them the truth," I hiss back.

In the back of my mind, I know we need to cool it. Fighting with Jasmine in the middle of my parents' party is not going to endear my request to my father and it will just upset Mom. At this point, she'd probably keep Jasmine and get rid of me. With a long breath in, I lean away from her, unclench my jaw. I slip my hand into my slacks' pocket. Because nobody who's got their hands in their pockets is pissed.

"But you're still here. You're allowed to be mad, but what you're not allowed to do, what I *won't* allow, is treat me like your verbal punching bag when the person you're really mad at is yourself."

Damn, I'm on a roll. But rather than take the bait and snipe back at me, she steps in close and trails her fingers along the button front of my suit jacket, like she read my mind about cooling it.

She whispers, her words like cirrus clouds, almost insubstantial against my throat. "I don't like you."

Because I have issues best explored with the guidance of a mental health professional, I get an erection.

With a hand pressed to the small of her back, I lean into her ear and whisper back, "You'll just have to fake it."

She scowls.

Her hair remains perfectly set, but I pretend like there's a loose strand, using it as an excuse to feel the soft curve of her ear. She's frozen in place, all but her lips, which part in response to the touch.

"Are you worried you won't be able to?" I ask. "You certainly didn't fake it this morning."

She clamps her mouth shut. Her eyes narrow and her nostrils flare. If possible, I think she'd happily wrap her hands around my neck, French tips and all, and squeeze until I turned purple. She's fuming.

It may be true; she may not like me. She may hate me after this. But she didn't hate me this morning. Didn't hate my hands, my mouth, or the words I spoke into her skin.

"You look a little warm." I rub my thumb along her cheek. It's pink because of me, not the temperature. "I'll get us drinks."

"Feel free to choke on one," she says cheerily.

I laugh as I walk away.

Between Jasmine and the bar set up at the kitchen island, I'm stopped by two couples, both friends of my parents' I barely remember, and I'm stopped once more on my way back with two flutes of champagne. They all want to know what I'm up to, then act surprised when I'm still "just a bartender." They double down on that surprise when I tell them I'm here with Jasmine. I get it, but also, rude.

Miranda and Claire have joined Jasmine by the time I get back to her, and the combination of her first few sips of alcohol and my sisters' embarrassing stories about me, specifically the crush I had on my first-grade teacher, Ms. Sarah—I still maintain I had an outside chance with her—loosen Jasmine's smile. Claire leaves to put her baby to bed, but Robert takes her place, with more champagne.

Charlie and Rashida join us, both exceptionally drunk. I'm not on the clock, but at this point, it's hard not to take notice of intoxication levels of the people around me.

Jasmine is incredible at small talk. She asks to hear Charlie and Rashida's engagement story, coos appropriately over the professional family photos that Robert and Alex have done every quarter, and expertly sidesteps too much detail about "us."

I'm in the kitchen, collecting waters for the group, when the familiar *ting, ting, ting* of a butter knife on stemware cuts through the conversations around the place. As my dad clambers up on top of the coffee table, the crowd quiets, and as he delivers his speech, Mom beams up at him from the floor. She isn't even pissed that he's standing on the furniture.

"I'm generally known as a man of few words." He pauses there, waiting for his audience to laugh. "But I want to thank you all for being here to celebrate what I can honestly say will never be enough years with my Mindy."

Pause for obligatory *awwwwws*.

The room is full, bright, warm. Alex and Robert stand with their arms around each other, Tilly half-asleep and clinging to Alex, her head on his shoulder like when she was a baby. Charlie hugs Rashida from behind, resting his chin on the top of her head. They're both glassy-eyed and swaying but at least they're doing it together.

Dad talks about how he thought Mom was gorgeous the moment he saw her and how she couldn't remember his name.

Pause for obligatory laugh.

I find Jasmine in the crowd. Her cheeks are flushed but not too much. A small smile pulls at her lips. She toys with the base of her champagne flute, drawing her finger back and forth around it. I'm tempted to go to her, grasp her hand, squeeze her fingers, take her to another room, somewhere private; I know all the best hiding spots in this house. I've spent the most time avoiding my dad. She laughs at something my dad says, then she looks at me. Like she could feel my attention like a caress. The remnants of laughter are still on her face.

"And finally, we want to thank all our children and their partners for joining us this weekend. Especially my son Nick and his new partner, Jasmine, who is such a lovely addition to our family."

More obligatory *awwwwws* and clandestine snickers from my siblings. My parents beam at me. So do their friends, people I don't recognize or remember but who knew me when I was Tilly's age.

Did Jasmine feel sick when we duped her co-workers? Probably not. But nausea builds as person after person turns my way. And as my father lifts his glass to toast, the champagne and finger foods sour in my stomach.

Jasmine is right. I am a faker. I'm fake. Is saving Moonbar worth lying for? Absolutely. But is lying to my family, accepting their pride in something that doesn't exist, worth it?

I am an asshole.

Around me people toast, clap, and turn their attention back to the party. Holding my breath and snagging a bottle of unopened champagne from the nearest ice bucket, I leave.

THE FIRST TIME Tilly saw the automatic pool cleaner, she cried and refused to get in the water. She called it a creepy crawly. So that's what we named it. Creepy Crawly chugs along the wall. Dad could have bought a new one by now, one that doesn't sound like an underwater combustion engine, but he'd rather fix this one over and over again.

The bottle of champagne is tepid in the humidity of the pool room but the lounger I chose is the comfiest one, more like a chaise longue than glorified patio furniture. Between the sudden bursts of laughter and the constant muted thump of bass, with my eyes closed, I can almost convince myself I'm home in the bed above my bar.

When the door opens behind me, I lie very still in case it's my parents. They're old so maybe if I don't move, they won't see me, like the T. rex.

No dice. Footsteps approach, heels. The newcomer puts a hand on my hip and pushes until I move over.

"What do you want, Jasmine?" I picked up her scent halfway between the door and this chair. Which I'll never admit. Makes me sound like a serial killer. She just smells so damn good, that rich, spicy-sweet scent.

When she doesn't answer, I turn onto my side, facing her. The lounger is big enough to fit both of us if we spooned.

"I say again, what do you want, Jasmine?"

"Why are you sulking?" She perches on the back of the chair, back straight, neck long. The glow from the outdoor lights softens the severity her tight bun and the sharp lines of her dress give her.

"I'm getting some air."

"It's like forty degrees in here."

"But there's *air*."

She rolls her eyes.

"What do you want?"

She fidgets, smoothing already smooth fabric and flattening already flattened hair.

"*Jazz.*"

She huffs. "Come upstairs with me," she says, attention averted.

"To do what?"

Another burst of sudden laughter reaches us. She watches me, lips pressed together, until it fades, as if I wouldn't be able to hear her otherwise. "Come with me and I'll tell you."

I huff a breath. Fuck. I am not in the mood for this. "Jasmine, tell me why now or I'll never leave this lounger."

"Nick," she says, stern.

"Tell me or I'll throw up."

"You're acting like a child."

"Tell me or—"

She covers my mouth with her hand. "Stop. And don't lick me, either."

She's lucky she's fast, because I was about to. When she removes her hand, she wipes her palm on my suit jacket hanging off the back of the lounger anyway.

"I've been considering what you said earlier and..." She sighs. "You're right."

Channeling my best Judd Nelson, I throw my fist into the air. She pulls it back down but rests my hand in her lap and holds tight with both of hers.

"It's not fair that I get to lie but you don't, or that I asked you to lie for me but then I'm upset about it. It's hypocritical."

She opens my fist, spreads my fingers out on her lap, tracing the outline with her index finger; goose bumps follow.

"I stayed because fairness is important to me. You helped me so it's fair that I should stay and help you, and honestly, the reason you need me is a lot more noble than the reason I needed you."

"We don't need to compare—"

She shushes me, though one side of her mouth tips up in a hint of a smile. I make a claw with my hand and squeeze her leg right above her knee, making her squeal.

"Anyway," she says after we catch ourselves staring goofily at each other. "You won't be my verbal punching bag anymore." Her voice is soft.

Creepy Crawly still chugs along the pool floor. Large windows line two walls of the room, but with the lights off, it's secluded, almost secret.

"Wait." I sit up. "Why did you need me to go back to our room for that?"

She ignores or doesn't notice my use of "our," so I ignore it, too.

She huffs again, frustrated.

"Did Grandma and Tilly set up a series of booby traps for you?" I ask. "Do you need me to escort you?"

"No." Tinkling laughter escapes her. "But I'm sure that could still happen." The fidgeting starts again. She shifts on the lounger, checks the collar of her dress, pulls at her sleeves.

"Jasmine, I swear to god..."

"I like things to be fair," she says, her voice echoing. She starts again, quieter. "I don't like owing anyone."

I wrack my brain. What could she possibly owe me? "You're staying. You're helping me. My hang-ups about lying to my parents aren't your problem. Trust me. I'm as surprised as you are."

She closes her eyes. "That's not what I mean," she says, her shoulders slumping. With a deep breath in, she zeroes in on me, like she's preparing herself. "I'd like to give you a hand job."

Other than the pool cleaner, there's no sound. Still, I'm not sure I heard her correctly. "Come again?"

"Yes. Exactly," she says.

"Ha ha," I say, deadpan. "No. I don't think I heard you correctly."

"I want," she says slower. "To give you." Her expression grows serious, her voice steady. "A hand job."

I glance around for the bottle of champagne I discarded. Maybe someone spiked it? "A hand job?"

"Yes."

Even as my blood pulses and my pants get tight, I narrow my eyes. Maybe she's confused. Maybe I'm confused. "I don't think that word means what you think it means."

"Please don't paraphrase kids movies to me right now."

"You're serious."

"Yes," she says, slapping her thighs in frustration.

I laugh. Even though it will piss her off, I can't help it.

"Stop laughing," she snaps.

I try to. I really do. "What," I say between gasped breaths. "Were you going." I wipe at my eyes. "To do?" I have to actively stop myself from keeling over. "Just..." I make a fist with my hand and move it up and down. "Dry?"

She crosses her arms over her chest and despite trying to look offended, the corners of her mouth curl up. "If you didn't have lube, I figured I could just use spit or something."

Holy shit. Are we seriously negotiating the terms of my hand job? What the fuck am I doing?

"So just use your spit here." Now that I've wrung all of the humor from this situation, my cock has taken over, anticipating what's next.

"I can't do that here," she squeaks, scanning the room as if we're surrounded by all the party attendants. "This isn't a bedding ceremony at the French court."

"You have to know I have no idea what you're talking about."

"Someone could see."

My damn heart stutters. Holy shit, she's considering it. I fall back on the lounger, resting my hands behind my head, looking up at the ceiling, at the reflections from the water moving across the glossy surface. "No one's even out here."

"We are," she says, like *duh*.

"Trust me, the only person in my family who'd consider coming here for a nighttime swim is me. And I'm already here." I'm half-hard already from this teasing and arguing. I'm not too proud to accept an IOU handie, and Jasmine wouldn't offer unless she wanted to.

"I can't do something like that," she says, almost to herself.

If I focus hard enough, I can feel where her hip is just inches from mine. "Why not?"

"It's just not...*me*." She looks down at herself, at her perfect clothes, her perfect posture, as if one look at her could explain it all.

"So don't be you. Don't be Jasmine, be Yasmin."

She barks out a laugh, but sobers quickly, her eyes turning serious again. "What..." She bites her lip, a flush crawling up her neck, painting her cheeks. "What would Yasmin do?"

I rough a hand down my face, close my eyes, search for a modicum of composure.

My suit jacket is already off, but I open the first two buttons on my shirt, cross my legs at the ankle. Can she see my heart thundering against my chest or the growing bulge in my pants? I've never dictated a sexual encounter before and now that the opportunity has arrived, there are too many options to choose from.

"Yasmin would start slow," I say. With my eyes closed, it's easy to imagine, a slow sinuous walk, her expression a mix of desire and contempt. "She'd start over the clothes, firm pressure. She'd like the feel of it. How quickly I get hard for her. It makes her feel good. It makes her wet."

Jasmine makes a strangled sound. A moment later, her hand lands gently on my thigh, slides up toward my dick.

"She'd rub me through my pants," I say, no longer smiling. My voice sounds different to my own ears, deeper. "Squeeze me."

She does. Her hand is hot through my clothes.

"Then what?" she asks, closer now, like she's hovering over me.

"Gimme a sec." I want to feel this right, just for a moment. Her slow gentle pressure, the soft whisper of her breathing.

On an inhale, she shudders, and with my eyes closed, I can't tell whether it's a good sound or a bad one.

"Hey." I stop her with my hand, open my eyes, meet her gaze. "You don't have to do everything I say. You know that, right?"

She nods.

I swallow thickly, blow out a breath. "Cuz I'm probably about to say some things you have no interest in doing."

She squeezes me beneath my hand. Impatient.

"Like what?" she asks, starting the slow motion on my dick again.

"Like...I stop you before I come." I release her and unbuckle my belt. Then pop the top button of my slacks.

She doesn't have to go farther than this, but I'll gladly continue if it's okay with her. She looks up, scanning the windows that face the deck.

"We can stop," I say, sitting up and closing the front of my slacks.

"No." With a determined set to her jaw, she swings one leg over the chair, straddling me. "Keep going," she says, her command strangely timid for a woman who's currently tugging on my pants. She pulls them down to my thighs. My cock is hard, leaking a wet spot into the fabric of my boxer briefs. "What happens if someone catches us?" she whispers, drawing her hands up and down my legs, dragging her nails through the hair above the elastic waistband of my underwear.

"We'll hear them coming." I can't stop watching her hands. "And then, I'll—"

She squeezes me, pulling a hiss from me, then pulls my Jockeys down, tucking them behind my balls in one surprisingly fast, shockingly proficient movement. My cock bobs between us, curving slightly to the left, begging for her attention.

She leans over me. "Then?"

"I'll throw you in the pool—*ahhh*."

She spits, and a silvery string drips down my dick. I gasp as she spreads it up and down the shaft, over the head. Almost pass out as she spits again.

"Wh-who are you?" I ask, shock coloring my tone.

"Yasmin." She grins, winks. "So." She settles into a slow, steady rhythm. Her fist and spit make wet sounds. If I were on my own, I'd never come at this pace. But with her? That sound? That wink? I could embarrass myself pretty quick.

"You'll throw me in the pool," she practically purrs, "and then what?"

"And then, I'll jump in, too."

She spits again. "A romantic night swim," she says. "Keep going. Tell me what happens after you stop me before you come."

Suddenly, a wave of embarrassment hits me. I don't think I've ever felt as vulnerable as I do now, revealing this little moment of fantasy to her, but she's going out of her comfort zone for me. The least I can do is return the favor.

"I pull down your top." I move my hips with her, searching for just a little more friction, more pressure.

In response, she squeezes harder.

I close my eyes in relief, lean back on my hands. "I drip massage oil over your chest, cover your nipples, your breasts, until you're slippery and shining."

Jasmine moans, the softest sound. Her hips move, a choppy rhythm. Like she wants that, my hands on her tits, covering her in oil until she's slick. Oh fuck. She's going to get my come on her dress.

"Then you." I huff. "Yasmin, let's me fuck her tits."

She groans. "Would you come like that?"

"I'd come so hard for you, baby." I'm going to come so hard for her right now.

She leans closer.

"Careful," I say. "Your dress."

Closer still, she ghosts her lips over mine, across my cheek, my chin. "Where would you come?"

Her mouth goes from soft to hard, substituting lips and tongue for teeth. She bites along my throat, my collarbone. Scratches across my thighs with her other hand, my stomach. I wrap my fingers around her throat, loosely. Her hand moves faster. She swallows, the sensation illicit against my palm.

"Here," I say. "I'd come here."

Pleasure pools heavy in my back, my balls. A cord pulled tight.

She snatches her hand away. Instead of snapping the cord, she leans away from me, leaving me cold. The pleasure coiled inside me comes loose, unravels.

I gasp. "Fuck."

Laughter, shouts from the party, drifts over to us and Jasmine tenses. The haze of our little game gone, snapping us both back to reality. Jasmine stands, pulling herself together again like she always does. I can't stop gasping, can't stop staring at my dick, hard and leaking.

She studies the mess she made of me, her mouth tipped in a satisfied smile. "Now, we're even."

16

———

JASMINE

"Are you fucking serious?" He breathes the words across the back of my neck. That, plus the blast of cold air from the open mudroom door, sends goose bumps along my spine. The door slams and I startle, but none of the partygoers notice over the din of celebration.

"Maybe we should mingle." I'm filled with anxious energy.

"Not a fucking chance." He holds me by my hips, pressing into my back. He is still hard.

I thought he'd finish himself off back beside the pool, but I can't deny the thrill that snakes up my spine knowing he didn't.

"How exactly does orgasm denial make us even?" he asks, his stubble rough against the shell of my ear as he crowds in closer. "You came." The strain in his voice makes me wish he'd bite me. A thought I've never once entertained before. I want to feel the imprint of his teeth on the base of my neck, draw my fingers across the spot later and feel the indentations.

I shrug, feigning indifference. "Consider it a tax."

It wasn't until he was laid out beneath me, his lower lip caught between his teeth, the flush in his cheeks visible even in the dark, that I decided to do it.

Or not do it, as it were.

It's hard to think of it as a punishment for him, more like a reward for me. Because I didn't want it to end and that's what letting him come felt like.

An ending.

He squeezes my hips more tightly and guides me toward the back steps.

"Someone has probably noticed we're gone," I say, stopping at the foot of the stairs, my hand on the banister, even if staying down here is the last thing I want to do.

"Get upstairs." His words are clipped, his tone impatient. "Please," he adds with a harsh breath.

I can't hide my shudder. Nick makes a satisfied sound that I feel against my back more than hear. Excitement propels my feet forward. That's what this anxiousness is: excitement, anticipation. Desire.

I glance at him over my shoulder. He's as disheveled as I feel.

I want to make more of a mess.

In the few moments it takes to reach his bedroom, I am breath-less, and not from the stairs.

We slip into his bedroom and before I can say another word, he has the door closed and my back pressed against it.

"Oh." My hands flutter in the air between us before they land on the shoulders of his Oxford shirt. "You left your suit jacket at the pool," I whisper.

With a shake of his head, Nick scowls. If I didn't know better, I'd think he was angry. But I've learned quickly that there's not much that makes him well and truly mad and besides, he doesn't have much reason to be upset right now.

"I want to eat your pussy, Jasmine."

"Oh." My heart trips over itself. When I was the fake Jasmine—Yasmin—this was easier. The urge to take the lead, to act out his fantasies and maybe eventually mine, was natural. Imperative. But I'm the real Jasmine again and there are rules, a binder's worth. "But then we won't be even."

Nick drops to his knees and takes one of my ankles in the gentlest hold, asking for me to spread my legs apart. "If you don't want me to, I won't," he says, his breathing harsh. "But I think you do. We can balance the books later."

"Don't you want—" I wave a hand at the bed, where sex usually happens.

"Jasmine," he grits out, his eyes blazing, "I swear to god—"

"Ugh, *fine*." The words escape me with a huff. As if I'm not aching to feel his mouth on me. "Just let me get this off—"

Nick doesn't wait; he lifts the thick, structured fabric of my dress and runs his hands up my legs.

My head falls back against the door. "Oh god."

As he rubs his cheek against the inside of my knee, my inner thigh, the roughness of his stubble sends a zap of electricity up my spine. He pushes my thighs apart, his breath hot through my thin, soaked panties. Suddenly, he bats at the fabric of my dress and pokes his head out. "Just tell me to stop and I will."

I grab him by the back of his head and push. "*Don't stop.*"

Nick needs no more urging. He sucks at the delicate skin of my inner thigh and runs his hands up the backs of my legs, urging me to spread wider. My kitten heels pinch my toes and I always get a blister from the strap, but I could be floating right now as Nick's shrouded head presses between my legs and he cups me in his mouth, laving his tongue over my panties.

Holy shit. I'm riding Nick Scott's face.

Groaning, he slides two fingers into my pussy, meeting no resistance. The noises we make as he pumps his fingers inside my drenched pussy are illicit. He nuzzles into me, pushing my panties to the side and finally his tongue makes contact with my clit.

"Fuck," I whisper, bearing down on his fingers and mouth.

He grunts a response and I wish we could be louder, messier. Moments ago, I wanted to use his bed, but now, I don't ever want to be fucked on a bed again. Not when a bathroom mirror, a pool lounger, and a closed bedroom door are this good.

My skin is hot, slick from sweat and desire. He has to be hot under there, between the skirt and my body heat, but like he could feel my mind wandering, he nips at my thigh, bringing me back to this, now, him.

His fingers are an unyielding force, keeping me open. His face holding me up. I grind on him, move over and against him. He encourages it, one palm planted on my ass cheek, gripping me hard enough to leave a handprint.

I gasp. My pleasure pools in between my legs. "I'm close."

Then he's gone and the tidal wave of desire ebbs. I whine in frustration and press my fists against the door.

Nick's face is flushed, his lips shiny and red, his hair wild as he stands. "I'll take care of you," he whispers into my neck, his mouth wet against my skin. That's from me. He loops his arms around me and fiddles with the buttons at the back of the dress.

Turning in his arms to give him better access, I press my cheek against the wood of the door. In my ear, the sounds of a party slowly dying are muffled. At my back, Nick breathes with a deliberate steadiness as he slowly works each delicate button free. His hands are gentle and careful, even though there's no way he could know that I found this dress in a bin at a garage sale and that over the span of three months I repaired and altered it. But he treats it like he knows as he finally undoes the last button and slides it gently from my shoulders.

I let it fall to the floor. Leaving it puddled like that for a few moments won't kill it. I turn to him, my hands crossed over my chest, which is silly. He already knows what my pussy tastes like.

"Can I see you?" he asks.

It's the vulnerability in his words, like he's worried I'll say no, that makes me drop my arms. His attention shifts to my breasts, then my tummy, my pussy, my breasts again. He reaches out, glides his fingers between my legs, holds them up for me to see. Absently, he rubs at his cock with the heel of his other hand, the thick bulge at the front of his slacks from when he tucked himself back in. He doesn't try to hide any of it, unashamed to be indecent and crude, maybe even proud.

"You wanted the bed?" he asks.

I shake my head. "I changed my mind."

He scans the room. "Here," he says, tapping the desk.

My breathing stutters. Desk sex? Okay.

When I perch on the edge of the wood he stops me, turns my body, sets my hands on the surface, spreads my legs apart again.

"Do you trust me?" he asks against the top of my spine, making me shiver.

I don't have the first clue what he wants to do with me. I've never let someone have this kind of control. Though that's likely because my partners have never seemed to want it. They wanted nice girls in nice clothes. They wanted a woman who looked good next to them. My orgasm was a check box on their to-do list of sex. They wanted missionary on the third date, blow jobs on my period. Mitchell wanted anal on his birthday. It hurt a bit, but it had the potential to be better, he just never took it and I had to get myself off in the shower without him.

No one has ever wanted this; looking just to look, bruised knees, the risk of suffocation in the pursuit of my orgasm.

Do I trust him? After what he did, the answer should be no. But I trust that if I laid my head on my hands on this desk and presented myself to him, for his use, nothing would hurt, *and* I'd still come hard enough to crack my molars. I trust him with my body, if not with my heart.

"Yes," I whisper.

He cups my ass, squeezes both globes, spreads me apart.

Flushing, I close my eyes. Even though we're alone, and he can't see me.

Nick goes to his knees again, his hands trailing down my legs.

My breath catches, and I lift up an inch. "What—?"

He licks me from clit to perineum. My head hits the desk with a soft thud. He sticks his thumb inside me, thick and hard, a decent substitute for what I really want. I moan, louder than I should, spread my legs wider, push back against him, seeking the pressure of his thumb inside me and his fingers on my clit. He laughs, smiles into the back of my thighs. Then he gives me what I want. Nick plays me again, like a stringed instrument tuned to him. His thumb slipping deeper in my cunt, his fingers rubbing gentle circles around my clit.

I come like that, fully open to him, on display, my toes curling in my kitten heels, clenching my teeth to hold back the scream that threatens to tear through me. My body convulses around him as he draws out my orgasm until I can feel come dripping down my legs, hear the wet sound of it as he fucks me with his hand. My clit pulses, flutters against his constant, steady rhythm. Tears leak from my eyes as I gasp, "Stop. Please, stop."

He obeys, moving his hands, but he keeps his skin on my skin. I don't know how much more I can take.

Palms on my back, he smooths them up and down in a gentle caress. "Not much longer," he says. "I promise."

I think I said that out loud. "Okay."

Standing, Nick presses his hips against me, his erection thick and hard between us. "Can I come on your back?" he asks, the question punctuated by the sound of his zipper.

"Oh god, yes."

"I'm going to touch you again, just a little." He gives me the warning, but doesn't move, waiting for my permission.

I nod, panting, chest heaving against the wooden surface beneath me. "Okay."

His fingers slip inside me again and I gasp, an aftershock of my orgasm like a conditioned response to his touch. He presses a hand on my back, holding me there. The sound of rustling is barely audible over the air sawing in and out of my lungs. The wet skin on wet skin is louder. Lewd and erotic, the rhythmic jingle of his belt buckle. Part of me wants to turn around and watch. Or offer my breasts and neck for him. Part of me wants to get on my knees and take him in my mouth and let him empty himself down the back of my throat so I can know what he tastes like, too.

But when he makes a sound, soft and high, aching, and the first stream of his come hits, warm against my sweat-slick back, my choice is made for me, and I'm exactly where he needs me.

Nick comes in three long spurts across my back, then presses the head of his dick to the top of my ass, leaving a small puddle there.

I am exhausted, my legs shaking, but I can't move, not when he's standing behind me, his hand on my hip, his breath warm gusts across my skin.

"Okay," he says finally. "*Now* we're even."

I glance at him over my shoulder. "Fair."

THE NEXT MORNING, it's as if nothing has changed between us. Except, when he wakes up first, he brings me coffee, black. Except, as we eat breakfast with his family, most of who are hungover, he rests his arm along the back of my chair the whole time.

Mostly, everyone is quiet, minus the kids and Nick's dad, who laments there's not enough time for a Scott v. Scott hockey game on the lake.

Nick packs the car, gently placing my brown leather bag in the trunk. After thirty minutes of tearful hugs from Mindy, hand-shaking back pat hugs from the other men, and squealing hugs from Tilly—especially when he rubs his beard into her neck—he walks me to the car with his hand at the small of my back and opens my door.

I send Jade a text letting her know we're on our way. Her only response is "Gucci."

Mindy waves until we can't see her anymore.

"She loves you," I say once the Scott cottage-mansion is out of sight.

"She loves *you*."

That sentiment causes a strange sense of pride to swell inside me. Until I remember that she won't love me if she finds out I lied to her.

He passes me his phone. "Want to pick the song?"

I scroll his playlist, hoping to spark the memory of the song he said could be "our" song, because it feels like a test to be given this honor. When I spend more than thirty seconds searching in silence with no luck, I pick a song at random and press play. He smiles at me as I set the phone down.

"I never asked you"—I shift in my seat to face him—"how the talk with your dad went."

"Yes, you did." He drives exactly the speed limit as we travel through town. It's a slow crawl compared to the street racing speeds most Toronto drivers get up to.

"I asked you if your dad gave you the loan. I didn't ask how it *went*." The distinction is important based on their relationship.

"It went fine," he says in a tone that sounds not at all fine. "He agreed to give me the loan."

He shrugs. That's it. Never before has a sign of indifference ended a conversation so definitively. Tapping his thumbs on the steering wheel to the beat of the random song, he hums. The humming turns to singing softly under his breath. I should have made a binder for the drive home. Without the anxiety and anticipation of the ride up, we don't have anything to say to each other, which is more disappointing than I'd like to admit.

"If I ask you a question," he says once we're on the highway, "will you promise to give me an honest answer?"

Straightening, I assess him. "What kind of question is it if you need me to promise to answer honestly?"

He grins. "It's not sex-related, perv."

I tip my head against the headrest, close my eyes. "Okay, ask, then I'll decide."

"Why'd you stay?" he asks, glancing over with a frown before focusing on the road again. "After you found out. Most people would have left."

Between the hum of the wheels on the road, the music, which has taken a folkish turn, the sun, bright through the windows, and the strangely quiet roads, we're in our own little bubble.

My chest constricts as I work through my thoughts to formulate the best response. "Have you heard of the Veronika Gervers Research Fellowship?"

"I've heard of the *Fellowship of the Ring*."

I shake my head. "Not everything is a joke, Nick," I say gently.

"I know." His words are so quiet I have to read them on his lips.

"I've always loved fashion. Everyone thought I should become a designer," I say, moving the conversation along. "But that wasn't really what I loved about it, and I can't draw anyway. In fifth grade, my class went to the ROM. I'd been so many times before but this time, as we were walking through the textile collection, a curator was talking about this robe, this really old robe. She wouldn't even touch it, she wouldn't take it out from behind the glass, to protect it. She was explaining what material culture says about a period or a society, or what we can glean about gender and race based on..." I pluck at my top, a green and pink crocheted cardigan with short sleeves. "The things we put on our bodies."

"Hmmmm."

My heart sinks at the subdued response. "Sorry."

"Don't be," he says. "I don't think I've ever seen you so excited before."

That makes me warm and sad all at the same time. "I wanted to study that, material culture, specifically fashion and the intersection of clothes-making, sewing, textiles, things that are historically seen as *women's work*, and capitalism, consumerism. That was my dream. I was going to be a Veronika Gervers Research Fellow."

He frowns at the road, then me. "Jade," he says, like *eureka*.

I shrug. "Jade."

"You had to drop out of school, right?"

"Yeah." Despite the many years between me and that decision, my throat still tightens with tears. "I don't regret it. Jade is brilliant. She deserves..." I shake my head, searching for the words to describe my little sister. Love isn't the right word, isn't *enough*. "Everything."

"So do you," Nick says quietly.

I glance out the passenger window, uncomfortable with the idea, although I'm unsure why. All I know is that I got a few good years with my parents before they totally gave up, whereas Jade was born into that relationship's sharp decline.

"Is that still your dream?" he asks.

"The Fellowship?"

He nods.

"No. Not really. Not anymore."

"Why not?" he asks, squinting at the road.

I shrug again. It's embarrassing to say out loud. It kind of sounds like giving up.

"Can you pass me my sunglasses?" He motions to the glove compartment.

"Sure." Relieved for the change in topic, I eagerly pull at the latch, but it doesn't open.

"You've gotta hit it," he says, eyes still on the road while making a pounding motion with the side of his fist.

I do, but it doesn't help. All it does is hurt. "Ow." I cradle my fist in my other hand.

He leans over, the scent of his deodorant or shower gel different than usual, though not unpleasant. With a quick bump of his fist against the glove compartment, it opens, and chaos spills out. Papers, manuals, hopefully a registration and insurance info. Cords of phone chargers dangle like vines, empty travel hand sanitizer bottles, one Band-Aid, and a tire gauge.

No sunglasses.

Nick notices the same time I do. "Fuck."

"Here." I pull mine out of my bag, wiping down the lenses with the microfiber cloth.

"Thanks," he says. "How do I look?"

Handsome, of course. The round frames are perfect for his face, though the glasses themselves are a bit small.

"Great," I say, and he smiles goofily.

I busy myself with putting away the glove compartment wreckage.

"Don't think I'm letting you off the hook," he says. "You still haven't answered the question."

Instead of answering him, I fight with the glove compartment again, slamming it over and over until it finally closes.

I sigh. "I don't want to be an academic anymore. Terrible pay, terrible job security, and then there's the debt."

I love to think about it; what the work would be like, what my life would be like now. But actually doing the job?

"It's just not realistic anymore."

Nick frowns, his brow climbing above the frame of my glasses. "So, now what's your dream?"

"I..."

My dream? For the last few years, my dream has been Jade's dream. My goals have been in service to hers.

"Well, I..."

This is embarrassing.

"You don't have to answer now," he says quietly, giving me an out that I don't want to take.

I'm goal oriented, motivated. How can I not have a dream? How can I not know what I want? To some, my dream might look like marriage to a rich man, but that's not the same as my Veronika Gervers Research Fellowship dream. That's not a dream just for me.

"Thanks," I say quietly. Ashamed, embarrassed. "I guess you could say I'm currently between dreams."

He nods. "That's allowed."

"Anyway," I say with a sigh, "I know what it feels like to lose your chance at your dream. That's why I stayed."

The song changes to the one he chose for us. Our song. Nick grips my thigh. There's the lightest dusting of dark hair across his knuckles. A scar between his thumb and index finger, on the soft fleshy skin there. I trace my finger over it.

"Jasmine," he says, his voice rougher, quieter. "Thank you."

I cover his hand with mine and keep it there.

Nick pulls into the parking lot of a small restaurant. The outside is painted black, and the sign on top is painted a striking black and white and reads *Baker's Burgers.*

"Hungry?" Before I can respond, he shakes his head. "You know what? I don't care. You're getting a burger." He throws the car into park.

"I told Jade we were coming straight home though."

He pauses, staring down at his hand on the seat belt buckle. "We'll get them to go."

As I climb out of the car, my phone chimes, alerting me to an email notification. Nick is already halfway across the parking lot, but I rummage through my pockets for it. The preview screen reads:

FROM: Nick Carmichael

SUBJECT: A Second Chance On A First Date

MY STOMACH SWOOPS. Nick Carmichael. Nick. The other Nick. The *real* Nick.

"Jazz," this Nick yells, spinning and walking backward toward the restaurant, his hands stuffed into the pockets of his jeans because he's the kind of Canadian man who insists he doesn't need a coat despite the temperature being below freezing. "Come on."

I school my expression, hide the confusion and panic bubbling inside me, but Nick starts back toward the car.

"Can you just order for me?" I hold my hand up to stop him. Somehow, his proximity will make all of this worse, wrong. "I...I don't want my clothes to smell like cooked meat."

Nick huffs, but without ridicule, he nods.

"No tomatoes," I call.

He holds his hand up in acknowledgment, jogging to the door. I don't open the email until I get back in the car.

DEAR JASMINE,

First, my sincerest apologies. For as ludicrous
as it must sound to you, I promise it sounds just as
ludicrous to me and I lived it. I keep thinking
about you sitting at Moonbar waiting for me,
believing I stood you up, and I feel sick. If you
decide you want nothing to do with me, I understand.

But I hope you'll give me a second chance. I
promise to avoid impacts with all moving vehicles
this time.

I was so excited when I first received our
match—99.338%! And I'm still excited.

X,

Nick

RATHER THAN CHARMED OR PLEASED, I feel nauseous. Sick and foolish. Until right now, I had let myself forget. Nick is not my match. This Nick. "Fake" Nick. He isn't supposed to be mine, and I let myself get distracted by what? Sex, a nice family, that stupid fucking smirk? Nick is complicated, this is nuanced. Yet I *like* him and the way he makes me laugh and lets me be myself. He almost insists upon it. But I don't trust myself anymore and part of that is because of him. If I want to take this seriously, maybe I need to give the other Nick, "real" Nick, a chance.

The car door opens, and I jump, my phone flying from my hands and landing with a muted thud on the floor mat in front of me.

"What the fuck, Jasmine?" he asks, laughing as he slides into his seat.

"Sorry." I pat around for my phone, throw it in my purse. "Thanks." I take the bags from him. And there are bags. Plural. "How much food did you get?"

"Listen, you have to get the full Baker's Burgers experience." Once he gets settled, he opens the bag on his lap. "Fries, onion rings, gravy on the side." He holds open his hand for the next bag and I pass it over. "Two hot dogs, two cheeseburgers, no tomatoes. Did you know you can get a bucket of burgers from this place?"

I can't stop the automatic grimace. "That sounds like a cardiac episode."

"But what a way to go. And then," he says tapping his fingers on the steering wheel in a drumroll. "Pass me the other bag," he whispers.

"Shit. Sorry." This is the heaviest one.

"Ta-da!" He pulls out a tray of drinks, presenting them to me like they're diamonds. "Milkshakes."

I raise my hands in mock celebration. "Yay."

"Whatever. It's your loss not appreciating good food."

I can't help but laugh as he organizes his haul. He somehow forgot napkins but luckily, I have some in my bag. By the time he gets it all organized, we could have just eaten inside. He doesn't pull out of the parking lot until I take my first bite, insisting he has to see my reaction.

"'S good," I say, holding my hand up to hide the mouthful of food.

"Right?!"

"Hey, Nick." I wash down the food with a gulp of strawberry milkshake.

He arches a brow. "If you're going to chirp my choice of strawberry you can stuff it. I like what I like."

"Oh no, I like strawberry. I have a question, and I need an honest answer."

"Okay," he says, side-eyeing me.

"Would you ever do matchmaking?"

He chews for longer than is probably necessary, examining me as he does. "Why?"

"Just answer." The car smells like fried food. I'm going to have to crank the manual window soon.

"Honestly, probably not." He sounds sort of sad about it.

I nod, using my own food as an excuse not to speak.

"But," he says. "I'm glad you did."

Nick keeps one hand on the steering wheel as he eats. We don't even come close to eating all of the food, but he insists the fries make great leftovers. As we approach the city and after I've organized the trash and food into separate bags, I send Jade a quick text.

She sends back a message filled with expletives and exclamation marks, which I do not dignify with a response.

"Nick," I say quietly, head lowered. "Will you take me to Underground Karaoke tonight?"

"It's not happening tonight," he says, pulling his milkshake from the cupholder. "And it wouldn't start for another few hours anyway."

Face heating, I swallow back my nerves. Nick is, almost assuredly, a sure thing. Even so, it doesn't make this request any easier. "Will you take me home anyway?"

He glances between me and the road, brows lowered in confusion. "My home?"

I nod and clasp my hands tightly in my lap. "Yes."

"Yeah," he says, releasing a deep, almost relieved breath. "Yeah. Of course."

"Wait down here for like five minutes, okay?" he asks, helping me onto a barstool like I'm a sickly Victorian child.

"Why?" I scan the empty space around us.

He winces. "I can't remember how I left my apartment, honestly." He makes a face of mock horror, then he collects our bags leaves out the swinging door labeled Employees Only. Under the one overhead light, Moonbar is a bit bleak. Without the cram of people in front of it, the paint on the stage is noticeably peeling. There are scratch marks on the floor from the tables and chairs, and the high-set windows are covered in a faint fog.

But the photos tucked into the frame of the mirror behind the bar give the place life. Nick and Bernie and a third person who is probably Rocco based on Nick's description of his friend. The man who owns the bar, Ed, in a faded photo that looks like it's from the early 80s at the latest. The room smells clean, which is a miracle in itself.

Every bar I ever worked in always had the lingering scent of spilled alcohol, vomit, or dirty dishrag—or a combination of all three. I haven't batted down any fruit flies either.

This place is well-loved and well cared for. Nick is, as well.

"Hey," he says from the doorway.

I hop off the stool and shuffle closer. When I reach him, he takes my bag out of my hand and sets it gently on the floor. Then he pulls me into his arms. He buries his face in my neck, his embrace gentle but strong. His chest expands against mine.

"You're right," he says, finally straightening. "You should always wait in the car when we get food. That way you'll always smell like you."

I press my nose to his neck, my mouth to his throat. He swallows against my tongue.

"Don't worry," I whisper. "You still smell like you."

With his hand around mine, he leads me up a steep, narrow staircase. Along the walls are posters advertising shows from years ago. Punk bands and all-girl rock groups who have performed at Moonbar. Nineties hip-hop, reggae, country musicians, and house DJs; a few names I recognize, though most I don't. Nick wasn't lying about the community here. At this point, I think he could apply for heritage designation for this building and get it easily.

There's a single door at the top of the stairs that must lead to Nick's apartment. The landing is just big enough to house a place for boots and a few hooks for coats. Above his door is a sign, one that likely used to sit above the front door of the bar. It reads *MOONBAR* with images of the moon in all its phases, and below: *ALWAYS FULL.*

I set my boots beside his on the rubber mat. He takes my jacket and hangs it on an open hook. The door sticks, then groans as he pushes it open. The space is small but bright in comparison to the darkness of the bar beneath. Several skylights across the room, above his bed, filter in soft, natural light. Unlike the deeply stained wood downstairs, his open-plan apartment is awash in birch accents. To the right, tucked into the corner, is his kitchen with a fridge that looks like it could survive a nuclear blast. A pine-scented candle burns on top of a small kitchen table with four retro chairs set up between the kitchen and the bed on the far wall.

He leans against the counter, watching me. His attention feels like too much, causing instinct to take over and urge me to hide.

"Do you have a bathroom?" I ask.

Pressing the heels of his hands against the countertop, he chuckles. "Uh. Yeah." He looks around the space. "Since like, the eighteen hundreds, I think."

Though I should be annoyed, I can't help but smile. "I meant, can I use it? And maybe could I have a shower?"

With a kiss to my temple, he guides me to the room on the left. The bathroom is surprisingly large and has been renovated.

He starts the shower for me. "The water needs a lot of time to consider heating up," he explains as he shuffles over to the washing machine. He gives me a quick rundown on how to use it if I want, then shows me where the towels are. They're plush and soft and I'm so thankful he's not one of those bachelors with only one always damp, thin as a tissue towel that I kiss him.

Once the water is hot and I've stripped down, I stand in the stream for several minutes, letting my muscles relax. I let my hair out of the bun and wash it twice, then scrub every inch of my body and shave despite having done it two days ago. I take my time drying my hair with a towel, finger combing it, doing my skincare routine, and moisturizing my whole body. Without dressing, I tuck my jewelry away into my toiletries bag, except for my pearl earrings, which I put back on.

I stand in front of the mirror, examining my reflection, my skin still pink from the shower and the heat, my nipples pointed and pert. I draw my hand across my chest, around one of my areola, between my breasts, over my stomach. Legs spread, I part my lips with two fingers. Despite the warmth in this room, the air feels cold against the delicate skin there. I brush my finger once across my clit and shudder.

"Jazz?" Nick knocks on the door.

My heart lurches, and I yank my hand away on instinct. "I'll be right out."

Nick lied, yes, but he also agreed to help a woman, a random stranger, when she asked for it. I've never thanked him for that.

Nick is on the bed when I open the door, one hand behind his head, the other tucked under the waistband of his boxers. His jeans are open, and his T-shirt is pulled up, revealing a patch of pink skin and dark hair. His eyes travel the length of my body, twice, as I stalk toward him, plant one knee on the bed, then the other, and straddle his legs.

"What do you want?" I ask. My heart pounds and blood whooshes in my ears.

His irises are black holes, void of all color.

"You," he says simply, reaching out.

I grip his wrist and push him back down. "No. What do you *want*? I'll give you anything."

He drags his hand down his mouth. Shakes his head. "Jasmine." But he says it like he might be a little disappointed. "Go over there." He pats the pillow next to him. "Lean back. Spread your legs."

My eyes flutter closed, and I flush. It's embarrassing how turned on I am by such simple words, how the rasp of his voice combined with the casual command make me wet. I settle myself against the pillow

Without a word, he frowns and gives his head a shake. He pulls me upright and shoves two more pillows behind me, until I can sit comfortably reclined with my knees bent, legs apart. He hops off the mattress, tugging his shirt over his head as he goes, then shucks his jeans. From a drawer in a cabinet next to the bed, he pulls out a condom and lube.

"I don't think you're going to need that," I say with a nod to the bottle of clear liquid. He must be able to see my arousal painting my pussy, my lips plump and shining.

He shrugs. "Can never be too prepared."

Oh god, even that is hot to me.

Finally, he settles on his knees at the end of the bed. His erection strains against the material of his underwear. He doesn't bother hiding that or the way he can't take his eyes off me.

"Touch yourself?"

Though I'd usually be mortified to do this in front of a man, Nick wrung any shame out of me last night. I follow the same path I found in the bathroom, my breasts, my nipples, my stomach. I circle my hole, my clit, paint my lips with my wetness. When I plunge my finger into my pussy, a flame ignites in my core and my toes curl.

Nick does nothing. He doesn't touch himself or me. He watches, his eyes huge, his face flushed, wearing an expression of sheer wonder.

It takes no time at all for my orgasm to gather inside me, an invisible string that I pull tighter and tighter. "Can I come?" I ask, the words choppy.

He touches me for the first time, a gentle hand on my knee, pushing it open after I let it fall too far closed for his liking. "Of course you can, baby."

He takes his cock out, squeezing the head, hard and shining, leaking pre-come across the bedspread. He holds himself as he watches me make myself come, my middle finger moving over my slick clit.

"You come so pretty," he says softly as my fist clenches and my back arches. "God, look at you." He's vocal where I am quiet, biting my lip, only allowing the softest moans and quietest whines to escape. "I can't wait to fill you up."

The image of that, his cock inside me, what it will feel like, the relief of it, sends me into another orgasm, or maybe it prolongs the one I'm already having. I can't tell.

"You like that?" he asks, his voice closer now.

I open my eyes. I don't know when I closed them. He kneels between my legs, the condom in his hand.

"Yes." My voice is high-pitched and needy. "Please."

"I'll give it to you, then," he says simply before opening the package with his teeth, rolling the rubber down his length.

"I have an IUD," I say. "Just as back up."

He nods, attention locked on my face. "Will you do me a favor?"

"Anything."

"When I'm fucking you," he says, almost sparking a third orgasm. "Will you be rough with me?"

My chest tightens, a frisson of unease working its way through me. "You want me to...hit you? Or something?" I try to school my features into neutral acceptance. I'll do whatever he needs and I'm not here to kink shame, but I've never hit a partner before.

He shakes his head, caresses my chin, the pad of his thumb rough, the sensation sending sparks down my spine. "Not if you don't want to. But I meant that you can scratch, bite, pull my hair. If it feels good, I want you to leave the marks on my skin that prove it."

He crawls up my body, kisses me, his lips moving slowly over mine, his tongue a warm, soft brush inside my mouth. I draw my hand up his back, into his hair and grip a handful. "Like this?" I ask, tugging his head back.

"Yeah," he says, his voice suddenly deeper.

"I love the way you kiss me." I kiss him back. "Will you kiss me one more time?" I push his head closer, gentle.

He grins. "You're so greedy. I love it," he adds quickly, clearly sensing that I might interpret that as a bad thing. "Keep your hand there." He drops onto his stomach, pushes my legs up, as far apart as I can go. He kisses into my cunt, his tongue and lips touching everything.

Exactly what I wanted.

I pull his hair, gently at first, harder when he grunts in response, when his hips start to move against the bed. I move his mouth where I want it and he grips my thighs tight, pinning me down. I'm the one on my back, but I'm still riding his face as I come, pushing, pumping my hips into his mouth. I'm still coming when he crawls up my body, his face wet, nose a little smushed, and slides into me without any resistance. We make sounds into each other's mouths. Grunts, moans, whines. I grab him, at his hips, his ass, scratch up and down his back as he thrusts into me. I bite his collarbone, shoulder, scratch and claw at his chest hair. We're a tangle of limbs, half on our sides, at an angle that doesn't allow him to get too deep yet still makes me feel so full.

"Can you come again?" He pants.

"No." I shake my head, tossing it back. "No."

"Do you want to try?" He slips his hand between us.

I push him onto his back, follow him over, hover over his cock. "Yeah."

He arches up into me, sits up, leaning on one hand, wrapping his other arm around me. He holds me close as he pumps into me, and I grind against him. He licks my nipples, sucks the skin between my breasts. He doesn't slow, even as his arms tremble. He's close. Nick grabs my ass, his hand spanning one cheek, his fingers edging into my dark cleft, pushing my hips back and forth, grinding me against him so that when my orgasm comes, it's a surprise. The sharp, short burst all my body is capable of now. Then he's coming, his cock pulsing, filling the condom, his body shuddering against mine.

For a long moment, we stay like this, heaving breaths, holding each other tight. He has to untangle my fingers from his hair when, eventually, he slides from inside me and rolls us to our sides. We kiss, touch, make sounds but no words. At one point, he gets up and wobbles to the bathroom. He comes back a little while later, the marks on his body apparent, his eyes wide and smile silly, blissed out. He holds a warm, wet cloth between my legs. I hiss at soreness I didn't know I had. He kisses me, my mouth, my shoulder, my back, my ass, and I try to stay awake for when he comes back to the bed, but I fall asleep before he slides in behind me.

17

NICK

The absence of my sound machine wakes me. I suppose that's counterintuitive, but in my exhaustion last night, I forgot to turn it on. Traffic out on the street isn't even bad, the silence is just too loud. I roll toward Jasmine, only to find she's not there. I stretch my hand out, keeping my eyes purposefully shut. If I don't open them, technically I'm not awake. The sheets are still warm, the pillow still smells like her.

"Jazz." My voice is scratchy and thin. "Jazz," I say again.

The mattress shifts, and then her warm hand covers mine.

"I'm here."

A knot in my chest uncoils. "I thought you left." I sound more relieved than I probably should; with those four words I give away too much of what I feel for her.

"Couldn't sleep," she says.

I roll back to my side of the bed. "I forgot the sound machine," I say, slapping at the milk crate nightstand I DIYed with a glue gun and two-by-fours left over from when we last repaired the stage.

"It's okay," she says, sliding a hand up my arm. "C'mere." She tugs.

I roll back to her, finally surrendering, and open my eyes. My heart catches. "Damn." I should have opened my eyes a lot sooner.

A combination of city and moonlight paints Jasmine in silver and shadows. Her hair is still down, a delight I haven't been able to luxuriate in yet. She leans on one hand, her breasts round and full, her nipples begging to be sucked, one leg curled over the other. Like this, she could easily inspire a Renaissance artist to create a masterpiece.

"What?" A small V of concern appears between her eyebrows.

"If I had any artistic talent," I say, grasping a strand of her hair between my index and middle fingers. "I'd paint you like one of those French girls."

She blushes, just like I hoped she would, and turns her face toward my hand, kissing my palm, first with her lips, then with her mouth open, sending a spark of arousal to my groin. She slides her hand across the bed and presses something hard and cold against my other hand.

It takes a moment to register that it's the lube I brought earlier. "Is it my turn now?"

She flushes again, the color barely discernible in the low light. "You'd want to do that?"

I walk my fingers up her arm, watch her skin raise in response. "Have you done it before?"

After a moment of intense studying, she nods. "Yes. Have you?"

With a chin lift, I let one corner of my lips turn up. "My motto is to try everything at least once. As long as we're all consenting adults."

Pulling her to me, I guide her so she's reclined on the mattress. I hook her leg over my hip, palm her ass. Jasmine is so proper, so good. I wouldn't be surprised to know that the thrill she gets from considering anal play is just as hot as the actual acts.

I brush a hand down her ass, over her pussy. "You were sore." I don't want to be overbearing, she knows her body best, but even with lube, penetrative sex won't make that any better.

"I don't want it for there," she says quietly.

I draw my hand back up her ass, pressing my middle finger to the top of her crease. She smiles, shaking her head. I reach for my own ass, but she stops me, places my palm over her breast.

"I thought we could do that," she says with such ease it leaves me confused. "I want you to fuck my tits, Nick," she whispers, her voice low and steady. The arousal I felt a moment ago is nothing compared to this, to my fantasy come to life. She tucks her hair behind her ear —she slept in her pearl earrings—drags her fingers down her jaw, her throat. "I want you to come here."

All I can say is "Yeah." Then, "Okay."

She laughs, her green eyes lighting. "Do you want to?"

I sit back so fast the bed shudders, and nod emphatically. "Yes. Absolutely, I do. Are you serious?"

"Yes."

"Okay. Yes." I'm hard, ready to go. I need to take a beat, slow down. With a deep breath in, I force myself to stop, then slowly reach for her. Jasmine said she'd never been kissed the way I kiss her. The truth is, I've never wanted to kiss anyone the way I kiss her. I could kiss her, only kiss, for hours, days. Her scent in my nose, her taste at the back of my throat, the weight of her jaw on my fingertips, the slide of her hair against them, and the sounds she makes, the huffs, the moans, the sighs. Every kiss its own little serotonin hit until I'm addicted.

That's how I kiss her now, with the urgency of addiction. We lie side by side. Kiss, mouths and skin. She rubs herself, hot and wet, up and down my leg. I lick her nipples, suck her until her skin shines. Pushing her to her back, I move down her body, remind myself to be gentle with her, take care. Kiss her pussy, fuck her with my tongue. Her taste, her smell, her hands in my hair, her skin on my skin, how wet she is, the way there will be a puddle on my mattress later, a wet spot we won't have to argue about.

I'm happy to lie in it.

I hold her open with my thumbs. She moans my name, and other words like *please*. Her thighs a vice around my head, pinning me in place. As if I'd stop or leave or not give her this, my mouth, or anything she asked for, if she'd only ask. Her body shakes as she gushes all over my tongue, coming with a sharp cry. I trail my lips across her stomach, her ribs and breasts, petting between her legs as her trembling slows. Eyes still closed, she pulls me forward. I crawl up her body, my knees sinking into the mattress on either side of her, my cock in one hand, the bottle of lube in the other.

"Ready?"

Her legs still saw behind me, but she nods, biting her bee-stung lower lip.

She hisses and her eyes widen as I dribble the lube across her breasts. "Cold."

"Sorry." I wince.

But she pushes her breasts together, drawing her finger through the lube, along her cleavage, around her nipples. When her skin is slick, I brace myself on one hand and hover close, kiss her.

"Hold yourself together," I say as I pull back.

She obeys, and as my cock slips against her skin, between her tits, my head peeking out, a wave of ecstasy washes over me. Fuck. I move slowly, unable to take my eyes off her, off us. It feels like my first time again. Like when I had to watch my cock enter a woman's body just to make sure it was real.

This isn't the most sensation I've ever felt. It's far from the kinkiest sex I've ever had. But the way she grips herself, when she traps her nipple between her fingers, how she watches my cock with the same intensity I do, then opens her mouth, letting my head kiss her lips? It's enough to have tingles building at the base of my spine far too quickly.

I clench the pillow in my fist. The sound of my cock, her skin, the lubricant; the gentle suction of her mouth, her lips.

"Is it okay..." I gasp. A string of pre-come trails from my cock to her tongue. "*Fuck.* If I come..."

She lifts her chin, presenting her neck, her collarbone. I can't hold back any longer. I barely gasp out a quick "Coming" before my orgasm barrels down my spine, hot and hard.

She whimpers as it hits her throat. With her chin tipped up, her earrings glint in the light, my come glistens across her neck. She whimpers again because this time my come paints her chin, her cheek. Her fucking lips.

"*Oh.*" She looks up at me, her eyes huge.

"I'm sorry," I say quickly. "I'm so sorry."

"It's okay," she says, so quiet, gentle.

She's covered in my come, a mess. Her eyes shining, her lips glistening.

All the air is stolen from my lungs. "You look so fucking beautiful."

She takes my face in her hands and lifts her mouth to mine. She stops short of kissing me, giving me the choice to opt out. She should know by now; I'll never opt out of kissing her.

When I press my mouth to hers, she hums a happy sound against my lips. I'll do almost anything to hear that sound again.

THE NEXT TIME I wake up, the bed is empty again, but this time, Jasmine is moving around the apartment. The floor is too creaky and old for anyone to manage stealth.

"What time is it?" I ask, sitting up slowly.

She doesn't answer right away, and when my sleep-logged brain catches up with my eyeballs, I understand why. She was trying to sneak out.

"You could have woken me up," I say, swinging my legs over the side of the bed and stretching. "Do you want a cup of coffee to go?" I grab a T-shirt from the floor, sniff it, and put it on.

She stands by the door, bags in hand. Fidgeting. That's not good.

"Jasmine." My tone is the same one I use when I find newly minted nineteen-year-olds doing bumps in the bathroom and want them to question their choices. "What's wrong?"

She sets down her bags, clasps her hands in front of her, transforms in front of my eyes into that controlled woman I first met. "Thank you so much for your help and for allowing me to help you."

My stomach bottoms out at her polite tone. "What are you doing?" I'm standing in the middle of my home, but I feel lost. Where is the woman I spent last night with? The one who was brave and beautiful and bare, not just of all clothing but pretense.

She swallows, her steely gaze faltering. "Now that we've helped one another, I think it's best for us to go our separate ways." With a deep breath in, she holds out her hand.

A laugh threatens to sputter out of me, so I do my best to hide it behind my hand, turning the move into some sort of masculine, jaw-working action she doesn't buy for a second. "You want me to shake your hand?" I close the distance between us, ignoring her still proffered palm. "Jasmine." I lean in close, drop my voice like we are sharing a secret.

She plasters herself against the door as if she's suddenly uncomfortable with our proximity. As if she's fucking scared of me.

"My tongue was in your pussy last night. You were wearing my pearl necklace hours ago." I thumb her pearl earring, understanding now why she wore them to bed. For me. "Now you want to shake hands. Like this was some sort of business transaction?"

Her skin flushes a deep red as she scowls. She pushes me away and I go, taking the space she needs because *fuck* I need it, too.

Teeth gritted, she says, "I'm sorry if my actions last night gave you the wrong impression."

I'm losing my mind. This is a dream. Whatever this is, it isn't real. "Are you a fucking robot? What the hell is going on?"

Finally, she drops her white-knuckle grip on the act. "This wasn't supposed to turn into a *thing*, Nick," she hisses.

"So fucking what?" I don't yell, but only just barely. My chest aches so acutely I worry I'll have a cardiac event right here and now. "It turned into a thing."

"All of the reasons I thought we wouldn't work when I thought you were the *real* Nick?"

Wow. *Real* was certainly a choice. What am I, a puppet from the imagination of Jim Henson?

"Those reasons still apply," she bites out. "Look at you. I have to go to work now. Meanwhile, you don't have to be up for hours because you work at a *bar*."

I throw my head back and laugh, mostly to push away the way those words slice into me. "Is it that our hours aren't compatible? Or is it something else? Like say..." I shrug. "My bank account balance?"

"Fuck you," she says quietly, looking over my shoulder. Her eyes shine with unshed tears.

I should stop, but something snapped in me back around the word *real*. I want her to hurt as much as she's hurt me.

"Everything is a transaction for you. Even sex."

"Fuck. *You*," she shouts, coming at me with both arms outstretched. "You." She pushes me back. Once, twice, again. "Lied." Until the back of my knees hit my bed and she pushes me down. "To me."

Her tears spill over now.

"You pretended to be someone you weren't. Do you know how fucked up that is? You're a fucking liar. A fake."

"I'm the liar? I'm the fake?" I snarl.

I stand, loom over her, but she doesn't back down. We're chest to chest, nose to nose. I hold my breath because the scent of her perfume will just confuse me.

"You've spent your whole life trying to convince everyone that you're the perfect girlfriend, the perfect sister." After years of arguing with my dad, I've gotten too good at the kind of retorts that cut to the bone. "Everything about you is fake."

It isn't until that last part is out that I register the pain on her face.

She turns away, dashing at her tears with the heel of her hand. "At least I don't live my life as if it's a joke," she says quietly. "Playacting as some Peter Pan man-child."

Back turned, she shuffles to her bags and picks them up. She takes a beat, her shoulders by her ears and fuck if I want to go to her, apologize. Fucking beg her not to go, not to choose him.

Choose me.

She faces me again, her face void of emotion. "And sex, by the way, is transactional by its very nature. Remember that the next time you judge me for the sexual partners I choose. Not all of us have the luxury of running to our daddy when we want to buy a fucking bar."

She opens the door, pauses at the threshold.

"That's why I did matchmaking in the first place. To find the person I wanted, not the one I needed."

My heart stutters, because I wanted her to want me. I thought she did, maybe she could.

"That's why I need to make things work with the r—" She stops herself. "The other Nick. He's my perfect match." She puts her hand on my chest, and my heart beats hard against her palm.

"I'm sorry," I say, fast and breathless.

"Do yourself a favor, Nick," she says, her words ghosting across my throat. "Save for retirement."

Wow. Low fucking blow.

Then she's gone.

DAD CALLS, because of course he does. This man has a sixth sense for the absolute worst time to pick up the phone. I let it ring, watching clouds collect above the skylight until there is nothing but steel gray above me, low and dismal and cold. Just as the snow begins, he calls again. Now the cloud cover and snow have turned the sky so dark I can't tell what time it is. If I blow through my opening shift, Rocco will come get me, so I stay where I am. Don't bother checking the clock. When Dad calls a third and fourth time in quick succession, my gut twists. I can't put this off any longer. Part of me hoped if I never picked up again, he'd just forget. About my request, about me.

"Hey," I say.

"Where were you?" he asks.

My mind is as blank as the sky above me. "I..." Why did I say that to her? What the fuck is wrong with me? "I was here."

Dad's pause is what *Merriam-Webster* might call pregnant. "Why didn't you answer before?" At his core, Dad is a businessman. He doesn't like to feel his time is wasted.

She's right, though. I am fake. I lied to my family to get access to my father's money. "I'm a fraud," I say.

Dad stutters, laughs uncomfortably.

"I'm sorry," I say. "Dad, I..."

"Listen," he cuts in. "I called to let you know that we can do a transfer of funds, in three installments—"

"No." Panic washes like cold water over my body. This cannot happen. I cannot do this. "Dad, no. I don't want the money."

He says my name, exasperated now.

"Dad. I lied. We lied." I take a deep breath, garner all my strength. "Jasmine isn't my girlfriend. She never was."

18

———

JASMINE

"So, how much money do you make?"

I choke on the mouthful of 2017 Napa Valley cab sauv. "*Jade.*"

She slurps loudly from the can of her gin cocktail, staring at Nick while, like an angel, he chuckles a little awkwardly.

"How about this?" he says, raising his own glass of wine to her can and giving it a delicate clink. "We'll see how the first date goes and then we'll talk finances."

"I'm sorry," I say, my face flaming and mortification threatening to snuff me out.

"Don't apologize for me," Jade says, aghast.

With a soft smile, he squeezes my hand. "It's fine."

"I'm vetting him," she says.

"Exactly." His smile is like an advertisement for toothpaste, and I feel a strange sort of swoop low in my stomach in response. "She's being a good sister."

Jade remains unswayed. In fact, she's glaring over the rim of her can. The can of her favorite premixed gin cocktail that *he* brought for her, because when he asked if we could have a drink at home first, mentioned that he'd love to meet my sister, I told him she didn't like wine. So, he asked what she liked and brought that for her, too.

Because he's *nice*. More than nice; kind, charming. The real Nick is a successful real estate lawyer, though he dresses like he moonlights as a runway model. He leans against the kitchen counter in a casual navy suit, with a deep green cable-knit sweater and a crisp white Oxford underneath. Running his hand through wavy blond hair, he smiles, making the skin around his green eyes crinkle. Meanwhile Jade eyes him like he's the poacher solely responsible for the endangerment of the world's cheetah population.

"You know what?" I swallow my last mouthful of wine. "Why don't we go. Jade has studying to do, I'm sure." I glare.

"Nope." She tips her head back and finishes her cocktail, then crushes it in her fist like a frat boy. "I'll just be here. Waiting up for my sister," she says to him. Then she belches.

"*Jade*," I screech.

Nick chuckles again. "I'm just going to use the little boys' room." One dimple appears in his cheek when he smiles.

"It's just through the living room." I point around the corner.

Once the door closes behind him, I round on my sister, my blood boiling.

"What are you doing?"

She takes my wine glass and his. "I liked the other Nick better." She pouts for effect.

"First of all, keep it down about the *other* Nick. Second..." Please. As if I need the reminder. I look over my shoulder in case Nick has snuck up on me. "This is the right choice."

She scowls, unconvinced, but I push on.

"You talked me into the matchmaking in the first place. *He's* my match."

"But what if he's not your only match. What if the other Nick—"

"The *other* Nick is a liar."

Jade's face softens, even more so when she says, in the gentlest voice, "Technically, so are you, sissy."

"Yes, thank you for the reminder," I mutter, my chest tightening painfully. While I'd never tell her, it hurts that she won't support me on this.

"Ready?" Nick asks, standing in the doorway of the kitchen.

I nearly jump out of my skin as I turn to face him and in this moment of panic, my brain spits out one word, *No*.

But I catch it, choke it back before it can escape, and say, "Yes."

Jade narrows her eyes, like she heard that moment of internal confusion. My smile is plastic as I follow him to the door, Jade trailing behind us. Nick helps me with my coat, a gentleman, a mark for the matchmaking scoresheet.

"It was a pleasure to meet you, Jade." A lie, but he holds his hand for her to shake.

Her face softens, just a bit. She makes a miffed sound though, offering a limp hand in return.

A gracious gentleman, another point for matchmaking.

Outside the building, he opens the car door for me and confirms that I'm buckled in before he pulls out of the spot. He made a reservation at a nice restaurant, one that typically has a long waitlist, and while we order drinks, discuss apps and entrées, he asks me about myself. He doesn't dominate the conversation, and he lets me order for myself. Then, despite claiming we'll share the dessert, he lets me have three-quarters of it.

As we wait for the bill, he makes an offhand comment about how it's the best meal he's had in a while, and suddenly all I can recall is the taste of strawberry milkshakes and cheeseburgers from a mom-and-pop place on the side of the highway.

"Are you feeling up for one more stop?" he asks after the server takes his credit card. "There's somewhere I want to take you, but it's kind of a surprise."

"Um..." I blink in the dim light of this lovely fusion restaurant that has not a single cheeseburger on the menu. "S-sure," I stutter, sounding about as sure as I feel.

"Only if you're comfortable," he says, as if he's worried I'm nervous about going to a second location with him. How could I be?

He truly is so perfect. The strange stomach swoop returns, one I *want* to identify as swooning but again, I'm not sure.

"Of course, I feel comfortable," I say quickly, covering his hand with mine. "I'm just going to run to the ladies' room." Standing, I grab my purse. "Have to touch up my lipstick."

The matchmaking scoresheet is a cornucopia of As, gold stars, ten out of tens, and one hundred percents. He's done everything right, everything I could ever want. He's exactly what I would expect from my perfect match, but something feels off as I look at myself in the bathroom mirror, wash my hands, and reapply my lipstick. The same lipstick I wore for Nick. My Nick. The *other* Nick.

"Pull yourself together," I whisper just as another woman walks in. I wave my hand underneath the automatic tap and wash my hands again unnecessarily so this complete stranger won't think I'm in here talking to myself.

My brain is a disorganized binder, emotions and confusion like loose paper and too many disorganized tabs. I pull my phone from my purse and send Jade a text so she knows I'm headed somewhere else, and promise I'll text our location when I get there. This small act of routine—sharing our locations for personal safety's sake—helps; like a page righting itself within three-rings, like confirmation that I am on the right path. Slowly, I make my way back to our table, reminding myself of why I'm here as I go.

Because I deserve to find my perfect match.

Because this is me taking things seriously. Because I am serious.

Because this isn't fake. *He* isn't fake.

"Ready?" Nick asks, standing next to our table, bill paid.

No. "Yes."

He holds out his hand.

Are you a robot? The question haunts me. Nick said it to hurt me, but maybe it's true. A robot is exactly what I feel like when I put my hand in this Nick's. A mechanical windup doll who nods and smiles, devoid of thoughts. Even as a riot of feelings that I can't control wreak havoc on me.

Nick helps me with my coat, a thrifted leather biker jacket that complements the silhouette of my close-fitting, long sleeved red sweaterdress and black over-the-knee suede boots. As he flattens my collar, his exhales are warm on the back of my neck. He's tall; my boots give me another two or three inches, but I'd still have to stand on my toes to kiss him. I could do that, kiss my perfect match. Maybe I should. I probably would if the thought alone didn't immediately make me feel kind of sick. If I kissed him now, he might taste a different man on my lips.

"I don't think I told you yet," he says quietly. "How amazing you look tonight."

You look so fucking beautiful.

I blush; the dress is shorter than I'd usually wear, especially for a first date. "It's Jade's," I say instead of *thank you.* "She insisted I wear it."

Something about it being a good luck charm, which I didn't ask too many questions about when it became clear the luck she was talking about was sexual in nature.

...so fucking beautiful.

The sound of his voice over my own ragged breathing, how those words were ripped from him, I wish I could cover my ears to the memory.

"Thank you," I say, strangled. "So, where are we going?" My voice is high, nervous. Obvious to me, if not him.

"Well." He elongates the word, his lips tipping up. "I promise, it's fun." He takes my hand again. "Okay if we walk? It's not too far. I wouldn't do that to your poor feet." He nods to my high-heeled boots. A considerate gentleman.

I'd put it on the scoresheet if I didn't feel so unstable in the heels in question all of a sudden.

He side-eyes me as we step outside. "And you might think it's a little kooky."

"Kooky is good," I say.

It pleases him, if the way his eyes light up in response is any indication.

We stop at an intersection and wait for the light to change. Nick takes his wallet out and discreetly presses a bill into the hand of the unhoused man shivering against the mailbox nearby. It should melt my heart. Endear him to me further. But at this point I'm numb to it. Detached from every feeling I should have for him, all the ways he's shown me exactly why we matched with each other so well.

He leads me down a side street and at the next intersection, we turn onto King Street. My stomach drops. King Street is a long street, there are hundreds of potential destinations. There's a good chance where we're going isn't even on King Street at all.

So what if we just so happen to be walking in the direction of Moonbar.

"Where are we going?" I ask, my steps slowing, thoughts racing.

He runs his hand through his hair, looking sheepish. "So, I got hit by a bus, right?"

"Yeah. How are you doing by the way?" I can't believe I haven't asked him about that yet; I've been so caught up in my own head.

The sidewalks are filled with inebriated twenty-somethings. Navigating King Street on a Saturday night is like playing a game of dodgeball where the balls are human beings with delayed reaction time who get in the way of your dodge. A man runs from a bar, cutting right in front of us, and Nick puts his arm out to stop us from colliding. The man pukes next to a perfectly empty trash can.

"I'm fine. Totally fine," Nick says. "Like, miraculously fine." He squeezes my hand, leading me forward again. "But the reason it happened is because I was rushing, not paying attention, you know?"

A woman screams directly behind us, the sound so bone-chilling the hair on the back of my neck stands up. My fight instincts kick in but are quickly doused when she follows the scream with a cackle and staggers past us with her friend on her arm.

Nick and I wince and laugh in tandem. "Sorry," he says. "I should have anticipated this."

"It's fine," I lie. Whatever it is, it is not fine. I am not fine.

"Anyway, I'm in this rush to get to our date," he says.

His hand is warm in mine, so warm I can feel him through my leather gloves. Not *my* gloves, actually. These are Nick's gloves.

"I'm crossing the street, jaywalking because who doesn't, right? And I get clipped, which sounds like no big deal, but turns out getting clipped by a bus will throw you into a car fifteen feet away."

My stomach lurches at the image he creates. "Oh my god."

"My doctors think the coma was how my brain protected itself, you know? And when I woke up in that hospital bed, I thought, *oh fuck*. I couldn't remember what happened, but by the look of all the machines surrounding me, I knew it must be bad. And then..." He shrugs. "It wasn't. They couldn't explain it, but honestly, I didn't ask any questions. It was a wakeup call. A reminder to slow down, stop taking things for granted. A real YOLO moment as the kids say."

I wince. I don't need Jade to tell me that the kids don't say that.

"Yeah, that makes sense. I'm so relieved." And I mean it. Nick is a good man and I hate to think what might have happened, or what his loss could have meant for his corner of the world.

The night is temperate for early March, but his nose and cheeks are pink from the cold. It's easier to watch him like this, in profile, than to look him in the eye. One degree of separation that gives me the space I need to calm myself.

"That's why I wanted to come here," he says, stopping on the sidewalk and taking my other hand in his. "It would be easy to say this was cursed or bad luck, but I wanted to come back. Or come for the first time. And what's more YOLO than karaoke." He points over my shoulder.

I turn, that sense of detachment and unreality back as I take in what I already knew I'd find: Moonbar in neon.

I'm going to be sick.

"I...I..."

He's already opening the door.

"Nick, I..."

He stops at the top of the stairs. Green, blue, and purple lights flash over my boots through crank windows set at ground level for maximum light into the basement bar. Music and voices compete from inside. He reaches for me. To not take his hand would mean having to lie outright and I can't do that. Not again.

Are you a robot? I slip my palm against his, let him lead me down the stairs. Follow like I'm programmed to. Maybe I am programmed, a robot. Following a path written for me, even written by me.

The bar is busier than when I was here last, louder. Hot.

"Do you want a drink?" He has to yell to be heard.

"I, uh, no thanks."

He frowns like he can't hear me, so I just nod. He points at the stage. "Start thinking about which song we're going to sing." With that, he turns and is engulfed by the crowd.

"Fuck," I say out loud since no one will be able to hear me anyway. "Fuck, fuck, fuck." I can't do this. I can't sing karaoke with my algorithm-approved perfect match in front of the man I let come all over me last week. At this point, my only hope is that Nick won't be here; my only hope is the coward's way out.

Since the universe relishes making a fool of me, I'm instantly struck by the sound of a familiar voice. Nick. The other Nick, my Nick.

"The first rule of Underground Karaoke is..." he says into the microphone as he adjusts the stand.

"Don't talk about Underground Karaoke," the crowd shouts back. There are too many people in here. There must be. No bouncer checked our IDs, who's to say Moonbar isn't over capacity yet?

"We have a packed set list tonight." The rough edge of his voice is amplified, the sound sending fissures through my heart. He looks the same. Of course he does. It hasn't even been much more than a week. But in that time, I've changed. I'm so different that there is no way I could look the same to him. But the longer I stand here, the bar howling around me, the more differences I notice.

His T-shirt is black, an image of Picasso-esque naked bodies and *The Tragically Hip* printed on the front; his wardrobe hasn't changed. But his eyes are bruised by dark circles and his ever-present five o'clock shadow is thicker than usual, like he hasn't kept up with the task of shaving with any regularity.

And I'm a terrible person. Because my first thought? I want to know what that feels like on the delicate skin between my thighs.

"Jasmine," the real Nick, the new Nick, calls across the crowd.

I wince, even though there's no way the other Nick could hear him over the din of the people in this bar. He makes his way back to me slowly, two short glasses with mixed drinks of clear liquor and lime wedges in his hands. Nick probably cut those wedges.

"Gin and tonics," he says, a little breathless. "I hope that's okay."

I take it from him and drink it down in three gulps.

"Are you okay?"

"I'm fine," I say, an outright lie, shuddering as the gin burns my esophagus.

"We don't have to sign up," he says, angling in close so he doesn't have to yell. His cologne is delicious; full-bodied and expensive. Not as light as citrus, not spicy like pine. "Are you nervous?"

Nick taps the mic again, a boon I don't deserve. I take the opportunity anyway, straightening and pretending to be enthralled with his next announcement. "Before we get started," he says. "Have some bad news."

The crowd quiets, the frenetic movement slows, stills, making him easier to see, but also likely making it easier for him to see me. Part of me wants to hide, but a much bigger, selfish part wants him to find my eyes in this crowd. To see the recognition turn to want, then determination. For him to make his way through this crowd. To me.

"This will be one of the last Underground Karaoke nights at Moonbar."

"What?" I whisper, my question lost in the echoes of the crowd. My heart sinks, my chest heavy with sadness.

He nods, but his expression remains blank, the opposite of the last time I saw him when his anguish was tattooed into his skin.

"Unfortunately," he says. His skin is far too pale. "Moonbar is closing."

The bar erupts in boos and groans, but the sounds are far away. There's a buzzing in my ears, like every noise is filtered through cotton balls. I'm numb as Nick leaves the mic, stepping off the stage.

Someone says his name. He looks up, and that's when he sees me. First shock, then recognition. Then, worst of all, nothing.

He disappears into the crowd.

I don't have any right to be hurt, but I am.

"Take me home," I say, and I walk out.

19

JASMINE

Three hours later and despite last call, the sidewalk outside Moonbar is still packed. I try the door, but it's locked, unsurprisingly. Do I knock? Nick led me in through the back when he brought me here. Unfortunately, this requires me to walk down the back alley, which is terrifying at almost three a.m. Dumpsters line one side, in between back doors to the various businesses on the block. The wall of the adjacent building is covered in tags and street art. There's one light on above the back door to Moonbar; the rest of the way is dark, a lighthouse in a sea of trash and dark corners. My only option is to run toward that halo of light as fast as my high-heeled boots will let me. I skid on gravel and salt and I grab the back door, jerking on it as hard as I can. Also locked.

Fuck.

The hair on the back of my neck prickles and I can't help but look over my shoulder, like Ghostface has been hiding in the shadows for a moment just like this. I try again, as if that's ever worked in the history of locked doors. It does not. I knock again. Maybe Nick's already upstairs, in bed. Maybe he's not even alone. A sound echoes down the alley, an unidentifiable noise that the closed captioning on my TV would describe as [loud scraping], and a chill runs up my spine.

Fuck. Fuck. Fuck.

I try the door one more time, jerking it back and forth, growling through the exertion, taking out my frustration on the metal handle and rusty hinges. Because I am the idiot who thought coming down a dark alley at night was a good idea, the idiot who couldn't let her literal *perfect match* woo her into a stable, loving relationship because I was too upset about this bar. I am the idiot who is outside, in the cold, in the middle of the night, desperate to find out why the hell all the work I did impressing his family, while being bullied by a child and an octogenarian, was worth nothing.

On my final pull, the door gives with an echoing screech, and I stumble back as it swings violently and slams against the wall.

Nick stands there, backlit by the hallway light. He wears his glasses, but any delight I might have from seeing him in them is overshadowed by the scowl on his face.

"We're fucking closed," he shouts. His voice echoes down the alley and along my skin, leaving goose bumps in its wake.

I shiver, not from the cold, but out of fear. He's never yelled like that before. Regardless of whether he knows it's me, I look away to get myself under control. I don't want him to see me cry. Ever since I was a kid, listening to my dad yell at my mom, all it takes is one well-directed shout from a man to have me in tears.

"Jasmine?" he asks, his tone laced with confusion. "What..."

"What happened to the loan?" I ask, erecting the barriers I need to get through this conversation.

He deflates, leans against the doorjamb and pinches his nose beneath the bridge of his glasses. "Jazz."

"Don't call me that." Now that I can't use the door as my emotional punching bag, I'll have to use Nick. "You said your dad agreed to the loan. The whole reason I went to Muskoka with you was so you could get that loan to save your bar, and now the bar is closing."

"Jazz," he says. "Jasmine." He holds out his hands like he's trying to calm a wild animal. "Will you come in? It's cold and—" He looks left and right. "You're standing in a fucking alley. Why didn't you just text me?" Standing to one side, he holds the door open.

Holding my breath, I brush past him, but I stop just beyond the threshold, unsure if I should go upstairs or into the bar.

"I didn't text because I didn't think you'd answer," I say quietly.

The door slams shut, and Nick stands directly behind me. Not touching, but just barely. He sighs, puts his hand on my waist, moving me gently to the side so he can pass in the narrow hallway.

"You can wait upstairs if you want. I've got to finish closing," he says over his shoulder as he pushes through the swinging door.

I linger here, butterflies migrating to the spots on either side of my ribcage where he touched me. It's because of those butterflies I don't go upstairs. I don't need to be in such close proximity to a bed right now.

I follow him into the low-lit bar. "You can talk and close."

The floors have already been swept and mopped clean, garbage emptied, and tabletops wiped down. Instead of closing, he leans against the bar, his arms braced on its edge, head down.

When he looks up, his face is gaunt. "Was that him? The guy you left with?"

"It doesn't matter," I say, fisting my hands. "What happened to the loan?"

"*Of course it matters*," he roars, his face flushed and chest heaving.

"Don't yell at me," I yell back, for once feeling brave rather than reduced to tears.

He turns his back to me, his hands in his hair. When he faces me again, he's calmer, controlled. "I'm sorry."

I cross my arms, a useless protection. "He wanted to do karaoke. That's why he wanted our first date to be here in the first place. I didn't want..."

Nausea churns in my stomach. I'm not sure how to even finish that sentence. I didn't want to tell him the truth, another lie. I'm not sure anymore.

"I didn't know how to explain everything to him," I say simply. "I'm sorry."

Under the overhead lights, the bar is cast in strange shadows. The graffiti wall looks harsh instead of cool, the mirror behind the bar revealing its cracks and water damage. Nick is strangest of all. His eyes a little wild, not a smart-ass smirk or grin in sight.

"I didn't take it," he says. "The loan."

"*What?*" I will not cry, even though I want to. He was close, so close to his dream. "Why not?"

He lowers his head, gives it a shake. Sniffs, like maybe he's also doing his best not to cry. "I couldn't take his money, Jasmine. Not like that. Not when it wasn't…"

Real.

He pulls a bottle down from the shelf and pours himself a finger's worth of amber liquid. Staring into the glass, he gives it a swirl then tips it back and swallows half of it. "I talked to Bernie and Rocco. We thought about pooling our money, going in together, but…"

"It's still not enough?"

He nods, gaze averted, but devastated. So, I go to him, take the glass from his hand, bring it to my lips.

"I'd have poured you some," he says, focus fixed on my mouth as I drink. "But it's not cab sauv."

The whiskey is smoky, spicy, a bit harsh.

"I can handle it." I hand him back the empty glass, relish the alcohol's burn.

His gaze is warm, as warm as the whiskey and his hand on my hip. He leans in close, his lips shine. I want to make him shine with more than just whiskey.

"I should go," I whisper. He closes his eyes, drops his forehead to mine. His erection presses into my stomach, hot and insistent. "Down boy." Even to my own ears, I'm not believable.

A smile spreads across his face, wolfish. So very Nick.

"Stay," he says. "A little longer."

"I…" Can't think of a reason not to. Actually, I can think of many reasons not to. They're just not very convincing. "I really should go," I say, a last-ditch effort. The words tremble in my throat.

Nick leans close, and I can already taste him, the whiskey on his lips. "So, he took you out for dinner?"

"Yes." I close my eyes in a fruitless attempt to hide my arousal and the shame that comes with it that I can't disentangle.

His fingers drift down my front, tugging at the buttons on my coat. "You wear this for him?" he asks, the faintest mocking in his voice.

Nick opens my coat, his fingers linger where the hem of my sweaterdress meets the thigh-high boots, long enough only to feel the brush of his skin on mine, then he pushes the coat off my shoulders.

"Nick, what the *fuck*—" I hiss at him, bending to grab my coat from the sticky, dirty bar floor.

He beats me to it. "I already mopped," he mutters, folding the heavy fabric over his arm and draping it over the bar. Despite still being fully clothed, I'm suddenly vulnerable. I grab his forearms, a crutch, a buffer, but he turns me in his arms to face the long mirror against the back wall of the bar.

The floor behind the bar is spotless as well, the counters and cupboards wiped. The garbage changed. The air smells faintly of whatever lemon-scented cleaner he uses and him. Each bottle has been returned to its place, the taps cleaned and plugged, the ice drained. It's as clean as a dive bar can get.

In the mirror, we're distorted, made worse by the low light. Because it's Saturday night on King Street West, the shouts and laughter of people still outside despite the cold and the late hour drift in from outside, but behind the bar is our own little haven.

The mirror is set higher on the wall than the one we stood in front of at his childhood home, cutting off my view of us below my waist, but I don't need to see what he does next. His hands return to my thighs, fingers curling into the dress, nails scraping gently. "You wore this?" he asks, his voice husky. "For him?"

Again, I can't look. I lean my head back against his shoulder, keep my eyes shut. "Yes." Then, quickly, "No." I meet his gaze in the reflection. "I wore it for me."

It's far more daring than my usual style, but I felt—feel—good in it. Sexy. And I don't feel bad about wanting to feel that way, either.

"Yeah," he says, more an exhale than a sound. His chin bobs against my shoulder as he nods. "Yeah, you did." He drags his thumb against my lower lip and it's easy, it's nothing to open my mouth, taste him, answer him with the drag of my teeth against his skin. He hisses when I bite too hard, pressing his cock against my ass.

Slowly, he pulls the hem of my sweaterdress up, higher and higher. He watches with me, over my shoulder, stopping only when the white of my panties is visible.

"And what about this?" he pets me there, through cotton already soaked with my arousal. I lean into him, spread my legs as he settles against the bar counter behind us.

"What about it?"

He brushes his lips against the shell of my ear, scarcely breathing the words when he says, "You were bare last time." He slips his finger beneath the fabric, rubs gently across my still-bare skin. "Did you keep it that way for him, too?"

My chest shudders with each breath. I'm desperate for more, his touch, the barest pressure, relief. Even if I don't deserve it, not after what I did to him. "No."

I ache between my legs, my nipples throb, the anticipation of pleasure almost painful.

"For who then?" he asks. "Me?" Still his fingertips skirt the edges of my panties, my slit.

I reach for him behind me, my hand tangling in his hair. "*Me.*"

He takes his hand away, pulls my hem of my dress back down in one swift motion. I cry out, biting off the sound with my fist in my teeth. In the reflection his face is hard, but his eyes shine.

I stumble away from him, grip the counter while I try to catch my breath. "First of all," I say, in my best impression of unphased. "It's for *whom,* not for *who.*"

Even his answering laugh, husky and low, turns me on; the sound moves through me like an electrical current. I hate him.

I hate him.

I wish that were true.

He's still pressed close to me. Despite his egregious orgasm denial, part of me wants to push him away and walk out, my head held high. Most of me would rather turn in the circle of his arms, pull the sweaterdress over my head, and let him live out his next fantasy all over me.

"Second." I take a deep breath to collect myself. "I'm sorry. For coming here tonight with him. And for what happened between us." His face softens at my words, but that only makes me feel worse. I press my thumbnail into the wood counter, stare at the crescent shape as I say, my voice cracking, "It's my fault you won't be able to buy your bar."

"Whoa." Nick cups my face, his fingers gentle on my cheeks. "Whoa. What? Jasmine, no."

Mortifying tears fill my eyes. "If I hadn't left," I say, doing my best not to let emotion bleed into my voice but failing, "you'd still be able to take the loan."

He shakes his head, like he can't believe what he heard. "Why do you think that?"

"You're obviously pissed at me." I'm embarrassed to even say it, more so by the fact that it only makes me want to cry harder. I never should have come here. "And I understand why. I've been…" I shake my head. "A jerk."

His eyes go wide, shocked. "Baby, no." He kisses me, his lips spreading mine open, like if tries hard enough he'll be able to kiss those words right out of my mouth. His stubble is a familiar tickle and scratch, and I moan from the reminder of it, leaning into the abrasion. I want his kisses to have their desired effect, to feel magically absolved of my guilt, but that's not what happens, no matter how hard I kiss him back.

If anything, they make me more guilty. I push him away again. "I have to go."

A perfectly nice man dropped me off at home earlier tonight. He was understanding when I told him I'd felt overwhelmed by the crowd, when I lied that I'd love to sing karaoke with him one day, in front of a smaller crowd.

Seemingly reading my mind, Nick scowls. He refills his glass with more whiskey.

He does not offer me any.

"Is he waiting for you?" he asks.

"What are you going to do then?" I ask, ignoring him and his flashy argument bait. "If the bar's closing, what will you do?"

He sighs, setting his glass down to run his hands through his hair, suddenly nervous. "I don't know. Maybe go back to school?"

While I know it's unfair, my immediate reaction is anger. "You're just going to give up then?"

He's worked hard for the last decade and now he's going to do the thing his father always wanted him to, anyway.

"It's not giving up, Jasmine," he says quietly. "It's growing up. That's what you'd call it, right?"

I flush, not embarrassed because I think security and stability are important qualities for partners to have, but because my words so clearly hurt him. No matter the terrible things we've said to each other, I don't want to hurt Nick. And I don't think he's ever really wanted to hurt me, either.

"Besides, that's what you did, isn't it?" he says. "Gave up."

Okay. Scratch that. I do kind of want to hurt him. I reach for Nick's bottle of whiskey and pour myself a glass, and take far too large of a mouthful, wincing through the burn.

"What," I ask slowly to avoid any slurring while the alcohol warms my blood, "am I supposed to have given up on?"

"Us."

"There was no *us*, Nick. It was made up. We were made up."

He cups my jaw, his thumb brushing my cheekbone, tender, almost pitying. "We were. Until we weren't."

I turn my face to break his hold, but my skin tingles and glows where he touched me, something I'm not sure I can blame on the alcohol.

"I guess we'll have to agree to disagree," I say primly. I will not let him get to me. I came here to find out why he didn't have the loan, and now I know. In fact, I don't need to be here at all. Not anymore.

Turning, I reach for my coat where he's laid it over the bar top.

"Is that what you'd call it?" he asks my back. "A disagreement? Cuz I'd call it trusting a computer over your own heart."

I turn on my heel before I can force myself to calm the fuck down. "You don't know what I feel for you." I jab him with my index finger, lean into the scant inches between us.

He wraps his hand around my accusing finger, squeezing, his skin warm. "There's no way I was the only one who felt that way, Jazz."

Outside on the sidewalk, the bar's last call leftovers have dispersed, leaving only the sound of passing traffic. It's late. Way too late. I should go home.

The first thing I told Jade when she turned nineteen and was legally allowed to drink was that nothing good ever happens after two a.m.

I really need to start taking my own advice.

"You were," I say. "The only one." But I can't take my eyes off his lips.

"Prove it," he says, like I conjured him, like he really can read minds, like he's the genie inside my magic lamp ready to grant my every wish.

I grip the fabric of his T-shirt in my hands and pull his mouth to mine. "Fine," I growl against his lips. "I will."

Glasses and bottles clink as I push him against the counter. The erection that has not abated since we started this conversation presses into my hip. He grips my ass cheeks in his hands, rough, pulling me into him more, until he's almost bent backward over the bar counter.

He tastes warm, like the whiskey, his moan is rough, satisfied as I fist his hair and pull his lower lip between my teeth. When we pull apart, he stares at me, his eyes intense, the curve of his lips teasing, as always.

He wipes his mouth with the back of his hand. "What was that supposed to prove, Jasmine?"

I don't have an answer for him, but this entire evening was doomed from the start and it's all his fault. Any chance I could have had with the other Nick was ruined because of this one, and my guilt. So, I'll fuck him, get it out of my system, then we can both move on.

Nick can call it whatever he wants, giving up, computer-generated love. I don't care. I call it making the smart choice, because what was the point of all this in the first place if I don't give my perfect match a real chance.

"Are you going to fuck me?" I ask. "Or talk all night?"

Gripping the hem of my sweaterdress in my fists, I channel the woman I was in his pool room and pull it over my head in one motion. I'm naked beneath other than my panties, and my skin pebbles and pinks from the cold, the exposure, and a little bit from the audacity. I never truly feel like myself with him, but in the best way possible. Not because I'm hiding, because I'm revealing parts I didn't even know about.

No longer can I make snide remarks about him making a joke of everything. Nick's face transforms from sarcastic to serious. If there's one thing Nick doesn't joke about, it's fucking me.

"Do me a favor?" He looks away, wipes his hand across his mouth, like he can already taste me on his tongue. "Take your hair down?"

I pause, only because of all the things he could have said, I hadn't anticipated that. But I do as he asks, pulling out the bobby pins and clear elastic bands until my hair unfurls from the bun wrapped on my head and falls around my shoulders.

He sighs. Shakes his head. "You're so fucking beautiful."

His words, the gravity in his voice, pin me to this spot. They reveal more than my nakedness ever could and I cover myself with my arms.

All my life I've heard that. I've known I was beautiful since I was old enough to pass for "old enough." But the words have always been said in the context of what they do for someone else. I'm beautiful and that made a man happy, made him look good to his peers, made me deserving of his time.

To Nick, I'm beautiful. Like art is beautiful. Beautiful like one exquisite line of poetry. Beautiful like it's his honor to behold.

He reaches for me, pulls me by my wrist into him. His body is warm, his T-shirt soft, the jeans a bit rough against my bare thighs. "Don't hide, beautiful girl," he says softly into my hair.

"Sorry," I say, a reflex, and he tips my chin up, a quiet *tsk* on his lips for the unwarranted apology. His other hand travels down my body, skirting the side of my breast, my hip, running along the top of my thigh-high boots, the combination of the suede and his warmth laying a trail of shivers on my skin. His fingers glide up the inside of my thigh and finally he touches me like I need. He pushes his hand down the front of my panties, stretching the fabric, glides the pads of his fingers along my lips, and inside me.

I press my face into his shoulder, my mouth open.

"You can bite, baby."

As he pumps his fingers inside me, rubs the heel of his hand against my clit, I do. More another reflex than a conscious choice. He sighs, grunts, as I bite, grip his waist beneath his T-shirt as I spread my legs further apart so he can fit more inside me, as I stretch for him, my body pliant. He takes his hand away a moment later and I cry out again. I can't take another denial, but instead of teasing me he holds me by my hips as he gets on his knees, his back against the cupboards along the floor of the bar, his mouth at my pussy.

"Hold on to the counter," he says, the gentlest command.

"Keep your glasses on," I say back, and I do, and he does.

I grip the counter. We watch each other as he closes the inches of space between us, his stubble the sweetest roughness on my inner thighs. His glasses tilt as he pushes his mouth deeper between my legs, his tongue stroking. I force myself to keep my eyes open. I don't want to miss a moment of him like this, on his knees for me, flushed with arousal, his own version of beautiful. But I break my promise in the next moment when he pushes three fingers inside me once again, and I cry out, rocking against his hand and his face, coming, shuddering, held up only by my grip on the counter and his hand on my thigh.

He stands slowly as I catch my breath, not ready to open my eyes yet. He takes hold of me again, places a wet kiss on my shoulder. "Can I take you upstairs?"

I nod, my eyes squeezed shut.

"Can you keep your boots on?"

I laugh, seeing him finally. His glasses are perhaps permanently bent, his hair a mess, his lips shining in a way I've grown too accustomed to.

"Yes." I kiss him. Because I can and because I want to taste myself on him and because if I don't, I might hate myself for the rest of my life.

He places my coat over my shoulders and carries my dress and purse over his arm, gently herding me toward the back door and up the stairs. The cold in the stairwell, the transition to a new location, pull me from the sex haze I was in moments earlier. I shiver, the wetness between my legs no longer slick and warm. The intimacy and vulnerability between us crumbles away, leaving only a strange sense of embarrassment. Who did I think I was to undress in Nick's bar, as if this was an audition for a low-budget *Coyote Ugly* remake. Maybe I can blame the whiskey.

"I'm sorry," I say, turning to face him as his apartment door shuts behind us.

"You're good, Jazz." He tucks my hair behind my ear. "Do you still want to do this?" he asks into my hair. "We don't have to keep going, if you don't want to." After a pause, one where he breathes so deeply his chest expands against mine, he says, "What do you want, Jasmine?" The question far heavier than just a discussion of sex.

I step out of his reach. I can't think with his fingers skimming the curve of my breasts and his exhales against my neck. He's left the lights off, other than the weak lamp from the hood fan above the oven. I walk around his apartment, trailing my palms along the minimal, mix-matched furniture, the few wood accents he—or his father—made.

What I want is for him to do whatever he wants to me, but it's moments like these, the ones I want the most, that are the hardest to let myself have. There are so many lies, omissions, and half-truths, and not enough time between us to make it possible for me to trust myself.

He follows me at a distance around the apartment. When I stop at the edge of the bed, he stops, too. Nick's T-shirt looks soft, worn, well-loved. I ache to feel it between my fingertips because I know it will be just as it looks. It will smell like him, too. The dim light casts us both in shadows, his skin turning silver and blue, but his eyes are kind.

His eyes are always kind.

"I want..." I say, spreading my hand across his comforter. He's changed the sheets from the ones we slept under and that makes me sad even if I applaud the hygiene.

I want a way for Nick to be my perfect match. If I was perfectly honest with myself, with him, that's what I would say, but since I can't be that I might as well settle for what I want in this very moment.

"I want you."

I drop the coat from my shoulders, sit on the edge of his bed, lean back on my hands. I spread my legs. If this is our last night together, the least I can do is be real, and the real me wants to get absolutely railed by Nick Scott.

He pulls his T-shirt over his head, unbuttons his jeans, closes the space between us to brush the back of his fingers across my cheekbone, follow my hairline from my temple around the shell of my ear.

He gets on his knees between my legs, slides his hands up my boots. His eyes follow the path his hands take, and when he ghosts his lips across mine, arousal and want burn in my core.

"Nick," I whisper. He moans his response, and I let myself fall back on the bed as he crawls over me. Together we push his jeans off his legs, he toes off his socks between kisses. His fingers find me again, wet, wanting. I push down the elastic waist of his boxers, his cock hard silk and soft, the flared head dripping pre-come.

He takes the underwear off and starts to roll away, toward the cabinet where he keeps his condoms and lube. I stop him, squeezing his forearm before he can leave the cradle of my spread legs. "I've never had sex without a condom before."

He searches my face. "Do you want to?"

I nod, my heart pounding from the proposal I've sent out into the universe. "Have you?"

"Yes. Does that change your decision?"

I kiss him. Gentle, lingering, then pull him back to me. "Not at all."

I still trust him with my body.

He rubs the head of his cock up and down my pussy, making himself wetter and wetter until the sound of our mutual slickness is an erotic rhythm between us. His cock bumps my clit over and over, until every pass pulls a moan from me, and I seek the contact with my hips. He slips into me that way, with my hips raised, my fingers spreading my lips wide to expose my clit to him.

We stop. Pleasure radiates through my body, from where my pussy sucks the head of his cock into me, up my hips, deep in the pit of my stomach. Pleasure reaches my toes, fills my throat.

Then he moves.

Nick is slow at first, though he doesn't need to be. I am so slick he could slide right out of me. He stares at where he disappears inside me, his eyes huge in his face. I'm jealous. I want to see it, too.

"What do you see?" I ask, my voice strangled from the words trying to fit around the pleasure inside me.

He meets my eyes for a moment before looking back, his glasses still a bit askew on his face. "You're wet. Glistening."

He thrusts into me again and I arch my back. I wish there was a way to take more of him inside me, all of him. I want to be stretched to the point of pain, go beyond full to overflowing.

"Your pussy is so pink and plump." His lips pop around the words. "And then, around here." He glides his fingers up and down my lips stretched around him. "You're pinker, darker." He bites his lip, like it takes every ounce of self-control not to pull out of me and lick my cunt.

"Like this." He skims his fingers across my nipples, then takes one nipple in his mouth as if to prove his point. I shudder, twist beneath him, fist his pillow, frustrated. His mouth feels good but it's not enough, not what I want.

"Can you come again?" he asks.

I nod quickly. "Please," I beg.

His thrusts come faster, harder. His fingers find my swollen clit. I spread myself further for him, guide his hand in the rhythm I need. I've never been this shameless for my own pleasure before. But it's not my fault. It's his. He lets me be this way, he *makes* me this way. He is unapologetic and he makes me think I can be that way, too.

I reach around his hips, grip his ass in my hands, angry with him, hating him. I leave handprints on his skin, nail marks down his back. I pull his head to mine by his hair. Kiss him with too much tongue and teeth, growl into his mouth. The pleasure builds until every part of me is swollen, until I'm choking on it. The bed shakes. He holds me in place, pinning me by my shoulder, his thumb playing a furious rhythm against my clit, the ridge of his cock dragging inside me. Pleasure pulls me apart, piece by piece, rips at my skin, seizing muscle. Frustrated tears fill my eyes, roll down my temples, because I want to come, so bad.

But if I do, *when* I do, this will be over.

"Hey," he says, his voice a whisper. "Hey."

His thrusts slow, his grip on my body loosens. He wipes the tears from my skin with his thumb, disentangles my fingers from his hair. Nick kisses me, his body almost still inside mine, tonguing me in the same gentle way he pets between my legs.

"I've got you, baby," he promises. "I've always got you."

With a rush of warmth under my skin, I come, like the gentle rasp of his voice is the last detail my body needed to fall over the edge. He pulls a sound, somewhere between a cry and a moan, from my lips as he fucks me through my orgasm. My clit and pussy pulse against and around him, but he doesn't stop his slow, steady thrusts until I shudder and goose bumps rise against my skin.

I gasp. "Stop."

He pulls out and the absence of him is almost as pleasure-painful as being filled by him, but I don't have time to complain because in the next moment he flips me onto my stomach, pulls my hips up, and spreads my legs. He pushes back into me, fucking with sharp, snapping thrusts of his hips, then stilling, groaning. His cock pulses inside me and the thought of his come filling me up sends something like aftershocks through me until I'm moaning with him.

Nick rests on his forearms over me, careful not to crush me completely in the bed, though that sounds nice. I don't feel capable of much more than this facedown starfish on Nick's bed. He kisses my shoulder, my hair, as his cock slowly softens inside me.

"I'm going to clean you up," he says, and I nod. Facedown starfish can't talk anyway.

He slips from me again and crawls down my body. I feel him behind me, kneeling between my spread legs and ass cheeks. He can probably see *everything*.

Who am I kidding? There's no "probably" about it. He can see everything. But I can't bring myself to care or feel ashamed, or embarrassed. Every time Nick puts his hands on me, it's with reverence, worship.

His hands are gentle as he palms my cheeks and kneads the muscles of my lower back. The bed shifts as he moves, but instead of getting off the bed like I expect, he settles lower between my legs.

"What are you doing?" I ask into the comforter. "I don't think I can take any more fucking."

"No fucking." His breath is warm on my cool, wet skin. Gently, like he's pulling apart the petals of a rose, he spreads my tenderest skin. "I'm just going to clean you up."

His nose bumps gently against my ass, then he laps at my pussy.

I squirm. Apparently, I'm fine if Nick looks directly into my asshole but my discomfort draws the line at him sucking his come out of me.

But then his chin bumps my clit, his tongue a soft brush against my skin, his beard a velvety rasp on my thighs. His kisses are sucking and wet, around my hole and inside of me. He grunts, the sound affirming his pleasure and mine. I wish I could see us. I open my eyes, my cheek pressed against his bedspread, the room dark except for the electric glow from the windows and the kitchen, and watch, out of body, my fist grip his pillow.

He thrusts his tongue inside me, his nose and chin bumping against me. I come in a wave rolling slowly down my back, his name a whispering gasp on my lips. I come around his tongue as he laps the last of his come from inside me, shuddering against him and biting my knuckles. When he finally pulls away, steadying me or maybe himself with a warm hand on my lower back, I bury my face in the linens.

Finally, Nick leaves the bed, returning with a warm cloth and some water. He lets me lie there as he pulls back covers and sheets, rearranging me so he can finally pour me into bed and slide in behind me.

Nick was right.

There was no way he was the only one to feel this way.

But as he pulls me against him, kissing the back of my head in such a casual way, I'm not sure I can admit that.

I'm a coward. I was a coward when I asked him to pretend to be my boyfriend, for not choosing this Nick in the first place. I'm a coward because I won't take a risk, even when it's not really a risk at all.

After long minutes of silence, Nick shifts, hugging me closer to him. "Do me a favor?"

"Okay," I say, my voice hoarse.

"If you're going to leave," he says, his tone matter of fact. "Don't come back here."

My heart crumbles, like ash. A pain so searing I can't speak, not yet.

"I think it would be easier that way. For both of us."

I can't respond, but he doesn't need one. He goes quiet and eventually his breaths slow, lengthen as he falls asleep, and I watch the sun rise across the wall.

AROUND NOON, Jade slams open my bedroom door and thunders across my floor before I have time to turn over in bed.

"Leave me alone, troll," I whine as she snuggles beside me. In response, she pulls one of my pillows away from me, pounding it into submission for her own comfort.

"You're late for work," she says in a creepily chipper voice.

"I called in sick."

I left Nick's apartment early yesterday morning, after sleeping almost not at all. I'd walked out onto the sidewalk on wobbly legs, my heart lodged in my throat. It wasn't until I was on our front doorstep that I was brave enough to pull out my phone, open my text chat, and typed the words I should have typed long ago:

> Me: I'm sorry. I can't see you again.

I haven't been able to look at my phone since.

"But you're not sick." Jade places the back of her hand against my forehead for confirmation.

"Haven't been sleeping well," I mumble, rolling deeper into my pillows. "Maybe I'm coming down with something."

Mostly I just don't want to go to work today. I can't muster up the energy and make myself, which is really messed up because if there's one thing I've always been able to do, it's walk into a job I hate with my head held high. The idea of having to do Anaïs's bidding, of looking Mitchell in the eye, makes me want to simultaneously scream and throw up.

Jade huffs and rolls me over with the kind of strength a little sister shouldn't have over her big sister. "You're real dumb for such a smart woman, you know that?"

"Hey." I reach for her forearm to apply a pinch to the tender triceps area, but she bats my hand away and I give up. I don't even have the energy for retribution. "That's rude." I pout.

Jade sits up, cross-legged. Her hair is a mess, sticking up at odd ends and flyaways clinging to unseen static. She bounces on her butt just to hear the mattress springs creak, and even though she's much older and there's only one of her, I'm suddenly transported right back to Nick's parents' house. His bed filled with niblings and the joy he gets from them.

"What's wrong?" Jade stops her butt wiggling when she notices the tears that have started to leak from my eyes.

"Nothing." I sniffle and wipe at my cheeks. "Nick is an excellent uncle," I say, my throat waterlogged. "That's all."

Because Jade is Jade, she doesn't bat an eye at my non sequitur statement. She cups my cheeks, looking into my eyes like a mother looks at her newborn baby. "Sure, he is, honey," she says, her voice kind and sweet just like her. "And that's exactly why you're such a dumb bitch."

"Wh— *Excuse me*?" I sit up to hit her with my pillow. "Language," I say primly even though swearing has never been prohibited. "Plus, still rude."

She cackles, lying on her side, hugging the pillow I smacked her with. "Rude. But true."

"I am not *dumb*."

"Yes, you are."

"Am not." I cross my arms and lift my chin, not really that offended but unwilling to admit it.

"You've never cared that a guy is a good *uncle* before, Jasmine," she says dryly.

"So?" I flatten and straighten the bedspread around us. "It's a good quality to have."

"One worth crying over?" She grips my forearms in her hands, suddenly serious.

"Don't." I pull away. "I know what you're trying to do."

"Make you happy?"

"It's not that simple," I almost yell.

"Except it *is* that simple," she *does* yell. "You like him. He likes you. Yet here you sit, crying into your pillow and calling in sad to work. What's the problem?"

"He's not my perfect match!" I yell back.

Jade's face falls. She wraps her arms around me in a tight hug, squeezing hard, and not releasing me even when the hug is clearly over. She rests her chin on my shoulder.

"I'm sorry, Jasmine," she says quietly in my ear, "that our parents' problems made you feel like you had to be perfect to be loved."

She squeezes again before climbing off the bed. "You don't have to hold yourself to such a high standard. It's an impossible standard, really." She looks at the floor instead of me. Probably because she knows I've already started to cry and don't want her to see. "I feel responsible. You're the best big sister and I know that part of that is because you've done everything in your power to ensure life is perfect for me." Now she meets my eyes. She's crying, too. "I should have told you a long time ago that I don't need you to sacrifice everything for me. You're allowed to put yourself, your needs, first."

Moments ago, I wanted to be alone. Now, as Jade turns to leave, I've never felt lonelier.

"What if I make the wrong choice?" I ask. She turns back to me. "What if I fuck it up? Or I hurt him more than I already have? Or he hurts me more than he already has?"

She frowns like that's the most absurd thing she's ever heard. "That could happen." She shrugs. "And I don't know what will happen. But I know you won't be alone."

I tumble off the bed in my hurry to get to her, squeezing her tight to me, her short, spiky hair prickling my chin, the smell of sleep—a concentrated eau de Jade—still clinging. "I love you," I mumble.

"Love you."

Jade leaves me for the bathroom, the whine of the pipes battling for sound supremacy with her off-key rendition of a Tragically Hip song that immediately takes me back to Moonbar, to Nick and his T-shirts.

I hurt him by choosing another Nick, leaving, and even if he doesn't blame me for it, I've contributed to the loss of his bar. His dream.

He was selfish when he decided not to tell me who he was, but so was I. In the end, all of this is my fault. My pride, my need for perceived perfection in the eyes of people I don't actually like, brought us here. If I'd just accepted the out Butch and Anaïs offered me, if I didn't need to save face in front of a guy that I didn't really love, I never would have joined Core Cupid. And yet, I can't make myself completely regret it, any of it.

All of those stupid, prideful decisions brought me to Nick—the other Nick, the one I wasn't supposed to meet.

Those decisions hurt him, his heart and his dreams, but if I hadn't made them, I wouldn't be able to trust myself now, to know all of it was the right decision.

Core Cupid might have a near perfect algorithm, but it didn't have my perfect match.

Moonbar did.

And I won't let him give up his dream.

20

NICK

The glass and wood façade of the Art Gallery of Ontario reflects the city back at me through the street-facing windows of the Core Cupid office. It's gray and dull, judgmental on this cold winter day. Or maybe I'm just projecting. The leather couch in the matchmaker's office squeaks and creaks whenever I shift. I try not to.

"Sorry to keep you waiting," the matchmaker, Chloe, says from the open doorway. She takes a seat in an armchair across from me. Beside it, an adjustable lap desk is equipped with a notebook and pen. Strangely analog for the person responsible for creating a near perfect matchmaking algorithm. She clicks her pen. "Are you ready?"

Despite my best efforts, I shift on the noisy couch.

Chloe reminds me of Jasmine, though they don't look anything alike. They're both gorgeous. Chloe is blond and tan. Angular where Jasmine is curvy. They both sit with their shoulders square, backs straight, necks long. Chloe looks like she'd enjoy that fresh binder smell.

"Yeah, I guess." If I thought pulling at my collar would help, I'd do it. "What should I be ready for, technically?"

She shifts in her chair, uncrossing her legs and leaning forward like we're sharing a secret. "It's pain free, I promise. I like to meet with all our clients first. Afterward, you can fill out your online interview at your convenience. It's a bit repetitive," she says, her tone apologetic. "But that's by design. Don't overthink it."

I'm so good at not overthinking, it is basically my job. Except today I think I might get fired.

Chloe asks easy questions first: what does a day in your life look like? And can you summarize your dating history? Tell me your ideal date? Then, tell me your ideal partner?

It's hard not to describe Jasmine.

What are you looking for in a relationship? Marriage, long-term commitment? Kids? Honestly, I'm just looking for Jasmine. I'm looking to prove to her that we're a match.

"You know," I say, scratching at my jaw. "Now that I think about it, maybe this isn't for me."

Chloe frowns, looking up from the notebook where she's taken copious notes. "If you're worried about finding a match, Mr. Scott, I can assure you—"

"Please call me Nick."

"Nick," she says, her eyes softening. "I can assure you, you'll have great success. Women outnumber men as clients, two to one, and I can already tell that you'll make someone very happy." She tries to be earnest, but she sounds like she's reading from a script.

"Listen, I'm not going to ask for the deposit back or whatever. I just..." I sigh. "Honestly, I'm falling for one of your clients, but she won't choose me because I'm not her perfect match."

The office is silent for a long, awkward moment. Finally, Chloe clears her throat. "You were going to pay for matchmaking services in the hopes that you'd match with the woman you're in love with to prove to her that you belong together?"

I laugh. "It sounds even worse when *you* say it out loud."

Blushing, she ducks her head. "Honestly, it sounds romantic to me," she says, which makes me blush back.

I run my sweaty palms down my thighs and stand. "I'm sorry to waste your time."

"You didn't," she says quickly. "You're not." She stops me with her hand up. "Can I ask, would you have signed up for matchmaking if it wasn't for this woman?"

I wince, running my hand through my hair. "Ummmm. Nah. Probably not."

"It's totally okay." She smiles. "Why not, though?"

I sit back down on the squeaky couch as the answer hits me hard enough to knock me back. "Because I never bothered to take it seriously before."

I say it like a question, but it's not. It's far too true a statement. I wish I could lie to myself and say it's because of the cost, but that's secondary at best. My face flushes with embarrassment, like this one confession tells her everything else she needs to know about me.

That I've always felt like the black sheep of the family and I thought that was their fault, or my dad's at least. But that's not true. It's a role I've cultivated. I'm fucking proud of it. At some point I started to lean into it. Anything to piss off my dad. Anything to prove to him—to myself—that I didn't need to follow his plans for my life.

But on the heels of the confession comes acceptance, because yeah, I make a joke out of a lot of things, but I wouldn't change it, not any of it. Not even if I thought it would have somehow saved the bar for me.

I like my life. I like my job. That I get to wear my T-shirts to work and that I live above the bar.

Maybe, if I had to, if I could, the only thing I'd change is Jasmine's first impression of me. I'd take that seriously, and her.

"Listen," Chloe says, folding her hands in her lap. "We don't usually do this. At its heart, matchmaking requires time. Even with a perfect algorithm. For the sake of anonymity, I don't need or want to know any more information about this client, but I'll sign you up for two weeks at half price. If the match happens, it happens. But if it doesn't..."

She looks around like a secret boss is hiding behind her chair or she doesn't want whatever she's about to say next to get picked up by whatever bug has been planted by Core Cupid's closest competitors.

"If you don't end up matching, I don't think you should let that stop you. If you love her, she needs to know."

I thank her, taking my time filling out the forms she needs to start the paperwork, her words echoing around this drafty office even if I'm the only one who can hear them. This is so generous of her. Clearly, she's the right person to help others find love if she believes in it this strongly.

The only problem is, I don't think Jasmine is as ardent a believer. Even if Jasmine knows for sure how I feel, it might not be enough.

THERE'S a strange man waiting outside the bar when I get back. This isn't uncommon. Some of our regulars have nowhere else to be. Sometimes unhoused folks will sit against the door for warmth in winter; our policy is to offer them water and a meal, then ask if they'll move out of the doorway.

What's strange about this man is that he's my father.

I stop in front of him. "Are you okay?" Maybe he's on a new cholesterol medication that causes him to enter fugue states and travel hours into the city. That reason seems far more likely than any other I can think of.

"Can you pour your old man a drink?"

"Old man?" I say, mimicking his offended tone when I used the label, but I open the door and let him in.

Dad takes his time, studying the graffiti wall, testing the stability of the stage, inspecting the audio system. By the time he takes a seat at the end of the bar, opposite where I stand prepping limes, I have a flight of three beers ready for him. All from local craft breweries and complementary in malt and hop flavors, bitterness, conditioning, body, and—Rocco's favorite tasting factor—mouthfeel.

Dad takes the first glass. "*Slàinte mhath*," he says in Scots Gaelic, echoes of his Glaswegian accent in his words despite not having lived there since he was eight years old.

The silence between us while I work and he sips is amicable. It isn't until he's finished his first beer that he straightens on his stool and clears his throat.

I put down my knife. Here we fucking go.

"I've been hard on you," he says.

I freeze. Finally, blink, breathe. Fight the urge to laugh and sling a petty retort, but the shock and sarcasm are quickly squashed by a rush of emotion. So, I keep my response simple, if not a little strangled. "Yeah."

"Of all my kids, you have always reminded me most of myself, and I wished I'd had more guidance when I was a kid."

"I'm not a kid anymore," I say, my voice still rough.

He nods. "Sometimes it's hard not to look at you—at all of you—and see the babies you were," he says. "I'm sorry, Nicholas."

I swallow to buy myself time, but in the end, I don't need it.

"I want to offer you the loan again."

I jerk my head up, all the air from my lungs leaving me. "Why?"

Dad's smile is familiar. "If you were willing to pretend you were dating a complete stranger who thought you were someone else, just to make me happy, you deserve it."

That statement doesn't make up for a lot of shit, but it's a start. I walk around the bar and Dad wraps his arms around my shoulders, patting my back with strong hands.

"Wait," I say into his shoulder. I push us apart. "How'd you know that? That Jasmine was a stranger and thought I was someone else?"

"Didn't she tell you?"

My stomach drops like a stone. "Tell me what?"

"Jasmine called us." He hugs me again. "She told your mom everything."

"How? When?"

He chuckles against my chest. "Your mother gave Jasmine her cell phone number."

"Oh. Of course she did."

My brain is blank. I don't know how this feels, how I feel about any of it.

He slaps my back, grinning. "So, what do you say? Ready to buy this bar?"

Dad sounds hopeful, because of course he does. He probably thinks it all *means* something, like Jasmine loves me, like all his dreams could finally come true: his second-oldest son will finally be a business owner and maybe even married.

He doesn't know what I know. Jasmine left me. Twice. What Jasmine feels for me is guilt for lying, for coming here with Nick, for "losing" the bar for me, but not love. This is just what Jasmine does, helps others instead of caring for herself.

"I appreciate the offer, Dad," I say, then take a deep breath. What I'm about to say next could completely undo our tenuous détente. "I think figuring out what's next is something I want to do for myself."

21

JASMINE

Moonbar is packed. Good thing Jade is with me this time. Apparently, the announcement from two weeks ago that the bar is closing has done nothing to dissuade people from coming in. Maybe they think if they fill the bar every night, they'll somehow save it from impending doom? Like this is a TV movie where the girl gets the guy and saves her family's farm in her small town from financial ruin all in one closing scene. I wish it was.

I hope.

Normally, I wouldn't invite my little sister to witness this, but she insisted. She's "invested now," she claimed. As if she hasn't been sticking her nose in my business since birth. I'm somehow lucky enough to have snagged the same spot I had the first time I was here. There was only one stool available but Jade insisted I take it while she uses the bathroom.

Bernie shoots a smile at me across the lacquered wood surface between us as she takes a customer's order. I wasn't sure how she'd receive me, if Nick had told her what happened between us, but it seems he didn't. Or if he did, they don't seem to care. Ed certainly hadn't been hostile when I showed up at his door earlier this week,

Rocco hovering behind him. Miraculously, I was able to convince them that a) I was not a weirdo, b) they should let me in to talk, and c) Bernie should probably be included, too.

After Mindy called me back to let me know that Nick had declined his parents' offer of a loan, I'd pitched the idea to Jade. She was immediately on board. Obviously.

But beyond all the rational reasons why this plan was flawed, it also required the rest of the Moonbar team to buy in, and I'd known that would be a long shot.

Apparently, not long enough though.

Rocco and Ed walk through the Employees Only door and Rocco helps Ed get settled at the other end of the bar.

I do everything I can not to throw up.

I wish I'd brought a binder for a situation like this. I just don't know all the resources I'd need when trying to apologize to a man whose heart you've broken while also suggesting you invest in his bar to save his dream of owning it one day soon.

Nick is nowhere to be seen. When we arrived, I'd double-checked with Bernie that he was in and she assured me that he's here, but it's been at least five minutes, maybe ten. Normally, he wouldn't leave his partner alone for this long. And he's supposed to host Underground Karaoke.

Jade comes bounding back from the bathroom. "They have genderless bathrooms," she says with an adorably happy grin.

I take her hand. "That's great, honey."

"I'm just saying." She shrugs. "This place is a good investment."

"Yeah." I scan the space for Nick for the hundredth time. "That's the plan."

It's a risk, a huge risk. Forget security and planning and perfect. This is a Hail Mary.

Finally, he pushes through the door.

"What took you so long?" Bernie yells.

"I was changing the keg." He lifts the collar of his T-shirt and uses it to dab at the sweat on his brow. "*Someone*," he says, staring her down, "stacked the Molson at the bottom again. It's like playing *Donkey Kong* with those barrels down there."

Ed laughs, the sound raspy but strong, startling Nick.

"What are you doing here?" He spots Rocco standing next to Ed. "Since when do you come in on your day off?" he questions as he slides behind Bernie at the bar.

Rocco shrugs and Bernie tries to distract Nick from the change in routine with her next words.

"There are a couple of customers down there I haven't been able to get to yet." She gestures toward Jade and me.

Still, he doesn't notice us, chirping Rocco and Ed, his voice light. He's clearly happy to be surrounded by people he loves. He throws a Labatt Blue coaster down in front of me still half-turned away, then finally, *finally*, he sees me.

The instant our eyes meet, he goes stock-still. After a heartbeat or two, his gaze jumps to Jade. Then he's taking in the scene behind and around me, checking for any other companions I may have brought.

"It's just me," I say.

"And me," Jade says. "Hi, Nick."

"Hi, Jade," he says, pointedly turning to her before turning back to me. "Hi."

Willing my pulse to steady, I give him a small smile. "Hi."

"What are you doing here?" His tone is hard enough that I fight the urge to wince.

"Ordering a cab sauv, if you have it."

"As a matter of fact, we do. Berns," he calls over his shoulder. "Can you open a new bottle of cab sauv?"

"Sure thing, boss."

Next to me, Jade practically vibrates with excitement.

I've made bad decisions with men before, a lot of them. Whether I was trying to take care of her or needed to be taken care of myself, I've let that cloud my judgment, and I've allowed myself to get hurt too many times. I'm still worried she'll think I'm making another bad decision.

Genuine affection shines in her eyes, though, as she looks at me.

"Okay." Nick turns back to me. "What are you doing here?" he asks again, more than just hard this time. He actually sounds angry.

Fuck.

"I...um..." I wipe my sweaty hands down my short black skirt and tights, my heart shuddering. I had a whole speech planned and suddenly I can't remember a single thing. "I'm here because..."

He cocks an eyebrow. There are marks on his nose from the pads of his glasses. He must have been wearing them right before work.

"I want to buy the bar," I blurt out.

His eyebrow only cocks higher, totally suspicious.

"Sorry. No. What I mean is." I take a huge breath, and I don't let myself hold it no matter how much I want to. "I have the money to invest in your business. And I think it's enough."

"Uhhh..." Nick looks more confused than ever.

"Enough for you to save the bar," I say quickly, then gesture behind him at Bernie and Rocco. "If we all went in together."

He turns back to his co-workers, his friends, his jaw set. "Oh, I see," he says quietly enough that I have to read the words on his lips. "So, you all schemed behind my back, huh?"

"For the record, I was not part of the scheme," Jade chimes. I kick her shin, and she yelps.

"Not. Helping," I say through gritted teeth. "There was no *scheme*." My hands are out to bat away any angry assumptions he may make. "I wanted to help. We all did."

He shakes his head as Bernie slides my glass of wine toward me, laughs like he's in disbelief. "You thought that would help me, Jasmine?" He leans over the bar, not crowding me, but so he can lower his voice when he says, "When it comes down to it, it's not the bar I wanted. It was you. And you left me." He leans back, his eyes dark, his mouth sneering. He raps the bar with his knuckles. "Twice."

With that he steps away. "The wine is on the house," he says. And he walks out from behind the bar toward the stage.

"Shit," Jade says.

Ed and Rocco watch me from the other side of the bar, but I can't bring myself to meet their eyes. Bernie keeps sending me gentle smiles; that just makes me want to cry more.

"Maybe we should go?" Jade tugs on my wrist, squeezing when I turn to her, the tears welling in my eyes visible. "Let's go," she says resolute. She knows I hate to cry in public.

Nick starts his intro to Underground Karaoke and the crowd thunders with the excitement and anticipation of alcoholically lubricated live performances.

He hates me. He might actually hate me.

My mind is numb, my ears filled with the sound of bees, even though I know that's incorrect. There are no bees here. Jade easily drags me from my barstool, collects my coat, pulls me toward the safety of the exit.

My god, I'm an idiot. Leading with a *business proposal* rather than the truth, that I'm falling for him. I fell. I fucking love Nick Scott. Bartender, son, brother; liar, boss, friend, best kisser I've ever kissed. I fell for him because he loves the things he loves without shame, and he feels judged by his father but still wants his approval, and because when a complete stranger poured her heart onto his bar top he didn't laugh at her or judge her, he helped her.

Nick helped me.

I plant my feet on the sticky floor before Jade can tug me through the exit. She whispers, "Come on, sissy. Every exit is an emergency exit if you try hard enough."

I shake my head, squeezing her hand, and turn back to the bar. "I want to sing," I say to no one in particular. Before Jade can persuade me not to, I march back to the bar, where Bernie stands with a clipboard in hand. "Bernie, I want to sing."

She looks at me, then over my shoulder. Presumably at Nick.

"Anyone can sing, right?"

She heaves a sigh and says, with a click of her pen, "Anyone. What song?"

Shit. I hadn't thought that far ahead. A crowd pushes in from behind me, the other karaoke-ers waiting to get their names on the list. I'm going to sing in front of all of them.

What have I done.

"'Night Moves,'" I hear myself say. "Bob Seger."

She scribbles the info down before nodding toward the stage where the band is tuning their instruments. "It'll be about five more minutes, but you're first up."

I walk on wooden legs to the side of the stage, lean against the wall. The cool brick and rough surface helps ground me in my body, the feeling in my limbs returning.

"*Jazz*," my sister hisses. She stands directly in front of me. Where did she even come from? "What are you doing?"

I rummage through my bag, looped around her shoulder, for my hand sanitizer. My hands aren't particularly dirty, it just feels good to control something right now, like the percentage of living bacteria on my hands. "Singing in public. Terribly."

The lights go down, but the volume in the bar goes way up. This is going to happen. It's happening. People whistle, the shrill sound making me wince and Jade clap her hands over her ears.

"Are you sure you want to do this?" she asks.

I shake my head. "No."

"Do you want me to come with you?" We're just inches from each other, but Jade has to yell to be heard over the noise and the musicians warming up beside us.

"No." My stomach rolls with nerves. "I have to do this myself. I have to do it *for* myself."

Jade smiles. She looks proud of me, and even though my hands shake and my heart won't leave my throat and I won't have a voice to sing with, even though I think I could pass out at any moment, beneath all of that, I'm proud of myself, too.

"It helps," I say. "To know you're here."

Jade hugs me, one of her better hugs. Tight, warm, vibrating with laughter, or love, or just pure energy, I'm never quite sure. "Always," she whispers in my ear.

The crowd erupts around us as Nick hops back onto the stage, Bernie's clipboard in his hand. "Our first performer," he says into the mic as he glances down at the sign-up sheet, "is..."

He pauses. Frowns. He scans the rest of the list, lifts the paper to scan the list behind it. When he flips the paper down, he looks at me. For the first time in what's felt like forever, his voice changes, soft, tender, warm, when he says, "Jasmine."

Jade has to shove me forward and the next thing I know I'm on the stage. The lights are brighter and hotter than I expected. The space cramped, with the band stuffed in tight behind me, carpet covering the wood flooring. Nick stares at me, his expression unreadable. He's not mad, at least not as mad as he had been.

"Hi," he says softly, away from the mic.

"Hi," I rasp.

He leans closer and for this moment I'm not on a stage in front of strangers, I'm just with Nick. I lean toward him, but he blinks and faces the crowd. "Jasmine is singing 'Night Moves' by Bob Seger."

The room erupts again, impossibly louder than before. So that's great. Apparently, there are a lot of Bob Seger fans in this bar.

"Oh my god." I grab Nick's arm before he can walk off stage and leave me here. "I don't know the words," I half-shriek, though I'm still barely audible.

Nick turns me slowly, his hands warm through my thick white fisherman's sweater, to face a screen with the lyrics.

Duh.

He's gone when I look over my shoulder, though, and it's not like I could have said anything anyway because then, the music starts.

22

NICK

Because I'm not sexism and a bag of dicks wrapped in a trench—and because I have living human sisters—I know that whole "women don't sweat, they glow" thing is bullshit. Except for right now.

Jasmine glows. Between her fiery hair, the flush in her cheeks from embarrassment and probably fear, the stage lights illuminating every corner, she's a freaking moonbeam. She's glorious. She's beautiful. For the life of me, I can't remember why I'm mad. She left. Twice. So, what? She can't make a decision to save her life, even when the right choice is literally right in front of her, or behind her, on top, beneath, between her legs. Who cares? She's stunning and she's brave and beneath the perfection she's compassionate.

She wants to invest in my bar. She wants to help me.

As the band begins to play the first notes, she holds the mic up to her mouth and says, her eyes on me, "This is for you, Nick."

Fuck. I love her.

And then she starts to sing.

I've never heard this room get so quiet so fast.

Jasmine Palmer, regal, beautiful, aflame, is a terrible singer. Like, absolutely horrendous.

She mumbles the words. The only reason I can hear them is because I know them by heart myself, but the mumbling is for a purpose: so we can't hear her.

Pitch? Never met her before. Someone has to be paying her to sing off-key. She's alternatively flat or sharp and nothing in between.

It's not until the end of the first verse that the first wrinkle of a frown forms between her brows, specifically when she sings about what Bob and a certain black-haired beauty get up to in a truck. She drops the mic in the few moments between verse and chorus and says, "This isn't a love song."

Around me, people chuckle. I laugh, too loud for the weirdly quiet room, but still she doesn't let this stop her. Through the chorus her frown deepens, especially when she's forced to sing the titular line.

"This is a song about sex," she says, aghast.

I jump on the stage, ready to put an end to this. "It's not a love song," I confirm. The band keeps playing for a few more notes then slowly fades. People chatter now, mostly sounding perplexed at why I've interrupted her.

"You don't have to do this," I say, my voice amplified by the microphone.

"I'm sorry." She grasps my wrists, my elbows. "I talked about business when I should have told you the truth. The most important thing."

"No, it's okay." I cup her face, rub her lips, her cheek with my thumb.

"It's not," she says, her voice high and strained. "I..."

"We're not a match," I say quickly.

She blinks, confused. "Y-yes we are."

I sigh. It's pretty embarrassing to have to admit this right now. "I went to Core Cupid." I follow her hairline with my finger as a distraction. "Told Chloe everything and she signed me up to see if we could be a match. But we're not."

She shakes her head. "That's the thing, I don't want an algorithm to tell me how I feel anymore. I canceled my Core Cupid membership. I decided to follow my gut."

The softest butterfly wings brush against my ribcage. I never thought of myself as a butterfly guy but it turns out I just needed the right girl. "And what does your gut say?"

"That I love you," she whispers, trailing her fingers through my hair, scratching her nails through my stubble.

"Jazz." I say her name like a sigh.

"I mean it though. I want to be a part of this with you. I know it's a risk, but I see the community you created here, how happy it makes you. I don't have a lot of experience running a bar. I might be bad at it at first, but I want to save Moonbar."

"I thought you didn't like doing things you're not good at," I tease.

She fights her smile. "Clearly, I've given up on that."

"O-M-G kiss already, please!" Jade squeals from the front of the stage. Jasmine turns bright pink at the realization that we are being watched by...everyone.

"We should give the people what they want," I say, pulling her attention back to me, tugging her closer by her hip. Tentative at first, as I run my nose along hers. Then not tentative at all when the spice of her perfume fills my nose, when all I can think about is being surrounded by her, feeling her laugh against my throat. Her lips are warm, her tongue soft. I taste her teeth because she can't stop smiling, her giggles turning to buzzing against my lips. Then the whistles start, the catcalls and the affectionate requests that we get a room.

She presses her face into my throat, my shoulder. I cup the back of her head. I want to hold her, feel her next to me forever. Until her fingers find the tender skin of my triceps and she pinches me.

"What are you doing?" I scrub my stubble across her neck.

"Just checking," she says, kissing my chin, my cheek. "Wanted to make sure this is real, you're real."

I kiss her again to a chorus of hoots and hollers. "Very real."

There's nothing fake about how I feel for her.

EPILOGUE: NICK

October

The wine rep standing on the other side of the bar frowns as Jasmine sets down her wine glass. His face falls further as she steps back, her face chalky.

"You okay?" I reach for her, but she sidesteps my grasp as she rushes past me, pushing through the back door of the bar.

"Yup," she warbles. She sounds anything but okay.

"Sorry," I tell the rep – I've already forgotten his name – and follow after her. "Be right back. I'm sure it's not your wine," I say over my shoulder when I catch a glimpse of panic on his face.

It could be the wine. It tasted fine to me, though. But then, I'm not the one trying to expand our wine list. I was happy with the merlot we already had. Or as Jazz likes to call it, "bar rail fruit fly attractant".

Light escapes underneath the door of the Employees' Only bathroom.

"Jasmine?" I knock but can barely hear her response over the buzz and clank of the fan which hasn't been replaced since the Industrial Revolution.

After a few moments, the door opens. In the harsh light of the naked bulb hanging from the ceiling, Jasmine looks washed out, her eyes are red, and she dabs at her mouth with a brown paper towel.

"You're sick," I say, lifting my hand to her forehead, but in another deke move that would get her a walk-on spot on the Maple Leafs, she avoids me.

"Yeah," she says. "No. I don't know." She plasters herself to the wall. We've been together long enough now for me to know she wants space because she's upset about being sick or feels embarrassed for puking or a combination of both and not because she's upset with me.

"Do you want to go upstairs and lie down? I can finish the tasting."

She shakes her head, but she's pressing her lips together and her color has gotten worse. I'm about to put my foot down about it when she says, "I think I'm going to go home actually. My home."

"Oh." Maybe I need to rethink if she's upset with me.

The last time she slept at her house was in August.

"Okay," I say, once I realize that I haven't said anything for an awkward amount of time.

"I'm probably just tired. Maybe burnt out a little?"

Fatigue could be a factor. I did wake her up after my shift so she could sit on my face for a bit. Even though she doesn't take bar shifts – we tried that, and she got way too flustered – she's still forced to be on my schedule.

Jasmine was the missing piece we didn't know we needed at Moonbar; she's got a binder for every possible situation; she's improved our marketing tenfold when it was previously zero. Gone are the days of forgetting to reorder vermouth or restock napkins with our logos on them. She even found a way to promote Underground Karaoke while still adhering to the number rule of Underground Karaoke: no one talks about Underground Karaoke.

We sell merch now, too, and she got us all T-shirts for us to wear on shift. Rocco was most excited about the fact that she got our names embroidered on them. She blessed Moonbar with all her

Jasmine-iest qualities, and we're thriving, but I can see how all that work could burn her out.

"Do people usually barf when they're burnt out?"

This gets me in trouble. She scowls and pushes me toward the door. "Tyrone is waiting. Go taste his wines. I wrote down our needs in the notebook on the bar." She points a stern finger at me. "Do not go over budget."

I hold up my hands in placation. "That won't be a problem."

"Don't go under budget either." Then she gives me one final push out the door.

TURNS out Tyrone is pretty chatty, so he doesn't leave until Rocco arrives and it's time to start opening. The bar fills up fast since it's a Thursday and Underground Karaoke is loud and fun but impossible to sneak away from to call or even text Jasmine to ask how she's doing. At two in the morning, I text her, knowing she won't see it until the morning. Then, I text Jade, because she's always up now.

> Me: how is she?

> Lil' sis: qué?

> Me: your sister

> Lil' sis: ????

> Lil' sis: why what'd you do?

> Me: NOTHING!!!

> Me: she was sick today. threw up and went home.

She doesn't respond until I'm out of the shower and in a bed that feels far too spacious.

> Lil' sis: just checked on her. she's snoring.

> Me: take a vid. we can use it for blackmail later

> Lil' sis: dude you are diabolical

She sends me the video, which is just a black screen since Jasmine's room is pitch black from her blackout curtains, but over the whoosh of her sound machine – a tool I got her hooked on – her breaths come in soft snorts.

She snores delicately. Because of course she does.

I fall asleep to the lullaby of her snores, rather than think about if Jasmine is okay, why she never told her sister she was sick. Or why she hasn't reached out to me once since she left.

"Remember Yasmin?" Jasmine sets down her fork with intention, not hard, not softly, but with far more concentration and precision than the action usually deserves. She dabs at the corners of her mouth with her napkin, even though she's barely touched her lunch.

I stuff my fork into my mouth, my fork laden with leafy greens and sweet potatoes and whatever other root vegetables she's stocked my tiny kitchen with. But even after I've masticated longer than necessary, I can't recall a single instance of meeting Yasmin. Best case scenario, this is a friend I've forgotten about. Worst case scenario, she's an ex I've forgotten about, though that seems unlikely. Even for me.

"No," I say around a mouthful so large Jasmine shakes her head huffing fondly. I hope. She smooths the already smooth red and white checked tablecloth that covers my kitchen table. I've never once owned a tablecloth before but one afternoon I came upstairs scrounging for a snack and there it was, along with her and the table set for two. Now we eat lunch together every day. Except for yesterday, when she stayed home claiming continued illness – and wouldn't let me come over at all to help – and the day before, when we were so busy we never even had lunch.

"You met her the first time we went to your parents'," she says shyly. "In the pool house?"

"Oh, Yasmin." Fuck yeah, I remember Yasmin.

I grin and I'm not even trying to make her blush but she does. Those are the best blushes, when they're unplanned. "Yeah. Love Yasmin. How's she doing?"

She shrugs. "Fine, I guess. I was just thinking…"

I place my fork down and reach across the table for her hand. "Thinking about what exactly?"

My hope is always that she's thinking about sex. Specifically, with me, though I'm not picky. But based on her inability to meet my eyes and the fact that ever since she got sick a few days ago something has been just a little bit off, my hopes are not currently high.

She mulls over her words quietly, her lips pursing, her brow crinkling until I want to reach across the table and smooth her out. Or maybe take her to the bed and keep her there until every muscle and nerve is relaxed, incapable of a single fold.

"I was thinking that –"

Rocco chooses this moment to fly up the stairs in three loud leaps. They kick the door once with their boot and don't wait for a response before they open it. "Beer delivery is here." They're breathless, hunched in the doorway hands on their knees.

I keep Jasmine's hand in mine as I turn to face them. "And you couldn't be the one to intake that because…?"

They straighten, flashing a notebook at me, like I'm supposed to know its contents. "Cuz me and Jasmine are talking about the new cocktail menu."

She squeezes my hand. "We'll talk about it later."

"We can talk about it now," I insist, but she smiles, pulls her hand away, and takes my empty plate to the counter along with her full one.

"Show me the menu," she says to Rocco.

So, I guess we can't.

ROBERTA, the beer delivery woman, spends most of the delivery talking about how October in the city is the perfect time of year. Cool without being cold, warm without the sticky, stuffy humidity. While I agree, I'm not a great conversation partner. My attention is stuck halfway up the stairs. Only when she asks after Ed do I pull my attention back to her. I'm always happy to share how he kicked chemo's ass and impressed his doctors with his recovery from surgery.

Finally, I sign off for Roberta on the dotted line and make my way slowly back up the stairs. My parents were ecstatic to learn that Jasmine and me were back together, or together for real, at least. Mom's scream nearly broke my laptop speaker when we FaceTimed them. Dad is happy but he's made his concerns about the intertwining of our professional and personal relationships abundantly clear.

And I get it, but goddamn would it kill him to be supportive for once?

I've tried not to let it bother me, and Jasmine and I have worked hard to create boundaries since the beginning, ones that will "create longevity for all levels of our partnership", according to Jazz. That's why we haven't moved in together; though, I don't think she's ready to officially leave Jade anyway. That's why we keep our finances separate. It's why we haven't even thought of words like fiancée or marriage license. But if she wanted to, I'd marry her in a fucking second.

For a guy who'd never really done commitment before, I feel like I'm kind of fucking killing it. Maybe that's why this sudden, subtle distance from her feels like a gap I can't help but mind. Things feel wrong, off, like the way Jade looks when she's forced to use a microfiber cloth: uncomfortable but suffering through it. I want to fix it for Jasmine, whatever concerns, worries, or god forbid, doubts she might have.

But what if I can't fix this.

As I reach the top of the stairs, Jasmine and Rocco's hushed voices drift through my apartment door, slightly ajar. It's all a jumble of high-pitched hissing until Rocco's whispered screech breaks through, "Aren't you on birth control?"

I stop at the top of the stairs, my last few steps quiet. I don't strain to hear what she and Rocco are talking about on the other side. I don't even hold my breath to hide my arrival. But I don't not do those things, either.

Yes. Yes, Jasmine is on birth control. She's had an IUD since I've known her. I can't hear her response through the ringing in my ears but I assume that's what she says.

Shit. Fuck. Damn. This is not what we need right now. It's not what we want; at least, not what I want. If I was ever going to consider the possibility of offspring, it would be with Jasmine, but I never got the sense she wanted them, either.

While it's certainly not the worst thing about a potential pregnancy situation, the fact that my father may now be able to employ his favorite saying, "I told you so", doesn't make it better.

"You guys haven't discussed this before?" Rocco asks, and while it's uncommon I'm surprised to hear judgment lacing their words.

Jasmine says something inaudible and then with a tremble in her voice, "Please don't tell Nick."

"Of course not, sweetie," Rocco responds.

A claustrophobic panic closes my airways like anaphylaxis. I nudge the door open with my foot. "Don't tell me what?"

If my heart wasn't hammering in my throat, I'd laugh at their twin faces of shock and shame. Rocco is frozen, the same look of horror on their face as when they unwittingly muttered shut up into a live mic during Underground Karaoke when a patron would not, in fact, stop talking.

Jasmine on the other hand almost seems relieved. She shakes out her hands and opens the door wider. "Come in and I'll tell you."

"You're pregnant," I say, testing the word. If I say it enough times maybe it won't feel so bad.

"No." She hugs herself. "Thank god," she mutters.

"But I heard you – "

"You were eavesdropping?" Rocco asks, aghast.

"Yeah, and I heard you colluding with my girlfriend to keep secrets from me." I chuck my thumb over my shoulder. "Scram."

They roll their eyes as we switch places, and I close the door behind them.

I'm mad. Or maybe sad. I'm hurt. It takes everything in me to turn and face her with a neutral expression.

"It's not what it sounds like." She takes my hands, but stays at arm's length until I pull her into me, trapping her hands between my back and the door.

"Okay. What is it then?"

Her sigh presses her chest against mine. "I thought I was pregnant. The wine tasted absolutely awful and made me sick immediately. When I went home, I started Googling and I came across all these stories about women who'd gotten pregnant with IUDs and I panicked."

"Cuz you don't want to have a baby with me?" I ask, even though I am so fucking relieved.

She sighs again, kisses me hard and quick. "I don't want to have a baby at all."

"Great, neither do I."

She smiles, kissing me again, slower, softer. "Yeah, but I didn't know that. I'm not pregnant. I took a test. I think my stomach reacted poorly to drinking the wine on an empty stomach. But once I realized all that, I was so worried because we'd never talked about kids. And..." She looks away suddenly, biting her lip, her eyes welling with tears.

"Hey." I cup her chin. "Don't cry."

"I didn't want you to leave me," she says in the quietest voice. "Because I didn't want to give you a baby." Her eyes are bright as the tears fall. "If I ever did want to have a baby, it would be with you though."

I lean my head back against the door, laughing as she speaks my own thoughts back to me. I squeeze her closer to me.

"Me too. And I'm sorry we hadn't discussed it sooner. Or that you felt like it was even an option that I would leave you because of that. Even if you were pregnant, we would deal with it together," I say. I want her to know she's never alone, especially in this. "We'd deal with it, whatever that looks like for us."

She flushes, pressing her temple to my cheek to avoid looking me in the eye.

"Wait." I lean into her, rubbing my stubbly chin into her neck until she squeals. "Why were you asking about Yasmin earlier?"

She huffs a quiet laugh into my shoulder. "I don't want to tell you."

"Why not?"

"It's embarrassing." Her hands slip beneath the back of my button-up plaid, a futile attempt at distraction.

"Now you have to tell me," I whisper, my voice huskier. I won't be distracted, but I am still just a man.

She glides her nails up and down my back, a tingle more than a scratch, before slipping her fingers beneath the waistband of my boxer briefs. I suck her skin in retaliation.

"Nick." She pushes me away, trying and failing to catch a glimpse of the spot on her shoulder.

"I didn't leave a mark." I press my thumb over the spot, because I wish I did.

She sighs, crossing her arms over chest. "I was sad because I thought about how I couldn't even keep a role play character alive, so I'd probably be a terrible mother to a baby I didn't even want, and then you'd leave me," she says, stern and matter of fact.

I wait for her to crack a smile. Because this has to be a joke. "Jazz."

"I know."

"That's..."

"I know..."

"You raised your sister," I remind her. "You don't want a baby. And you're not even pregnant." I throw my hands up in the air.

She lifts her chin, unwilling to break. "I never said it made any sense."

I pull my phone out of my pocket, checking the time, before placing it on the table beside my door where I put all my mail. "Well, if you're feeling sad, there's only one way to make you feel better." I stroll past her toward the bed, unbuttoning my shirt as I go.

"What's that?" she asks, her voice rightfully suspicious.

I sprawl on the bed, my legs spread wide, leaning back on my hands. Her gaze lands on the exposed skin and hair of my stomach and chest as she slowly follows me.

"We'll have to resurrect Yasmin." When she gets close enough, I hold out my hand. She takes it for balance and sets one knee on the mattress, then the other. She hikes up her long skirt until her thighs are exposed.

"You're right." She splays her hand over my stomach, up to my chest.

I hold her hand over my heart, pressing my skin to her skin to mine. "Should I be someone else, too?" I ask. It only seems fair that if she has a sex role play character, so should I.

She pauses, midway through pulling her hair out of its bun. She leans over me, her hair falling around us, a silky shroud. "Absolutely not," she says, resolute, against my lips.

"Why not?" I whisper.

She pulls her shirt over her head, unhooks her bra, holds her breasts in her hands, nipples peeking between her fingers. As she grinds against the growing bulge in my pants, I raise my hips to meet her. My mouth waters to taste her where she teases me, her fingers plucking and pulling, caressing where I want to suck her most.

"Why not?" I ask again, my voice hoarse, my dick hard, my heart thumping. She could break me into a thousand jagged pieces and I'd still get hot for her, love her.

She smiles, softly, running her hands through my hair. "Because in every possible plot, you'll always be my Nick."

THE END

ALSO BY RUBY BARRETT

The Friendship Study

The Romance Recipe

Hot Copy

ACKNOWLEDGMENTS

As always, writing books is hard, writing Acknowledgments in harder which is why I've put this off so long. And since this is my first self-published book, there are even *more* people who deserve acknowledgment. I'm going to do my best to make sure I get to all of you without making this it's own novel.

MA Wardell, KD Casey, Zoey York, and Nellie Wilson have been invaluable resources answering all of my (often panicked questions) and wonderful friends.

Sam Palencia of Ink and Laurel, Beth Lawton of VB Edits, and Kaila Desjardins of KD Editing, thank you for your time, effort, and care with these characters. This book felt so safe and so well represented in your capable hands.

Meg and Darryl, thank you for answering questions and filling in subject matter gaps.

To the readers who make any and all of this possible, there are no words for the gratitude I feel for you, but thank you nonetheless; especially, Ada for her sharp eye for vibe checks, and the funnest (big Nick word choice) book club ever: Monica, Dani, Shelby, Kate, Erica, Allie, Kaitlyn, Brittany, and Callie.

This book would not be what it is without the people I trust most with my words: Esther, Lyssa, Stephanie, Kiki, and Rosie; you make me better and I love you.

Finally, Karou and Mike, thank you for the gift of time, support, and most of all love.

ABOUT THE AUTHOR

Ruby Barrett writes steamy, smart, and tender romances, inspired by the intimate details of everyday life and always being the thirstiest friend in the group chat. She lives in Ottawa, Canada with her husband and child. *The Match Faker* is her fourth novel.

If you enjoyed *The Match Faker*, please consider leaving a review. And don't forget to sign up for my newsletter.